T0335315

WALTZING MONTANA

MONTANA

A NOVEL

Mary Clearman Blew

University of Nebraska Press · Lincoln

Part of chapter 19 previously appeared as "The
Balky Horse" in *High Desert Journal*, no. 28 (Spring
2019). Parts of chapters 13 and 14 previously
appeared in *Hive Avenue*, no. 1 (2019): 36–41.

Library of Congress Cataloging-in-Publication Data
Names: Blew, Mary Clearman, 1939– author.
Title: Waltzing Montana : a novel
/ Mary Clearman Blew.
Description: Lincoln: University
of Nebraska Press, [2021]
Summary: "Set in central rural Montana in
1925, Waltzing Montana follows midwife
Mildred Harrington as she grapples with feelings
for her old sweetheart while also trying to
overcome the horrific abuse that she suffered
as a young teenager"—Provided by publisher.
Identifiers: LCCN 2020025980
ISBN 9781496225054 (paperback)
ISBN 9781496225641 (epub)
ISBN 9781496225658 (mobi)
ISBN 9781496225665 (pdf)
Classification: LCC PS3552.L46 W35
2021 | DDC 813/.54—dc23
LC record available at https://
lccn.loc.gov/2020025980

Set in Whitman by Laura Buis.
Designed by L. Auten.

Waltzing Montana

Mildred Harrington rode west. The trail grew indistinct as the sunset faded, and she felt weary beyond her years. But her good horse, Smokey, knew the way home, and she could sit in the saddle and let her mind rest and her thoughts wander. Mrs. Svoboda's labor had gone on and on until she was exhausted and Mildred resorted to forceps to draw the baby boy from the birth canal. But he was healthy, and she had bathed and dressed him and held him for a long moment of private grief before she left him squalling in his mother's arms. She could have stayed the night with the Svobodas. But her own cabin and her own bed called her, and she would have a full moon to ride by.

She and Smokey followed a trail that angled down from the Svoboda ranch buildings through shale and bunchgrass and skirted the hawthorn brush that choked the creek bank. As she came to the Svoboda crossing, she could see the willows on the other side of the creek reaching for the current with their long leaves, and she could smell the water and the fetid mud where cattle had been coming to drink. With luck, she would have only another hour's ride ahead.

Smokey suddenly shied and snorted. Mildred reined him in sharply and laid a hand on his mane while he quivered and blew rollers through his nose but stood still for her.

"What's your problem, Smoke?" she asked him.

She got a voice in reply: "Is somebody there?"

"Yes."

"God, I'm glad."

Hawthorn branches heaved and leaves shuddered as a shape crawled out on all fours. Mildred would have thought she was seeing a bear coming out of the underbrush, except for Smokey's reaction, which now was mild interest, and, of course, the voice.

He raised his head, and by the last of the light, she recognized the young man.

"Pat!"

"A piece of him," he said.

She saw that he was hurt, and her training responded, as she swung down from Smokey and ran to him.

"What happened?"

He rolled over and sat up, gritting his teeth with the effort. "Mil," he said, "I'm damn glad to see you."

Mildred tied Smokey's reins to a hawthorn branch and knelt down. Pat winced when she touched his left boot, and she could tell by the taut leather of the boot that his ankle had swollen inside it.

"Mil," he said.

"How long have you been out here?"

He shook his head. "I don't know. Since the middle of the afternoon, anyway."

Long enough that it was going to be impossible to get the boot off without cutting it. Without getting it off, she couldn't tell if a bone was broken or if she could hope it was only a sprain. In any case, she wasn't going to be able to do much for Pat out here in the gathering dark.

"What happened?" she asked again.

He looked skyward, and for a moment she thought he wasn't going to answer. "Fool that I am, I was riding along the creek, trying to head off some yearling calves, and my horse stepped in a badger hole and fell head over heels, and me with him. I managed to kick out of my stirrups and land on my feet, but I came down hard, and now my leg won't hold me."

"Where's your horse?"

"Last I saw, he was back on four legs and headed out on a hard lope. I was hoping he'd go home and somebody would come looking for me. Mil, I don't suppose you've got any water with you?"

She untied her canteen from Smokey's saddle and held it for him when she saw his hands shaking, and he gulped gratefully until she took the canteen away.

"That's enough for now, Pat. I want to make sure you can keep it down."

"I'd crawled farther into the hawthorns hoping I'd find a stick stout enough for me to hobble out on, but of course nothing but hawthorn twigs. But it was shady in there, out of the sun, and I must have slept for a while—"

Or been concussed, she thought. If anybody had come looking for him, they'd surely have been here by now. Of course, if he'd been lying concussed in the underbrush, he'd be easy to miss.

"I can leave you here and go for help, or I can try to get you up on Smokey. What do you think?"

He would know as well as she did that no help was closer than her cabin, an hour's ride away and at least an hour back with the help. "I'll try Smokey," he said. "Do you think he'll let me mount from the Indian side?"

"He's pretty good," Mildred said. She was thinking how best to go about getting him on the horse. Even though the moon had risen, it was too dark down here in the creek bottom to find sticks for splints or a crutch. But she thought if Pat could get himself up on his good right leg, she could steady him enough for him to reach the stirrup and mount. She led Smokey down the slight slope and dropped his bridle reins, trusting him to stand ground tied with his right side turned uphill.

"Ready to try it?"

By hanging on to the stirrup with one hand and Mildred's hand with the other, he was able to stand on his right leg, although she could tell from his breathing what it was costing him. Now the hard part. Luckily, he was cowboy spare, all muscle and bone, and she was young and strong. She wrapped her arms around his left thigh and braced herself and lifted him until he could grip the saddle horn and cantle and take part of his own weight long enough to get his right foot in the stirrup and swing his injured leg up and over. He sat bowed in the saddle for a moment, recovering himself.

Smokey snorted at the unfamiliar right-side mounting but thankfully stood for it. Mildred gathered his reins and patted his neck and led him to the level ground by the creek crossing, and Pat raised himself enough to slide behind the cantle so she could swing into the saddle in front of him. She felt Pat's arms close around her waist, steadying himself, as she turned Smokey toward the creek and the long trail on the other side.

It was fully dark by the time they cleared the last swell of prairie and Mildred could see the widening bend of Plum Creek and the outline of her cabin roof. She had been thankful the past hour for the full moon and Smokey's sure footing. No light showed from her cabin, of course, but farther down the creek a window in Renny's shack glowed and Mildred rode toward it with Pat's head resting on her shoulder. Except for his grip around her waist, she would have doubted he was conscious.

"Renny!" she shouted at the closed and shadowed door. "Renny!"

What to do. Renny's dogs had roused from the shadows, but they recognized her and Smokey and weren't barking. She couldn't dismount without risking another fall for Pat, and she couldn't lift him down from Smokey by herself. She was considering riding closer and pounding on the door with her canteen, when it suddenly opened on Renny holding a lamp in one hand and pulling up his suspenders with the other. Of course. He'd been going to bed and had to pull on his pants before he could answer the door.

"Mildred? What the hell?"

Then he took in Smokey's double load, set down the lamp, and hurried to lift down Pat, who cried out sharply in his exhaustion.

"It's Pat Adams! Is he hurt bad?"

"I can't tell yet. If you can carry him inside, I'll take care of Smokey and be right with you."

Renny lifted Pat from Smokey and turned, burly as an old bear, toward the shack, with the young man over his shoulder, and Mildred rode down to the corrals, feeling the absence of the warm weight behind her and the arms around her waist. She dismounted and fumbled in the shadows for the familiar gate bar, led Smokey into the corral, and unsaddled and brushed him and grained him by moonlight.

The early June night was young. The Big Dipper hung overhead, and moonlight glazed the corral poles and the roof shingles and the leaves of the cottonwoods her mother had planted around the cabin before Mildred was born. And now Mildred's twenty-eighth birthday was coming up in August, and she felt old, and the cabin was still her home.

She could smell smoke from Renny's chimney and knew he would have started a fire to heat water. Patrick Adams. Too much history there.

Inside the shack, she saw that Renny had laid Pat on his own cot and was helping him with a cup of drinking water. He turned at the sound of the door closing behind Mildred.

"We got to get that boot off," Renny said.

Mildred knelt to look. Pat's left boot was tight as a drum over the swollen ankle. "Renny, have you got a pair of wire cutters here?"

"I think so."

He shuffled off to hunt for wire cutters, and now, by the light of the lamp, Mildred noted for the first time the nasty oblong bruise across Pat's forehead and wondered how he'd taken such a blow to his head from the fall from a horse if he'd landed on his feet. His face was beaded with perspiration. From the pain, or was he feverish? She laid the back of her hand on his forehead and found it hot, and he opened his eyes and reached for her hand.

"Mil."

"We're going to have to cut your boot," she said, pulling away, and just then Renny returned with the wire cutters.

Pat's boots were old, but they had plenty of use left in them, and Mildred hated to ruin them. "If I cut straight down the front," she said, "and across the upper foot, Renny may be able to lace it back together with rawhide."

"Do it," Pat said, and he grimaced as Mildred took the first snip.

"Maybe something a little stronger for him than water," Renny rumbled. He shuffled off again and rummaged and returned with a mason jar of his own hooch, golden brown and sharp smelling when he unscrewed the lid.

Pat took a gulp. "God, that's bad," he said, and took another.

By the time Mildred had snipped all the way down the boot and started across the top of the foot, Pat had raised himself from the cot, and his arms were rigid with his effort not to push her away from his foot.

"Just another few inches," she said. There might have been history between her and Pat, but she hated hurting him. Then she reached the toe of the boot, and Renny laid a hand on Pat's shoulder as she eased off the mutilated boot. By the light of the lamp Renny held up, she saw the blood-sodden sock and the wound where the bone had broken through the skin. Renny was shaking his head.

"It's going to be bad, Pat."

"Yeah." He lay back.

Mildred went to pour water from Renny's kettle into a basin and scrub up, and Renny, joining her at the washstand, asked, "What are you going to have to do?"

"It's broken just above the ankle. Once I get that sock off, I can tell how bad it is. The bone's got to be set and splinted if he's going to walk again. We could load him in the back of the truck and take him to Fort Maginnis to the hospital, but that long trip in the dark, and all that jolting—"

"I'd trust you farther with my leg than that damned sawbones they got there."

"I'd trust myself farther too."

She finished scrubbing up and poured fresh water into a clean basin. "Cut me some real thin slats of kindling and tear some strips of rags for bindings. If you don't have rags, I have some at the cabin. And you can give him a little more of that hooch."

The bloody sock wouldn't yield to the wire cutters. Mildred had scissors in her black bag, but Renny was handing her his sharp skinning knife, so she used it to slice and peel the sock back and drop it into a bucket. With the knife, she slit Pat's pant leg to the knee, and then she could see that the break was above the ankle, which was the only fortunate thing about it. She bathed away the blood with a cloth and used a little of the hooch to clean the wound, hoping it would disinfect it, although she had known it would sting.

Renny was back with the rag strips and the splints of kindling. "This is the bad part, Pat," Mildred said, and he nodded.

"You'll have to hold him and brace him, Renny."

Renny nodded. Otherwise, she'd pull Pat toward her and off the cot when she pulled back his leg to set the bone. On one knee at the head of the cot, Renny gripped Pat under his arms and held Pat's head and shoulders against his own chest. Braced himself.

Her trained fingers found the break, and she took a moment to think through what she needed to do and when. Not her first broken bone, she reminded herself. And then she caught his foot and ankle and wrenched back with all her strength while Renny held firm against her force, and she felt the bone move and meet itself where it should. Pat arched his back on the cot, struggling against Renny and thrusting upward, and uttered an inhuman sound through his clenched teeth that woke Renny's dogs and brought them barking outside the door.

"It's done," she said, and went about bandaging and binding the splints to the leg.

Pat lay back, breathing hard. "Mil, Jesus Christ," he gasped, and took another breath. "I love you, Mil," he whispered.

Renny found a couple of relatively clean glasses and poured himself and Mildred each an inch of hooch. They sat at his table with the wick of the lamp turned low and listened as Pat's breathing evened and slowed.

To sit in the same room with Pat. To hear his breathing. "He'll sleep now," she said. "Best thing for him."

"You need to sleep."

"I suppose we need to let Ferrell Adams know?" Mildred ventured.

"That can wait for morning. Ferrell will want to come and get him, the bastard."

Mildred sipped her hooch and let her mind skip over what she knew about Pat's relationship with his father. She was beyond tired, and she was seeing, with a deceptive clarity, the board walls of the shack and Renny's bearded face across the table from her and Pat on Renny's cot with his eyes closed and his leg elevated on a stack of firewood topped by a pillow. Pat's whispered words had jolted her, and she hoped Renny had not overheard.

And not that she blamed Renny. She shared his disgust for Pat's father. Renny, whom she had known all her life. Renny, who had saved her. Renny's face across the table blurred and receded.

"Good God, girl, go up to the cabin and go to bed!"

"But . . ." she glanced toward the cot.

"Don't worry about him. I'll get up with him if he needs me."

"Where are you going to sleep?"

"Don't worry about me, neither. I got a mattress in the back room."

Mildred let herself out and followed the familiar trail back up to the cabin. The cooling night air cleared her head, and she paused halfway to listen to the quiet lapping of the creek current and a cry, unrepeated, from some night bird on the hunt. The moon was moving on, but she could see the outlines of the cottonwoods along the creek and the bluffs on the other side. Below her, obscure in the shadows, were the shack and barn and corrals just as her father had planned and laid them out and Renny had helped him build.

She shook herself. Renny was right—she needed to get some sleep.

Two steps up to the front porch. A door opening into the front room. Kerosene lamp waiting on the table by the door. Mildred felt for the matchbox and took out a match and lit the lamp and saw paneled walls and river rock fireplace and sedate old furniture come back to life.

Feet, keep walking, one step at a time. Hands, set the lamp on the table by the bed. Mind, think about undressing fully, washing—no. Boots kicked off, belt and Levi's dropped on the floor. Mildred fell across her bed, and that was that.

2

Daylight through the uncurtained window woke her. The time! She rose on an elbow and saw by the clock on the top of the dresser that it was past eight. When had she slept this late? She swung her bare legs over the side of the bed and sat for a moment, collecting herself. The Svoboda baby, the long ride home. Pat Adams. And she had been dreaming.

She pulled her Levi's back on, buckled her belt, and padded barefoot through the cabin's front room to the kitchen, where she thought about starting a fire in the range and boiling water for coffee and a wash. No, she decided, it would take too much time. Renny probably had made coffee, and she needed to know what had been happening while she slept. She poured cold water from the kettle into a basin and rinsed her mouth and washed her face and hands, and then she found her old moccasins under the kitchen table and hooked them over her bare feet. About to leave the kitchen, she caught sight of herself in the little mirror on the door with her hair stringing about her face, and she took another minute to comb and rebraid it and throw the braid back over her shoulder.

Full sunlight and cloudless blue. Another dry summer ahead of them in what was beginning to seem like endless drought. As Mildred started down the trail toward the shack, she could see Smokey asleep in his corral with one hock comfortably raised. The calf had been turned into his pen, the milk cow into her pasture. So Renny was up and had done the chores. Probably somebody had gotten word to Ferrell Adams by now, and he had come and fetched Pat home.

The last time she had seen Pat would have been about this time a year ago, she thought. Word was that he had come home from law school for his mother's funeral. Renny had talked Mildred into going to a bull sale with him, out at the Bodleians' ranch. Neighbors stood around the corral, getting ready to bid as one of the two-year-old Bodleian Hereford bulls was led out, and she had seen Pat on the other side of the small crowd just as he caught sight of her and started around the corral toward her, and she had ducked away and found Renny.

Pat's bloody face . . .

She shook her head to clear it. When was she going to rid herself of that image?

She opened the door of the shack to the scents of a pitch pine fire in the stove and coffee and to the sight of Pat propped up on Renny's cot and Renny sitting on a chair beside him, both of them drinking coffee and looking downright companionable. That was something, she supposed.

"He won't let me get up," said Pat.

"He'd better not."

"Told him I'd break his goddamn neck if he tried," growled Renny.

She laid the back of her hand on Pat's forehead and found it cool. "Any coffee left, or did the two of you drink it all?"

"There's plenty," said Renny, "and there's oatmeal in the pan. Better have some."

Mildred found a cup at the back of a shelf and wiped out the dust and poured coffee from the pot on the stove and sat at Renny's kitchen table, not quite with her back to the two men.

"We was thinking," said Renny after a few minutes, "the best thing might be to take him to Fort Maginnis and have the sisters put some plaster on that leg."

"We could do that," said Mildred. She was thinking that at the hospital she would see Sister St. Paul. Suddenly she very much wanted to see Sister St. Paul. "Sure, we could do that."

She turned to find Pat's eyes on her. "Do you want to go home first?" she asked him. "And ask if your father can take you to town?"

"No."

Something she couldn't read was written across his face, and she had to look away. Trouble there.

"Okay," said Renny. He drank the last of his coffee and stood. "You want a smoke?" he asked Pat.

"You got the makings?"

Renny dug his can of Prince Albert and cigarette papers out of his shirt pocket and tossed them to Pat. "What do you think, Mil? Can he ride in the cab, or would he be better off in the bed of the truck?"

"The bed, I think. I want to keep his leg elevated."

And Renny nodded and went off to drive the truck up to the shack.

"Mil."

"I don't want to hear it," she said. "I just don't want to hear it."

And she meant to keep her eyes on the table, with its frayed oilcloth with a pattern of cherries and leaves almost worn off by use—where had Renny come by such an oilcloth?—but her head seemed to turn on its own, and Pat smiled at her, Pat's smile that could light a room.

"Hell, I was just going to tell you thanks for dragging me out of the weeds," he said. He took a deep pull on the cigarette he had rolled from Renny's makings and smiled at her again. "Mil. It always going to be like this with you and me?"

"Maybe," she said.

"Maybe."

Renny came back and got his mattress from the back room and carried it out to lay in the bed of the truck. Came back again.

"Ready?" He lifted Pat from the cot, and Mildred followed with the firewood and pillow to elevate the leg.

"We could prop him up a little," said Renny, and went back into the shack for a couple of sugans, which he rolled up and slid behind Pat's shoulders.

"Mildred, are you riding up front or back here to keep an eye on him?"

"Back here."

Renny looked from Pat to Mildred and shook his head. "Guess you're more liable to kill him than the other way around," he told her, and shut the tailgate and climbed in the cab.

The dirt road, deeply rutted with truck tracks after spring rains that had fallen too briefly, climbed out of the creek bottom and teetered its way up the side of the bluff, where little grew but sparse bunchgrass, and shards of quartz sparkled where the sun found them. Once on higher prairie, the road angled through sage and shortgrass and met the county road, where it passed a collapsed and scavenged heap of rubble and weeds that had been the Seniffs' homestead shack. Renny turned east on the county road, where he could make better time without jolting Pat so badly. At thirty miles an hour, they were still an hour from Fort Maginnis.

Sagebrush country all the way to the mountains. Sagebrush sprouting back across fields that once had been ploughed and seeded. It was a worn-out country, Mildred often thought. Old before its time, empty and getting emptier. Long ago when it was young, it had teemed with deer and antelope, and Mildred wished she could have seen it then. Renny said that when he was a boy, a patient hunter in hiding often could lure a curious antelope within rifle range by fluttering a white handkerchief.

Pat drew on the last of his cigarette and stubbed out the butt on the truck bed. Now that they were on the graveled and graded road, a little color had returned to his face. He reached for her hand and drew her toward him—"You might as well lean on these quilts of Renny's"—and didn't let go. Now her shoulder was an inch from his. Her hand in Pat's was browner from the sun than his, although law school hadn't honed off all his cowboy callouses. His fingernails, cleaner than a cowboy's would be. Knowing he was looking down at her, trying to distract herself from the warmth of his hand, Mildred gazed out at the passing prairie and caught a glimpse of something white—trash caught in a sagebrush root, she thought, as it fluttered and grew smaller in the distance as the truck rumbled along.

"Maybe," said Pat. "But maybe not."

Think about the antelope, she told herself, drawn step by hesitant step toward the fluttering white rag. But the deer and antelope and even the rabbits had been hunted out by hungry homesteaders; the homesteaders themselves, a depleted population from the drought that came and came again and starved them out. Mildred was luckier than most. Her father had settled here before the Montana Territory got statehood, and he had had a little money and years to establish himself in his prime creek bottom ahead of the big land boom and flood of emigrants in 1910. She had been lucky, even—she pulled back from the dark edges of that thought—that her history with Pat had brought her to Sister St. Paul.

Fort Maginnis, nestled in the bottomland along Spring Creek and overlooked by low mountains, had been a town for nearly fifty years, and the Hospital of the Good Samaritan and St. Rose's convent and church and school had stood on Upper Main Street for forty years, although the dressed sandstone buildings always felt as eternal to Mildred as the mountains beyond the town, and somehow just as reassuring. Been there all her life, after all, the mountains and the hospital and the convent. Renny parked by the front entrance and got out to hunt up a nun and maybe some orderlies.

Pat had not let go her hand, and he and Mildred sat side by side in the midmorning sun that bounced off the sandstone hospital walls and heated the metal of the truck bed. Mildred felt sweat crawling under her hat and through her hair and down her neck. What had become of Pat's hat? Renny was returning, followed by a nun in a white nursing habit and two men with a stretcher between them.

Pat's shoulder touched hers. "My brown-haired girl. Will you kiss me, Mil?"

She understood he was saying goodbye to her, and she turned to him and felt the light brush of his lips. Then Renny was helping transfer Pat to the stretcher. Mildred watched the nun in the white habit walk ahead and hold the hospital door open for the orderlies who carried Pat away. Saw the door shut behind them.

"So," Renny said. "You wanted to visit Sister? What, a couple hours, and I'll come back for you?"

Mildred nodded, thankful he'd said nothing of the kiss he'd seen. He gave her a hand to jump down from the truck bed. "Couple hours, then," he said, and drove off.

Mildred walked past a fenced yard where chickens chased a black-habited young nun who was scattering feed. Mildred didn't know her; sometimes the nuns came and departed. But she called out her question, and the nun nodded, yes, Sister St. Paul was in her study.

The familiar door, the familiar foyer of the convent. The familiar painted statues—Christ with his crown of thorns, the Virgin with her child in her arms, St. Rose with her crown of roses—just as they had encircled the foyer during the years Mildred had lived here and gone to school.

Her father had protested, "High school? For a ranch girl? For *this* girl? A girl like her shouldn't show her face away from home."

Sister St. Paul answered him in a tone Mildred later would see priests quail before, "She will live here with us. She's a very bright young girl, and she will go to high school."

Four years living at the convent during the school year and attending the new Catholic high school. Her surly father claimed her in the summers and put her to work. But Sister St. Paul had her ways and means, and he brought Mildred back to the convent every fall. Three more years, interrupted by the flu epidemic of 1918 and then resumed, to earn her nursing diploma under the tutelage of the nuns at Good Samaritan. Her father had not lived to see her receive the diploma.

"Mildred!"

Sister St. Paul embraced her in a rattle of beads and a flurry of black habit and stiff coif. She smelled of laundry starch and ink, and she kissed Mildred on both cheeks and embraced her again.

"Come along to the kitchen! That's where the coffee is. Have you eaten? How is everything at the ranch? How is Renny?"

Her voice was faintly accented. Her dark eyes took in Mildred's stained old hat, Mildred's hair falling out of her braid from the ride in the back of the truck, her rumpled and dirty men's clothing, her old moccasins that had been beaded by Renny's aunt Josie Archambault, whom Sister St. Paul knew well. Mildred wished she had had time to change into a decent dress and shoes.

Fresh curtains at the convent kitchen's windows, a little breeze blowing through. A young nun taking loaves of bread from the oven of the wood range turned and smiled, "Mildred!"

"Sister Boniface!"

Another embrace—Sister Boniface and Mildred had graduated together from the Catholic high school—and then Sister Boniface was setting out cups on an oilclothed table and pouring coffee. Just like any ranch kitchen, the coffee pot always at the ready at the back of the range. But the convent kitchen had a sink with a drainboard and cold running water, and it had a light bulb in the ceiling with a cord and a switch hanging down from it.

Sister Boniface slipped away, and Sister St. Paul pulled out chairs. "Sit! Have you eaten? What brings you to town?"

She sliced bread and cheese and set a plate in front of Mildred while Mildred told her the news she knew would interest her. Mrs. Svoboda's long and difficult labor and how in the end Mildred had to use the forceps, so the little boy would have dents on each side of his head for a day or two, but that would pass. The garden Mildred had planted this spring and was keeping alive with buckets of water poured into little ditches between the vegetable rows. Yes, her water well was good—she was lucky there. A couple of days ago they'd even had a little rain. Maybe the drought was finally easing. And Renny had gotten a little bounty and some cash from last winter's trapline, and yes, Renny himself was just fine and probably was visiting Josie right now.

She knew Sister St. Paul was waiting to hear the rest of the story. Sister St. Paul, with her curiously unlined face framed in white, her dark eyes and arched brows, her hair of course hidden under her coif. Sister St. Paul, who once had held fourteen-year-old Mildred on her lap and rocked her and crooned to her. *Sweetie. Sweetie. They won't hurt you again. And you have not sinned.*

So. Finding Pat Adams after his horseback wreck. Helping him on Smokey, riding with him to Renny's shack. Mildred and Renny patching him up and bringing him to town for plaster. Then the part she most dreaded to tell and most needed to tell. How she had let Pat kiss her goodbye and the strange way she now was feeling.

"Patrick Adams."

A pause. Mildred came back to the tranquil kitchen. Her coffee cooling before her, curtains moving slightly at the open windows. A clock ticking from the hallway. So peaceful. So many of the Catholic girls she'd gone to high school with had wanted to become nuns. One of them had become Sister Boniface. That door had been wide open for Mildred, and she had turned away.

"How old are you, Mildred?"

"Almost twenty-eight."

"Do you have a young man?"

She shook her head, thinking that Sister St. Paul already knew the answer to that question. If there had been someone, Mildred would have told her.

"Are you going out at all? They've surely started holding the dances again at the community hall, haven't they? Do you go to the dances?"

"Not really." She couldn't remember how long it had been. No, the last time she had gone to a dance was after the flu epidemic of 1918 finally burned itself out. Pat had mustered out of the army, and word had it he was living in Missoula. But he had been at that dance.

Sister St. Paul took her hand. "Mildred. Mildred."

The ticking clock.

"And now Patrick Adams is laid up with a broken leg, and he's over next door?"

3

Renny drove south to a neighborhood in Fort Maginnis that lay along Spring Creek where it ran through town and eventually joined Plum Creek on its way to the Judith River. Here were the cabins of the old Métis settlement. Tired-looking cottonwood trees and rutted dirt streets where dust rose behind his truck. No sidewalks here. He parked the truck by a chicken wire fence and got out and opened a board gate with a flapping hinge that he reminded himself to fix before he left, also the loose plank on the porch step. And there was Josie at the screen door, peering out to see who her visitor was.

"Renny! My baby!"

He lifted her off her feet in a hug, making her giggle.

"Come out to kitchen, have a glassa my wine! How come you in town, this time a year, Renny? Thought I might not see you till fall!"

Josie was tiny, not quite five feet tall and bird boned. Her round brown face was deeply seamed; her hair, nearly all white except for a few black strands and pulled into a bun. Renny thought that as she aged, she showed their old part-Cree heritage more than he or his father ever had. Dark print dress falling nearly to her ankles, silver cross on a ribbon around her neck. Moccasins, of course. She tugged him out to the kitchen and poured them each a jelly glass of her own chokecherry wine, chattering the whole time. "And I ain't seen you since you brung your furs to town. You got a nickel or two for them, I bet! How you been? How's the little girl?"

"Not so little anymore."

Her black eyes suddenly were watchful, and he knew she wouldn't let him rest until she heard the story.

"Lemme drink some wine first, will you?"

But she kept her eyes on him as he drank. She was past eighty, he knew, and still spry, and her memory went way back, all the way to Canada and the days when their people had followed the buffalo just like the full-bloods. We're Métis, he remembered explaining to Patrick Adams, who as a kid wanted to know all about everything. *Métis* means "mixed." We're mostly mixed French and Cree. Down here in Montana they call us "breeds."

"That goddamn Pat Adams," he said. "The reason we come to town. Goddamn him to hell. He took a fall and broke his leg, and we brung him in to the Good Samaritan."

"Don't swear."

"No. Guess it's the old man I'm swearing at, more than Pat," Renny said, and saw Josie cross herself.

What a country, thought Sister St. Paul. Montana. Too new and too raw.

She had seen Mildred and Renny off from the front steps of the convent, and now she stood with her hands folded in the sleeves of her habit, looking across Main Street and beyond, as far as the deep-blue line of the Snowy Mountains against a pale-blue sky. What this country did to women. To Mildred's mother, dead before her time from overwork. Mildred living out there now, such a pretty girl, and miles from town with no company for weeks on end except for Renny and a shrinking scatter of neighbors whose babies she delivered and whose scrapes and bruises and coughs she doctored. Sister St. Paul wondered how many of those neighbors Mildred and Renny, between them, had nursed through the flu epidemic that had closed the schools and canceled the community hall dances. People in this country didn't talk about their ailments. They either got better and lived, or they didn't. These things happen, they were likely to say to a sympathizer.

What else they didn't talk about.

Mildred's mother dying just when Mildred needed her the most.

Fourteen years ago Sister St. Paul had been angry beyond angry, angry enough to murder. She had confessed her anger to Father Quinn and done penance and received absolution, and still the anger lurked around the edges of her mind.

Well. She was also a count-to-ten woman.

She turned her back on the convent and walked over to the hospital, nodding to one or two nursing nuns she met as she entered the double doors into the familiar hospital hush, and followed the wide corridor to the stairs and climbed them to the second floor. She tapped on the third door and opened it.

The fair-haired young man looked up from his book as she entered. "Sister St. Paul," he said, surprised. So he remembered her.

"Patrick Adams. How are you feeling?"

"All right."

She sat in the visitor's chair by the bed, and he laid his book aside and didn't look away or try to avoid her eyes, although she knew he would be on his guard with her. He had taken a savage blow to his forehead, she noted. But the nursing sisters had cleaned him up and put his leg in traction.

"I hear you had bad luck last night."

"No," he said. "I had damned good luck—I beg your pardon, Sister. I had beautiful luck last night. If Mil hadn't happened to be riding home along Plum Creek, and if her horse hadn't spooked at me, I'd still be out there."

Propped up in his hospital bed with his left leg encased in plaster and elevated, he smiled at her, and although she was suspicious of his charm, she couldn't help but smile back. And she saw him relax against his pillow.

"It's good to see you, Sister."

"How long will you be laid up?"

"Couple months, they're saying. Then they can take the plaster off, and I can walk in a brace."

His youth and health would help heal him, of course, if the forced inactivity didn't kill him first. His physicality was obvious. The wide shoulders, the muscled arms. She had a feeling he was going to make a difficult patient. And she still hadn't found an opening to ask the questions she wanted to ask him.

"They tell me that you finished law school this spring?"

He nodded, and she could tell he was trying to divine her direction. He had a good face. Handsome even, except for the off-kilter nose that had been broken and never straightened properly, and now of course the deep welt across his forehead.

Intelligence in the blue eyes. A day's growth of stubble that no one had shaved for him. She made a mental note to leave instructions for the evening shift.

"Before law school, you were in the war? In France?"

"Yeah. I was in Black Jack Pershing's army. Gesnes—"

"So close to where I grew up," she burst. She knew from letters from home that the fighting had been terrible and the town, ruined.

"Yes," he agreed, as though he read her thought. "The last time I saw the town, it was pretty bad."

The destruction of Gesnes had been in late September 1918, almost seven years ago now. Her grief still felt fresh. And then had come the November armistice so shortly after.

"And then you shipped home?"

"Yeah. And finished college and started law school."

"Well," she said, and stood. She wasn't getting what she wanted. "Dr. Naylor won't keep you here the whole two months if you have somewhere else to go. Once he's sure there's no infection and you're healing, he'll discharge you, and your folks can take you home and wait on you there."

"I don't know what I'll do, but I won't go back to the ranch," Pat said.

Then he surprised her again.

"Sister. What happened. I would do anything if I could make it not have happened. And I'll never let Mil be hurt again if I can help it."

His blue gaze burned her. "And yeah, Sister. I want her. Is that what you wanted to know?"

"Thank you for not hurting her," she said when she found the words. She felt drawn to touch his stubble-roughened cheek with her fingertips, but instead, she nodded and left his room.

The day after she and Renny returned from Fort Maginnis, Mildred saddled Smokey and rode back along Plum Creek toward the Svoboda crossing. She had strapped her black bag to her saddle, along with her canteen, thinking that as long as she rode as far as Svoboda's creek crossing, she might as well ride farther and see how the new baby and his mother were doing.

It was another perfect morning. The grass had perked up from last week's rain, enough to give everyone hope. Clear blue sky, slight breeze, the sound of the creek current talking to itself. Berries hanging in green clusters from the chokecherry bushes to be picked when they ripened and given to Josie Archambault for her wine making. Mildred heard a meadowlark's liquid six-note whistle from somewhere above her on the bluff, and once she saw a hawk riding a thermal stream. But for the most part, she gave loose bridle reins to Smokey and sat back in the saddle and gave herself to the rhythm of riding horseback, the sense of being one with the big animal, his moving muscles, his regular gait, his belly rumblings, and the saddle creaking under her.

After an hour they came to Svoboda's crossing, and she let Smokey drink before she rode across the creek and located the place where she had found Pat. She led Smokey into the hawthorns for the shade and the protection from flies and tied him to a branch, and then she found herself a boulder that must have tumbled down the bluff in some past eon to rest above the creek.

And she sat and listened to the current and wished it would tell her what was worrying her. Think, she told herself.

Pat had said he was riding to head off yearling calves when his horse stepped in a badger hole and cartwheeled head over heels and threw him. The horse recovered its footing and headed for home, leaving Pat with his broken leg.

She could picture the scene well enough: the horse and rider tearing along at top speed to head off cattle, the horse stepping in the hole and cartwheeling, and the rider kicking out of his stirrups before he was flung headlong.

Hole. Badger hole. What badger dug holes down here in the hawthorns?

What rider took a horse full tilt through hawthorn brush? Smokey was a good brush horse, knowing when to duck his head and plough his way through, but she wouldn't think of trying full tilt with him. They both would have been slashed by thorns.

She had seen no scratches on Pat's face or hands.

That horse and feckless rider would have left a trail of ripped thorns and broken branches. It had been less than two days since she had come upon Pat, and she could see scuffs and crushed grass where he had crawled but no signs that any creature, let alone a horse and rider, had torn through these hawthorns at a gallop. She got up from her boulder and walked farther up the creek and saw branches that were doing just fine with their menace of thorns and their leaves drooping with trail dust. Haw berries just setting on.

She did make a discovery, about twenty yards deeper into the hawthorns from the place where Pat had startled Smokey. A stained and battered cream-colored Stetson hat that once had been expensive.

Pat had not been wearing a hat when he crawled out of the haws. She turned it over in her hands. His hat.

Then some instinct sent her crouching down among the hawthorn roots. A shod horse was jogging down the trail. As it came closer, she heard the jingle of bridle chains, and she flattened herself, not daring to look up for fear of drawing the rider's eyes. Then she did look up quickly and down again, because she had recognized the rider.

Ferrell Adams. The unmistakable bull face and bull shoulders of the man. The dark mustache. How she knew that face! From the sounds of his horse's hoofs, she guessed he rode as far as the creek before he turned and rode back, more slowly. After he passed her hiding place, she raised her head again and saw that he was leaning from the saddle, examining one side of the trail and then the other. Looking for something.

She was pretty sure she had led Smokey deeply enough into the haws to be hidden, and she prayed he wouldn't whinny at the other horse. He hadn't so far, her good horse Smokey.

The sounds of the shod hoofs faded, and still she crouched in the haws and counted to a hundred. She heard nothing but the creek current and a cow bawling for her calf from far upstream, and she dared to crawl over to Smokey and untie him and ride for home.

"Don't make any sense," said Renny. He'd carried a jar of his hooch up to Mildred's cabin and poured them both a little. Now he was sitting across from her in one of the old leather armchairs by the cold fireplace.

"Nother thing that bothers me about that story," Renny went on, "when I come to think about it. What the hell was Pat doing, working cattle at the crossing? That's Stan Svoboda's bottomland there."

Mildred hadn't told him about the hat, which she had brought home and set on top of the dresser in her bedroom, next to the clock. If it held any secrets, it wasn't telling.

Renny sipped his hooch and thought about it. "Whatever Pat was up to, I don't spose he was rustling Stan's cattle. A course, I never knowed Pat to be a liar, either."

"No," said Mildred. But she knew Pat had lied to her. The only part of his story she was sure about was his broken leg. That and the welt across his forehead.

"I woulda thought," said Renny, "from a fall like he told it, he'd a been more liable to break his neck than his leg. And that welt on his head."

She nodded. She had thought of that.

"So you never got up to see the Svoboda baby? Tell you what. If you want, I'll saddle up Pink tomorrow and ride with you. I wouldn't mind visiting with Stan."

4

The best time to catch Stan in the house would be early evening, which meant the Svobodas would invite her and Renny to stay for supper as a matter of ordinary ranch courtesy. So the next morning, Mildred kneaded bread dough and covered it to rise, and after she had helped with the chores and watered her garden, she fired up the kitchen range and baked the loaves so she would have a couple to carry in a pillowcase to Mrs. Svoboda. By the time the loaves were brown, the kitchen was uncomfortably warm, so she went out and sat on the porch with a glass of water from the Red Wing cooler and let her thoughts roam from Sister St. Paul to Josie—Renny had handed Mildred a paper sack when he picked her up at the convent, saying, "Here! Josie said to give these to the little girl," and Mildred had opened the sack and found a new pair of beautifully beaded moccasins—but inevitably her thoughts returned to the hat on top of her dresser, which kept a silent presence of its own.

Pat, damn him. It wasn't as though she and Pat even knew each other now. It had been too long, and they had been children when it happened, or at least she had been a child. Fourteen. Pat had been sixteen and boarding in Fort Maginnis to attend high school, so she hadn't seen much of him until that summer and their month of nights. And he hadn't quite hated his father yet.

Pat's bloody face—damn it! Forget it!

She hadn't even realized he was lying to her until she tried to fit together the pieces of his story. That was how well she didn't know him.

Renny's mare, Pink, was a rangy part Thoroughbred, part Hambletonian he'd picked up as a filly years ago from a racetrack somewhere. Maybe she had a strain of mustang in her to explain her strawberry roan coat and her mean streak, but she had the long Hambletonian stride and probably was the fastest horse in Murray County even at her age. Well, Renny needed a lot of horse to carry him, and he wasn't so young himself. Mildred, already mounted on Smokey, watched as Renny threw his saddle, one-handed, across Pink and cinched it and led her around the corral a time or two to get the hump out of her back before he heaved himself up and astride her.

Once in the saddle, of course, he was a deft and natural rider. Born with horse sense, like all his people. And he had taught Mildred to ride and passed some of the horse sense on to her. But she hadn't noticed that his rifle was in his saddle scabbard until they rode out of the corral together.

Last night she had caught herself fantasizing her way back into the hawthorns, where she had crouched and watched Ferrell Adams ride away from her, and this time, she had her rifle with her and took aim. It would have been an easy shot. She could see the squares of his plaid shirt through her rifle sights and feel her finger tightening on the trigger as vividly as though she really were drawing a bead on him—which plaid square to pick? She had to shake her head at herself, fantasizing about shooting Ferrell Adams in the back.

Renny's dogs started to follow as he and Mildred rode away from the corral. But he shouted something guttural in his patois, and they slunk back under the steps of the shack. Warm day. Mildred felt the sun on her back and shoulders and the trickles of sweat starting under her hat as she and Renny spurred Smokey and Pink into easy trots. How often they had ridden together, for miles sometimes, often with the comfort of silence between them, after caring for their neighbors during the flu epidemic.

The epidemic had taken a lot out of everyone, but it was behind them now. She hoped it was behind them. Only luck had kept her and Renny healthy as it ran its course.

At the crossing, they let the horses drink before riding upstream. Renny's eyes were on the trail, and Mildred looked where he pointed and saw the hoofprints of the shod horse.

"Looks like he rode back and forth a couple a times," he said. "Wonder what he was looking for."

The sun was lower when they reached the Svoboda house, but the air on the benchland was scorching. Stan Svoboda likely had spotted the two riders when they emerged from the creek bottom, half a mile away, because he was waiting in the open door.

"Ren-nee! Mild-reed! Tie up tha horses! Come een! Mama, we got compan-ee for supper!"

The Svoboda house had started as a tar paper shack and then had been added to and sided with boards salvaged from the shacks of departed neighbors. Now it had solid shingles on its roof and glass windows with curtains. Inside, a good-sized room with an iron cooking range and a woodbox at one end and a door into a bedroom at the other. A ladder to a loft for the older children. Bare studs on the inner walls, layers of newspapers pasted between the studs for insulation. An embroidered cloth on the table, crocheted white doilies pinned to the backs of chairs. A crucifix hung from one stud, a small framed picture of the Virgin and child from another. The Svobodas were Catholics, of course, like all their eastern European neighbors who had poured into the country fifteen years ago and tried dryland farming and mostly starved out in the drought.

Catlickers and bohunks, their more established and mostly Protestant rancher neighbors had called them. Mildred's father, for one, although as far as she knew, he'd never objected to the beads Renny always kept in his shirt pocket.

And here was Mrs. Svoboda, smiling and wiping her hands on her apron before embracing Mildred and kissing her on both cheeks. "And you brought bread! Ag-nees! Set plates for Ren-nee and Mild-reed!"

Agnes, the ten-year-old, hopped to obey, and Mrs. Svoboda returned to the stove to stir her pot. Supper would be beans with chunks of beef, canned last fall at butchering time. Mildred looked around for something to help with, and then the baby cried from the bedroom. Mrs. Svoboda pushed her pot to the back of the stove and went to rescue him, and Mildred followed.

She leaned on the foot of the bed while Mrs. Svoboda unpinned the little boy's diaper, and then she laid a finger in each starfish hand and tested his grip. And she felt his elbows and knees and pedaled his arms at the shoulders and his legs at the hips.

"He's perfect," she said, and watched Mrs. Svoboda pin a clean diaper in place while the baby stopped crying and looked up at his mother with unfocused blue eyes. Four days old, and already his mother was up and cooking meals and keeping a spotless house. Dr. Naylor in Fort Maginnis would have told the nursing nuns to keep her in bed for ten days, and when they did let her on her feet, she would be almost too weak to walk.

"What is his name?"

"Joseph!"

Mildred felt the familiar pang. Sister St. Paul had told her it was unlikely she could conceive again.

After supper, Mildred heated a pan of water and washed the dishes, over Mrs. Svoboda's protests, while little Agnes dried them and Renny and Stan sat at the table and stretched out their legs and rolled cigarettes and smoked them and talked about the weather.

"Cattle doing all right?" she heard Renny ask.

"Pretty good. That little rain helped. And the grass is still good along the crick. Not so good here on top."

"Hm. Neighbors doing any riding?"

"Ain't seen them two cowboys of Adams's for a spell. I think they drove his cattle over east. Maybe better grass that way."

Silence. Long drags on cigarettes, puffs of smoke.

"Seen old man Adams himself, though—when was it, Mama? You remember I remarked on it?"

Mrs. Svoboda gave him a look. "It was the day Mildred came and helped little Joey into the world. You don't remember that, Stan?"

"Yeah, Mama, I remember that. And I remember I seen old Adams yesterday too. Wondered at the time what it took to get the old bastard on horseback twice in one week."

"*Stan!*"

"What he is."

Renny stubbed out his cigarette and shook his head. "Have to wonder what he's up to."

Pat Adams already was fed up with lying in bed with his left leg hoisted, and not a damned thing he could do about it but shift his back and butt the little he could on the mattress. Too much time to think was the worst of it. He knew he needed to talk to somebody trustworthy, and he knew of one. So he scribbled a note and folded it and asked the night nurse if she'd see that Sister St. Paul got it.

Sister was sitting at his bedside when he opened his eyes the next morning. Her practiced eyes took him in.

"You're looking better," she said. "Maybe a little worse tempered. How do you feel?"

"All right. Well, no, I don't, but . . ." He couldn't think how to continue. Complaining wasn't him.

She turned the hand crank on his bed so he could sit partway up. "Is that better?"

"Thanks."

"The morning nurse will be bringing your breakfast tray soon," she said, and then she folded her hands into her sleeves and listened while Pat told her how he'd really come by a broken leg and a dent in his forehead. She didn't interrupt but let him finish, and then she got up and walked to the window overlooking Main Street and beyond. Blue line of the Snowies, lighter blue early morning sky. She stood at the window long enough to count slowly to ten, Pat thought, before she turned.

"That's not what you told Mildred had happened," she said.

"No. I don't know why. To protect her, maybe. Don't know why I'd want to cover for him, but—Sister, nothing was exactly clear to me that day."

"No," she said. "I don't suppose so."

Sister St. Paul controlled her anger long enough to get out of Pat's room, but counting to ten or even ten thousand wasn't going to do it for her now. She strode along the corridor and down the stairs, taking an unholy satisfaction at the sight of nursing nuns ducking around corners or hiding in patients' rooms at the sound of her shoes on the tiled floor. She fumed out of the hospital and over to the convent, down the hallway, and into the kitchen, where, at the sight of her face, Sister Boniface, who had been peeling potatoes, thought of somewhere else she had to be and dropped her paring knife and vanished.

Sister St. Paul picked up the paring knife and went back to the hallway. "Bonny!" And Sister Boniface reappeared.

"Please be so kind as to tell Father McHugh I need to talk to him," she said, and Sister Boniface nodded and fled in a rush of skirts.

Sister St. Paul, still carrying the forgotten paring knife, walked down the hallway to the convent's parlor to receive Father McHugh, where she sat and remembered the rage that had overcome her fourteen years ago.

"He should be arrested and prosecuted for murder!" she had shouted at Sheriff Tull, while poor Father Quinn, God rest his soul, wrung his hands. "For murder, and for attempted murder! She's *fourteen*!"

"Sister," Sheriff Tull had said. "Sister. With all due respect. I know. I know. And you're absolutely right. But if you bring this story out in the open, that little girl's life really will be ruined. This way, if everybody keeps quiet, at least she has a chance of growing up and marrying a good man someday."

Now in the convent parlor, Sister St. Paul remembered that she was holding the paring knife by its blade—the things little French farm girls learned to do!—and she stood and flung the knife at the heavy wood parlor door, where it stuck, quivering.

She felt better from the force of her own arm. Well.

The door opened, and in walked the new young priest, Father Hugh McHugh. He took off his hat, turned to hang it up, and saw the paring knife stuck in the door. Looked from the knife to Sister St. Paul.

"Pray for me, Father," she said, and he laid his hand on her head, over her veil, and began reciting the familiar Latin words.

In the comfort of the parlor, over coffee fetched by Sister Boniface, Sister St. Paul told Pat's story to Father McHugh. At least, what Pat could remember, which wasn't everything.

"What do you make of it?" she asked Father McHugh, who had set aside his cup and saucer to listen.

The priest shook his head. He was a fair-haired man, almost as fair-haired as Patrick Adams and not much older. He'd been living in the rectory only a month, but he somehow seemed to have his feet more firmly on the ground than poor Father Quinn ever had.

"It's worrying," he said. "For one thing, do you think his father knows where he is? Now?"

The hospital corridors, so quiet at night. Hardly anyone awake except the nun at the admittance desk and the nursing sisters on the floors.

"I hadn't thought about that."

"I'll talk to the police chief in the morning and ask him to have a car parked in front of the hospital at night. And when it comes time for Patrick Adams to be discharged, we'll find somewhere safe for him."

"I do have a thought about that."

Josie Archambault's little back room. Nothing much in it but egg crates and canning jars and Josie's top secret winery. And Josie's strapping grandniece, Evangeline, who'd be glad to earn a few dollars doing whatever heavy lifting and care Pat might still need.

"And Sister, the county prosecutor must be notified. And the sheriff. Even if young Adams wants to keep quiet for whatever reason. Because what about the girl?"

"He said he was afraid for her. And there's more I have to tell you," she said.

And she told the priest what had happened to Mildred, all those years ago, and why nothing had been done about it, and she saw the change in his face.

"I'll drive out to the Harrington ranch tomorrow," he said, "if you can tell me the way. And doesn't René Archambault live out there? Josie's nephew?"

Ren-aye, he pronounced Renny's name, accenting the last syllable. A pronunciation Sister St. Paul had cured herself of, years ago. Everybody else, even his people, said *Renny*.

"Yes. He does."

"Thanks for the coffee," he said, getting up. "And may I borrow this chair?"

"Of course. But why?"

"To sit on," he said, "outside Patrick Adams's room tonight."

"But what if Ferrell Adams does turn up?"

"Sister," said Father McHugh, "there you do me an injustice. If he comes after me with his crowbar, he'll rue it. In fact, I kinda wish he would."

Then he laughed at her expression. "Sister, back in Boston I was a boxing champion."

He added, "Of course, we can always get you to throw your paring knife at him," and left her speechless.

5

Mildred dropped the pump handle and straightened with a full bucket of water in each hand. She opened the gate in the chicken wire fence she and Renny had built around her garden, poured her water into the ditches between vegetable rows, and was turning back to pump more water when she saw the unfamiliar black automobile rumble around the bend in the road and stop in front of Renny's shack. Renny's dogs hurried out to bark and bristle as a man in a black suit and a round black hat got out of the automobile and knocked on the door. Of course, Renny wouldn't be home at this time of day. Renny had saddled Pink and ridden out early to bring in the workhorses for haying, but maybe this man didn't know much about ranchers. She didn't know when she'd ever seen a man in a suit this far from town. And so she set down her buckets and walked down a few yards where he would see her.

"Can I help you?"

He looked up. "Are you Miss Mildred Harrington?"

"Yes."

She watched him walk up the rise in the road toward her. He had a spring to his step, whoever he was. Then he stood opposite her, removing his hat and smiling down at her, and she saw his dog collar and his gold cross, and he was offering his hand.

"I'm so pleased to meet you, Miss Harrington. I am Father Hugh McHugh. And Sister St. Paul sends her regards."

So he was the new priest at St. Rose's.

"It's a fine day," he said, and she saw him take in her garden and her cabin and the big cottonwoods that shaded the cabin.

"It was a fine day last week when it rained," Mildred said. "But please, Father McHugh, come inside."

"Am I keeping you from your work?"

"It's all right. We don't get company out here very often."

She led him up the porch steps and into the big front room and then to the kitchen, where she set down cups and saucers and poured, without even asking him if he wanted coffee. Apparently, he'd lived in ranch country long enough to understand that pouring coffee right away was what people did, because he accepted the cup and sniffed appreciatively.

"We can sit in the front room." She led him to the old leather chairs by the fireplace where she and Renny had talked last night.

"It's a lovely room, Miss Harrington."

She saw him note the big leather chairs and the leather sofa and the glass-front bookcases, the inlaid table by the door, and the walnut pump organ with its carved panels and brackets and its ivory keys and stops, old family furniture that her father had had shipped all the way from Pennsylvania to the Montana Territory, first by rail and then by steamboat and then in a wagon drawn by oxen.

"That's a fine organ," the priest said. "Do you play, Miss Harrington?"

"A little. Please, Father McHugh, call me Mildred. Everyone does."

He sipped his coffee. "Mildred. *Mil*. That's what your friend calls you."

Her eyes shot up in surprise and found him watching her face. "No one calls me that but Pat!"

"Pat and I got well acquainted last night." Father McHugh smiled at her. "I like Pat. I think he and I'll be friends."

Mildred opened her mouth and shut it. It was bad enough to be sitting in her front room in her men's clothing while she drank coffee with a priest, but to be talking about Pat . . . She couldn't think of what to say, and her face felt hot and she was afraid she was blushing.

He set down his cup. "Mildred. A lot is happening. And we have a lot to talk about."

"Is Pat all right?"

"He'll be all right, Mildred. And I don't know for certain who is on the other side, but I'm on your side. And all my friends call me Father Hugh."

A thunder of heavy hoofs down the road by the cabin. Renny riding past the window on Pink, bringing in the workhorses.

"René," said Father Hugh. *Ren-aye.* "I'll need to talk to him too."

"He wasn't hurt by being thrown by a horse."

"No," said Renny. "We didn't think so, either."

They were sitting around the table in the kitchen with the remains of the meal Mildred had scrambled together with what she had on hand. An omelet with bits of bacon and onion, fried potatoes, last summer's canned green beans. Fresh bread. A dried-apple pie.

"I wouldn't a thought Ferrell would do something like that," said Renny. "A course, I wouldn't a thought he'd do some of what I know he done."

"What do you want to do?" Sister St. Paul had asked Patrick Adams.

"I don't know," he said, and heard his own frustration in his voice. How much more to tell her?

"Sister, you know I haven't been home much. I came home summers while I was in college to see my mother, and okay, always hoping I might see Mil, and a time or two I did, which didn't work out well. Then the war, and then . . ." he turned his head restlessly on his pillow. "Then I decided on law school, and he— my father—was angry as hell about it."

"Why, for heaven's sake?"

"I have no idea. Maybe he just saw something he wasn't in control of. Which was me, and which he wasn't, by that time.

I'd saved my army pay, and I knew where I could find work in Missoula. And I was outa here. Last time I came back was last summer, when my mother died, and he was worse."

A white-habited nursing nun poked her head around the door, saw Sister St. Paul, set Pat's breakfast tray hastily down, and scooted away.

"Drink your fruit juice," Sister St. Paul told him. "Why did you come back now?"

"Because—" He drank some juice and felt steadied by the sweet citrus. "That was the strangest part of the whole god-damned circus. Sorry, Sister. I'm not the man I ought to be. Because he wrote me a letter! Begging me to come home. Wrote that he had to see me, had to talk. And I thought—for my mother's memory—that I had to find out what was going on with him."

He drank more juice. "When I got here, the cowboys he's got working for him told me he'd been behaving way, way worse since my mother's funeral. Tantrums. Rages. They were starting to get afraid of him. What they thought he might do."

"Liquor?"

"Yeah. At least, that was part of his temper. And I don't know where he's been buying it, but it's not hard to get."

"No," she agreed, and sat quietly for a moment before she asked again, "What do you want to do about it, Patrick?"

"I don't know. I don't know. All I know is that I'm rigged up here in this goddamned bed—sorry—and I'm afraid for Mil, what he might do. And I can't do a damn thing. All I can do is think it through and think it through again. I had to talk to somebody. I don't know what I ought to do, Sister."

"You should tell Mildred the truth when you see her. Then . . . Let me think about what you should do, Patrick. You can't do nothing. I will pray about it for you."

"Pray for Mil," he said.

"I always do."

"Mildred, Sister St. Paul thinks you should come back to town with me and stay at the convent for a while."

She saw Renny's quick assessing eyes move from Father Hugh's face to hers. "What do you think, Mildred?"

Her garden needing water. The chickens needing feed. Renny couldn't do it all. The milk cow. The cream cooling in the creek for butter. And the haying starting tomorrow.

"Or else," said Renny, "I'll carry my mattress up and spread it on the porch, and I'll sleep there for a few days. Ain't like it's cold. Or you can come down to the shack and sleep on my cot, Mildred, and I'll sleep in the back room. And there's the dogs."

"That's what we'll do," she told the priest. "Give Sister St. Paul my love."

"I'll be on my way, then," he said. "Thank you for lunch, Mildred."

Renny followed him out, and Mildred watched through the screen door as he and the young priest paused on the steps and conversed in voices too low for her to hear. Burly, bearded Renny. The slim young priest, nearly as tall as Renny. A priest who walked—like what? Like a dancer might walk. With springs in his feet.

As she watched, Renny knelt on the trampled grass in front of the porch while the priest blessed him and gave him a hand back to his feet and then walked alone down the hill to his car.

What were they not telling her?

"Some of the story is Pat's to tell," Father Hugh had said.

His father—"I'm having a hard time saying those words," Pat told Sister St. Paul—sent the two cowboys to drive the cattle farther east, where the grass might be better. Then he asked Pat to help him rebuild a stretch of fence below the corrals, and Pat agreed. He was using posthole diggers to scoop out dirt where his father had driven through the tough sod with his crowbar as deep as he could. And his father was waiting for Pat to finish with the diggers so that he could strike deeper.

41

"I was almost finished," Pat said. "Just another couple of scoops with the diggers. And I was scooping and thinking about another summer day a lot like that one and, well, thinking about Mil, when something hit me a hell of a blow just above my ankle. I looked back as I went down, and he was standing over me with the crowbar. And I think that's when he gave me the dent on my forehead, but I don't remember."

Sister St. Paul and the doctor had puzzled over the dent, which didn't seem consistent with a fall from a horse, and they had worried that Pat's skull was fractured but finally decided it was just a deep, bad bruise and swelling. Clearly he had been concussed, though. Who knew for how long.

"Next thing I remember," Pat said, "I was draped over the front of his saddle, and we had come almost to the creek crossing, and he was pushing me off his horse, and I hit the ground hard. Played dead, best I could. And he said . . ."

Pat paused for a long moment. "He said, *You can crawl the rest of the way to your moccasin squaw.* And then he—strange what I remember and what I don't—he had my hat, and he flung it as far as he could into the hawthorns."

"Why?" she asked, meaning not just Ferrell's flinging the hat but the whole episode. "Why?"

"I don't know. Maybe because he knew I wouldn't stay on the ranch with him? That I was going to leave again?"

"If Pat really fears for her safety, we have to talk to the county prosecutor," Father Hugh had repeated to Sister St. Paul after hearing Pat's story and before he left Fort Maginnis for the Harrington ranch. "I talked with him for a long time last night—he couldn't sleep—and he clearly does fear for her."

Patrick Adams would have been beating his head against a wall in his frustration, except that he was in a shape too sorry even to get to a wall to beat his head against. He'd had to bite his lip to keep from snarling at the night nurse who helped him with a bedpan and then brought him a basin and water to wash his hands and face and brush his teeth. As it was, he thought he'd frightened her, when none of his situation was her fault. Whose fault? His own, for starters.

Mil. Where are you?

Now, tethered to a pole on his hospital bed, Pat began beating his head on the only surface he could reach, which was his pillow and unsatisfactorily yielding, but what else could he do.

"Patrick!"

The overhead light snapped on. Later he realized he'd frightened the night nurse so badly that she had run to the convent for Sister St. Paul.

"Patrick Adams, if I have to tell you one more time. Your leg must heal. You know that."

"Yes, Sister. I know that."

"What were you trying to do? Work yourself into a fever? Are you trying to undo all the work we've done for that leg?"

"No, Sister."

She stamped off, muttering that it wouldn't surprise her at all if he didn't end up spending an extra six weeks in that cast.

6

Before dark Renny carried his mattress and a pillow and his fiddle up from the shack and spread the mattress on the porch, and Mildred brought him sheets and a quilt, which he told her he didn't need in this heat.

"Oh, maybe it'll cool off before morning," he finally agreed, and took the quilt. His dogs curled up beside his mattress and went to sleep, and Renny took his fiddle out of its case and sat on the porch steps and played for a while. Mildred listened from her bedroom to tunes she had heard before but had never known the names of, old tunes brought all the way from the Red River country by the Métis.

"Two ways we folk different from the full-bloods," Josie had told her. "One, when we followed the buffalo, we always taken a priest with us, and two, we always taken a fiddler with us."

After a while Renny stopped playing, and Mildred heard his faint snore. But she still couldn't sleep. A three-quarters moon rose in her open window, and she got out of bed and looked out.

Silhouettes of cottonwood trees, stars as peaceful as though nothing bad ever happened.

"We don't know enough about what happens inside a mind," Father Hugh had said, "and maybe someday we'll have medication for the mind like we do for the body. But something goes amiss—in Ferrell Adams's case, his son wasn't doing what Ferrell thought he should do, and then Ferrell's wife died, and whether her death was a last straw or whether it was brooding out there on the ranch with nobody but cowboys to talk to, brooding about Pat, brooding about the drought, about having to sell off cattle—

and men like Ferrell turn to liquor, because it makes them feel better before it starts to make them feel worse."

"Never thought a little hooch would hurt anybody," Renny said.

"It's not a little that hurts."

Pat. Whatever tethered Mildred to him? Why did she see the three-quarters moon and wonder if he saw it through his hospital room window?

How he must hate being tethered to that hospital bed.

The first time she ever saw Pat was on her first day of school. She was nearly eleven years old, and her mother had been teaching her at home because she didn't think Mildred was old enough to ride horseback all that way by herself. But her mother hadn't been feeling well that summer. She could barely summon the energy for housework and cooking and chores, and Mildred's father put his foot down. Other kids rode to school, lots of them younger that Mildred. He took her to the office of the county superintendent of schools in Fort Maginnis and had her tested, and when the superintendent of schools said she could start in the sixth grade, he bought her a new tablet and some pencils and a black lunch box that she could tie to her saddle.

On that first day, her father rode beside her to the Plum Creek school. Afterward, she would ride on her own, but that day he showed her where she could tie her horse in the barn—not Smokey, of course, it was a mare named Banty, before Smokey's time—where a tall fair-haired boy had just tied up his horse.

The boy glanced at Mildred and nodded at her father on his way out of the barn, and her father gave him a cold nod back.

"That's the Adams kid," her father said as he and Mildred walked up to the schoolhouse so he could have a word with the teacher. "Spoiled rotten."

And now it was years later, and she couldn't sleep.

Pat had asked her to kiss him goodbye in the back of the truck, and she had. And now she couldn't keep from returning to the moment, living it over and over, every detail, every sensation, a gentle kiss but with his lips and teeth and the taste of his cigarette lingering on his tongue. *Stop!* She was being as foolish as she had been during the summer she was fourteen and had just graduated from the eighth grade, when her father said that was enough schooling for a girl and Pat had burned his way through high school early and said he was going to college in the fall and wasn't coming back. But he rode down to meet her every night at a place they'd found in a pine grove, and he had lain with her in the pine needles, and Pat called her his brown-haired girl, and they kissed and explored each other's bodies, and, well . . . Later that night, in her own bed in the cabin loft, she would relive every detail, every sensation, over and over. *So stop!*

She hadn't felt the conviction to enter the novitiate, but she thought she might as well have. What was she now but a nun without beads or a habit?

She had kissed Pat goodbye. Goodbye meant goodbye. A stop. And that was that.

Renny had sharpened the sickles on the mowing machine, and in the morning, he harnessed the quick little crossbred Belgian work team and hitched them up. Then he climbed to the seat of the mowing machine and slapped his lines over the Belgians' backs and trotted off to the lower hay meadow, where the grass wasn't good but probably better than the grass on the upper meadow.

Mildred stood from her garden watering to watch him drive the Belgians away from the corrals and saw what she never had seen before—Renny's rifle in its scabbard hanging from the seat of the mower.

She had fired up the kitchen range and set water to heat before she started the chores, and when she returned to the kitchen, the heat was like a blow to her face. She lifted her copper boilers from the top of the stove and carried first one and then the other to the porch and poured hot water into the galvanized tubs she had set on a bench. Carried the boilers, one and then the other, out to the pump and refilled them and carried them back to the kitchen. Added her soap shavings and the washboard to one of the galvanized tubs and, while the water was at its hottest, scrubbed the sheets and a pillowcase from Renny's makeshift bed and sheets and a pillowcase from her own bed. Once the sheets were rinsed in the other tub and wrung out, she set the rest of her whites—underwear, a couple of shirts—to soak in the washtub while she carried the sheets in her basket to the clothesline behind the cabin and pinned them up to dry.

Then the rest of the whites. Then the colored clothes. Finally, when the water was at its coolest, the darks. Levi's, dark shirts, socks. Out to the clothesline with her basket of wet clothes and back again. By this time the sheets were dry and ready to be put back on the beds.

Work. A lot of work. That was what life on a ranch was.

Want a chicken dinner? Take the chicken hook out to the chicken yard. Catch a squawking chicken by its leg. Cut its throat and let it flap until the water in one of the copper tanks is boiling. Scald the chicken in the boiling water and pluck its feathers. Gather the wet feathers to burn in the burning barrel. Hold the chicken over the fire in the burning barrel to singe off its pinfeathers. Go back to the kitchen and gut the chicken and throw its entrails into the yard for the dogs to fight over. Save the heart, liver, and gizzard for giblets to chop and cook in the gravy. Leave the chicken whole if it's to be roasted. Cut it in pieces if it's to be fried. All that's left to do now is cook the chicken.

Want vegetables to eat during the winter? Pull the carrots, dig the potatoes, and store them in the root cellar. Dig the onions and hang them up in strings. Pick the green beans, pull the beets, and shell the peas. Wash and trim and slice and cook. Hot fire in the range, stifling kitchen. Dig out the canning kettle from the cellar. Scald the jars, drain the cooked vegetables, fill the jars. Process the jars in the canning kettle. Cool the jars and listen for the little *pop* when the lids seal. Line up the jars on shelves in the cellar.

Want a bath when the work is done? Well, the work is never done, but the day eventually will come to an end. And Mildred will want a bath after washing clothes all morning and raking hay all afternoon. She'll heat water in the copper boilers. She'll set one of the galvanized tubs on the kitchen floor and fill it with water. She'll undress and sit in the tub with her knees under her chin and a sheet pinned around her neck for privacy.

How tired Mildred's mother had been toward the end. Then it was Mildred's turn to do her mother's work.

Mildred had finished her wash and brought most of the clothes in from the line before noon, which was when Renny would tie up his team and come back to the house for dinner. Dinner made from what she had. More eggs, more potatoes, the rest of the green beans from the jar she opened yesterday and kept over in the water cooler.

She looked forward to raking hay. Driving a team of horses around and around the meadow while she sat on the seat of the dump rake and had only to think about keeping her rows of hay straight. Although the meadow would be hot, of course, and unshaded.

So she washed her dinner dishes, and then she pulled on her boots and took her hat from its nail and walked down to the corrals to harness the calm old half-Percheron work team and hitch them to the dump rake and trotted them down to the hay meadow, where the hay Renny had mowed that morning already was curing and ready to be raked into long snaking windrows of hay.

Renny was mowing on the other side of the meadow by the time she rattled up with the team and rake, and he gave her a little wave to show he'd seen her. And Mildred slowed the big Percherons to a steady walk and headed them down the meadow and settled back in the seat of the rake.

Driving a team happened in a whole different realm from riding horseback. A line in each hand, for a start. Molded metal seat, metal footrests that spread a driver's legs apart. The feel through the lines of the big horses working their bits. The muscles of their rumps and hind legs moving in their own slow rhythm. The sun beating down on her hat and on her shoulders. Slow, slow. The stink of horse sweat, the fragrance of freshly mowed hay drying in the sun. The whistle of a meadowlark from the fence post she was passing. Mildred could relax into a kind of stupor, raising and lowering the teeth of the dump rake and knowing she'd be instantly alert if anything alarmed the horses, until she reached the bottom of the meadow and turned the horses to start her next round.

She had finished that windrow and was halfway down the next when she noticed that Renny had halted the Belgians and was watching something on the crest of the hill above the meadow, and she pulled up her team and turned to look.

A horse and rider on the crest of the hill, a dark silhouette against the bright blue sky. Motionless. Across the meadow, a motionless Renny. His team, resting with their hips shot and their hocks raised, waiting until the lines slapped their backs and told them it was time to go back to work. Silence, until one of Mildred's Percherons, the mare, snorted and stamped and shook off a fly.

She knew the rider, of course. No mistaking his seat on his horse, the angle of his head and shoulders, his bulk. And Renny had his hand on his scabbard.

No. Renny would never shoot over the brow of a hill, no matter who was in his sights. But maybe the rider didn't know that, because she blinked and he was gone. The crest of the hill as empty, the blue sky as unblemished as though Ferrell Adams had never waited there and watched her and Renny making hay.

From across the meadow Renny made a palms-up, what-is-there-to-say gesture and slapped his lines on his team. Might as well keep working.

That evening, after a supper of fresh corn bread and more eggs and potatoes, Mildred waited until Renny went out to his fiddle and his mattress on the porch, and then she changed her bloody pad of folded rags for a fresh pad and put the stained pad to soak and rinse out in a basin of cold water before she hung it out to dry. Her blood and moon was nearly over. She would only need the pads another day or two, she hoped.

She had been twelve the first time and baffled and frightened to find blood in her underwear, and she ran down to the horse corral and made herself small in the comfort of horses standing head to tail and switching flies for each other. She was sure she was going to die. First her mother and now Mildred.

Then Renny came out of the granary, carrying a bucket of chicken feed in each hand, and almost walked past where she was crouched but stopped at the sight of her tears. When he set down his buckets and stood looking down at her, Mildred was stricken not only with fear but with horrible embarrassment, and she tried to make herself even smaller.

Renny waited. Waited.

Finally, she raised her face from her knees. "I'm bleeding. *Down there*," she blurted, and burst into more tears.

Renny said nothing for a moment. Pondering what, she didn't know. Then he took a handkerchief out of his pocket and folded it and handed it to her. "Use this," he said. "I'll be right back."

When he came back, it was in his truck. He got out and scooped Mildred out of the corral dirt and set her in the cab, and then he got back in the cab himself and put the truck in gear. When she could stop crying, Mildred saw that he was driving them up the teetering track that led to the county road.

"Where are we going?" she asked.

"I'm taking you to town to see Josie."

"Does Dad know?"

Renny nodded, then glanced briefly away from the track and reached over and patted her knee. "Cheer up, honey. You're not gonna die today."

When they reached the little house by the creek, Renny spoke briefly to Josie in the patois Mildred didn't understand. Then he hugged Josie and patted Mildred on her shoulder. "Cheer up, honey," he repeated, and climbed in his truck and drove away.

Mildred stayed with Josie for a week. Shared Josie's meals of porridge and wild berries, eggs from Josie's chickens, stews of canned meat and vegetables from Josie's garden. Slept at night in Josie's lumpy bed while Josie snored softly beside her, and outside an open window, the creek current chuckled in the dark. Met Josie's grandniece, Evangeline, who was Mildred's age but already taller than Mildred and much, much taller and wider than tiny Josie. Evangeline brought along a Sears and Roebuck catalog for herself and Mildred to look through together, and she told Mildred what she had studied at the Catholic elementary school and how she would be starting at the new high school soon. And Mildred felt envious. High school wasn't necessary for a ranch girl, her father had said.

And Josie, in her lilting and sometimes topsy-turvy English, explained to Mildred what Mildred's mother would have told her if her mother had lived.

"No! You not gone bleed to death, Mildred! You gone be fine!"

She gave Mildred a bundle of rags that she could take home with her to make pads, and she showed her how to use the pads and change them and wash them in cold water to use again, and to make sure no man ever saw them. Gave her strange-looking dried leaves to brew into a tea to help with cramps.

"Blood and moon make you a woman, Mildred!" And Josie had hugged her and kissed her goodbye when her silent father, not Renny, had come to take her home.

Mildred roused herself from the past. She carried her clean pad out to the clothesline and pinned it up in the dark.

In the morning, she walked down to the corrals to harness her Percherons for another day's work with the dump rake. Renny already would be mowing what scant grass grew in the upper meadow.

"No! You not need sit! You not need lie down!" Josie had assured her. "Do what to do! You not mind blood and moon—blood and moon not mind you."

She had not seen Josie often after that week. Probably never would have seen her again if not for Renny. Strange shutters seemed to go up in people's faces. Keeping to their own kind. Her kind and their kind. Decent white folks here. The catlickers and bohunks and breeds there.

What Josie had not told her. What her father, silent but observant, had known when Mildred did not pin up her pads one month.

She drove the Percherons to the meadow and, with a horse on either side of the first windrow, headed them toward the bottom of the meadow. Lines in her hands, her feet on the iron rests. Between her legs, the lever that raised or lowered the teeth of the rake. The morning air, cool compared with what it would feel like by afternoon.

No horseman watched from the horizon. The only human activity in sight was Renny with his team in the distance, mowing the upper meadow.

"Sure hope we didn't make a mistake not taking Sister's advice," Renny had growled.

Mildred raised the teeth of the rake and dumped hay, lowered the teeth, and drove on. Too much she didn't know.

Pat's story to tell, Father Hugh had said.

7

The summer wore on, and the heat settled in, shriveling the hopeful grass and crops of early June. One of Renny's nephews, Joe St. Pierre, came out from Fort Maginnis to drive the Percheron team on the hay stacker while Mildred and the quick Belgians bucked the haycocks from the teeth of the buck rake to the teeth of the stacker, which rose on its pulleys as the Percherons plodded forward with Joe walking behind them. Renny, atop the growing stack with his pitchfork, spread the fragrant hay that the teeth of the stacker carried up and dumped there. And then Joe lowered the teeth for another load of hay as he backed up the Percherons, walking backward himself behind them. Hot work, dusty work, and thankfully, peaceful work. Not a lot of hay, but some. Hopefully enough.

Mrs. Len Barta went into labor, and Mildred saddled Smokey and tied her black bag to the saddle while the nervous young husband could hardly sit still in his own saddle. She rode back with him to the Barta place and delivered a baby girl without much difficulty, considering the baby was Mrs. Barta's first, and the Bartas insisted on giving Mildred a chunk of fresh beef wrapped in newspaper. He'd butchered a calf, Len Barta explained, rather than listen to it bawling and hungry.

Renny looked at what oats he'd planted and told Mildred he thought they'd be better off cutting it for hay. Not enough oats to be worth threshing. But Mildred's garden was doing fine. Her early peas were ready, so she and Renny could have fresh peas for supper. And she would can the rest. The beans would be next, and then the beets. All well, and no watching horseman on the horizon.

Pat Adams had finished his book, and maybe tomorrow one of the sisters would bring him another. But tonight he had nothing to do but look at the ceiling or think about Mil or damn his left leg for tethering him with a pulley and rope to a pole on a hospital bed like a coyote caught by one leg in a spring trap. To think about anything else, to give his muscles something to do, he raised his right leg, flexed it, and lowered it. Raised it, flexed it, lowered it.

After a while, for a change, he reached up and, with each hand, gripped one of the iron bars in the frame that formed the head of the bed. Used the bars as resistance to squeeze, squeeze, as though to force them closer together. Felt his muscles begin to wake, as though they had been sleeping too long. Squeeze, squeeze.

Then he tried using his grip on the bars to raise his shoulders and upper body from the mattress and felt the neglected muscles of his abdomen start to respond. Raise, lower. Raise, lower.

He had found a means, over the years, to keep track of Mil. Not from his mother, who would have been too frightened of his father—no, Pat was damned if he would ever call Ferrell Adams his father again. His mother would have been too frightened of Ferrell even to write news of Mil. But neither of Ferrell's cowboys liked Ferrell, and the cowboy with the long Dutch name, Albert Vanaartsdalen, had graduated eighth grade at the Plum Creek school with Pat, so Albert kinda liked writing letters to Pat. A couple of times a year, maybe. Not too often.

Who you writing to? Ferrell once asked Albert, and blithely Albert replied, *To my girlfriend in Texas.* Pat started drawing hearts with arrows stuck through them on the envelopes of letters he wrote back to Albert. Ferrell must never have caught on, because Albert still was working for him when Pat came home this time.

Albert wrote that old Thad Harrington was none too happy about the nuns keeping Mildred at the convent in Fort Maginnis and enrolling her in the Catholic high school, and Pat took some heart from that news. How Mil had longed to go to high school!

The questions she asked Pat about his studies, her infinite curiosity about the world beyond the mountains that framed the prairie.

Then Albert wrote that the nursing nuns at Good Samaritan were training Mil to be a nurse. In three years, she would get her diploma and be an RN. Old Thad had fumed and tried to yank her home, but that head nun they got at Good Samaritan, Albert wrote, is one tough nun, and she wouldn't let him. Yes, Renny Archambault was still living out at the Harrington ranch, running a trapline and working for Thad. Albert ran into Renny from time to time, which was how he got his news of Mil.

Pat wanted to write Albert from France but thought such a letter, even with hearts and arrows drawn on the envelope, would invite suspicion. In the last letter Albert wrote him was the news of Thad's death, heart attack they thought, also that Albert himself was shipping out to France.

Albert made it through the war and went back to cowboying for Ferrell. On that last terrible visit home, Pat had a chance to talk briefly with him before Ferrell sent Albert and the other cowboy, Frank Bates, driving the cattle east in search of grass.

"You still carrying a torch for her after all this time?" Albert asked.

"Yeah."

Albert shook his head. "She's real withdrawn now. Only time anybody sees her is when she's riding to deliver babies or such. I tell you, though, Pat. Everybody respects her for what she does, specially the folks she pulled through the flu epidemic."

Albert punched Pat on the shoulder, and Pat punched him back, the only expression of sympathy that had ever passed between them.

Raise, lower. Raise . . . Screech! Creak!

Jesus Christ, he'd pulled the head of the bed off its brackets. Tilted over Pat at an alarming angle were the white-painted bars of the iron frame. Pat himself was suspended by the rope and pulley that raised his left leg and fastened it to the pole, while one end of the mattress hung from the foot of the bed and the other end touched the floor. Now he really was tethered like a coyote with one leg in a spring trap, although at least the coyote could gnaw his goddamned leg off and escape.

The night nurse looked in to see what had caused the crash and screamed for the orderlies. The orderlies had arrived and were standing around Pat and the broken bed, discussing how best to raise the mattress and bed frame and repair the bed while Pat was in the bed, when Sister St. Paul burst in.

She stood over Pat, fuming, and Pat looked up at her from an almost-upside-down viewpoint.

"Patrick Adams! How many more times are you going to make me run over here? What's the matter with you?"

One of the orderlies said he thought if they could raise the frame and mattress, they could drill new holes for what looked like stripped screws and reattach the head of the bed where it belonged.

"I believe," said the other orderly, "that if we got some of them nursing sisters in here, maybe get three, four sisters on each side of that bed frame, we can help the sisters lift it to where they can hold it up with him on it until we can straighten out that head-frame and change its brackets and screw it back together again."

"Yup."

The night nurse ran to fetch more nuns, and the orderlies set down their toolboxes and chewed their chaws while they waited for the reinforcements. Sister St. Paul glared at them, but they were used to her. She redirected her wrath at Pat.

"Of all the boneheaded, brainless . . ." there was more, but Pat was intrigued by his new upside-down view of the world—his world, his new boundaries, what he'd come to—where Sister St. Paul had become a monolithic black pillar that had a voice and towered over him and where he could see the bottoms of door-knobs. The door took on fresh significance when viewed from its bottom and looking up. It was as though Pat's hospital room itself had been turned upside down and into a new room.

". . . unforgivably stupid *stunt*. Who knows how much damage you may have done to your leg under that cast?"

Suddenly, the room was full of white skirts that swirled past Pat and around him. He now was surrounded by a white curtain with women's faces looking down at him from over the top of the curtain.

"Ready, Sisters? One, two, *three*," and Pat found himself rising on his mattress and bed frame until he lay level again and could see, from their waists up, a row of white-habited women on either side of him. Their carefully controlled faces.

"Can you hold it like that, Sisters?"

And all the heads nodded.

Pat couldn't see what the orderlies were doing behind him, but he guessed from the sounds that they were drilling new holes in the headframe for screws and replacing its brackets.

"We're going to stand it up now, Sisters. Hold on."

A *clank* under him as the bed frame met new brackets.

"Just about done, Sisters. Hold on a little longer."

And then the orderlies were reemerging from behind Pat and packing up their toolboxes, and the sisters were dusting off their hands and swirling out of the room and disappearing with lilts of laughter trailing behind them.

Pat's room returned to its old self, the shapes of doors and doorknobs back to banal. The coyote came back to his trap. Pat was reflecting on his entertainment value for nuns when Sister St. Paul said, "*Why*, Pat?"

"Because I'm losing it."

"Are you worried about Mildred?"

"Partly that."

Sister St. Paul's sharp dark eyes measured him. "Father McHugh drove out to the Harrington ranch. He told me that Renny Archambault is sleeping on the cabin porch with his rifle at hand and that Renny's dogs won't let anybody near, especially at night, without barking."

Pat nodded. "That's good. I'm thankful for that. But Sister—"

"Father McHugh and I have prayed for guidance, and while I doubt anything will come of it, he plans to talk with the county prosecutor—"

"Sister. What I did to Mil. Back then."

"Ah," she said. After a moment, she said, "Can you tell me about it?"

He couldn't imagine saying what he needed to say to Sister St. Paul. "I don't think so."

He saw by her face that she probably already knew.

"Would you rather talk to Father?"

"Maybe. Yeah."

She stood. "I'll speak to Father in the morning."

She added, "And I want that leg to heal," in a voice Pat imagined his leg hearing and obeying.

One of Renny's dogs barked in the night, a single warning, and Mildred woke from what might have been sleep and went in her nightgown to the window. She could see the outline of the dog, a big shepherd-collie mix, bristling at the top of the porch steps and looking out into the dark. And Renny, up on one elbow. Then she heard the chorus of howls from the bluff, and the dog barked once more.

Coyotes, out hunting for what they could find in the dark. Insulting the dog, hoping to tempt him far enough from the house that the pack could bring him down. She saw Renny lie back down on his mattress, and she returned to bed herself.

The hat on the dresser by the clock. She guessed she'd gotten used to seeing it there. Then, as if in rebuttal, *Pat*, as vividly as if he really were standing at the foot of her bed instead of tethered to a hospital bed. She almost reached her hands for him, even though she knew she would reach for thin air.

The scent of pine needles in the dark. Pat's hands. By inches over a month of nights, his hands moved from her hair to her back and shoulders and unbuttoned her dress and cupped her breasts until she trembled in a way she had never dreamed of, and when her hands followed the curve of his back as far as his beltline, he breathed *oh yes* into her hair.

Pat's hands between her legs, touching her where she never had been touched. His mouth and tongue touching her there. He was unbuttoning the fly of his Levi's, and she supposed she had known what men and boys had under the flies of their pants. After all, she had seen the cows getting freshened, and she knew why the mares were taken to the stallion and how the stallion put foals in their bellies. But she had never seen a boy's or known the word for what a boy had, and when she touched Pat's, he gasped *oh God, Mil,* and parted her legs, and she gasped, and he touched her *there* with *it,* and she gasped *yes.* And that was when he said *no* and rolled off her and sat naked with his back to her for a moment before he said in a more or less normal voice, *We don't want to do that now, Mil. We don't want to take that chance.*

Turned out, they already had.

"The life force is so strong," Sister St. Paul explained, "that sometimes it doesn't need complete penetration. And you both were young and healthy."

Mildred shut her eyes and opened them again on the dark shape of his hat on her dresser, keeping its secrets.

Father Hugh answered the rap on the rectory door to find Sister Boniface standing on the step and out of breath. "Father! A man came to the convent and asked if Mildred Harrington was there!"

Father Hugh didn't really know Ferrell Adams but thought he'd seen him on the street once. "He didn't give his name? Was he a big burly man, maybe in his late fifties?"

"Oh, no! He was a younger man. From the way he walked, I thought he might have been a cowboy."

He felt a shadow lift that he hadn't known had settled on him. But it was way too soon to feel relieved, he told himself. "What did you tell him, Sister?"

"That I hadn't seen her." Her eyes dropped. "I lied, Father. I said I hadn't seen her all summer."

"You can say one Hail Mary tonight for lying," he said. "Or maybe two, if you feel like it."

When she looked up at him, startled, he smiled at her until she gave him a tentative smile in return and fled for the convent.

Father Hugh wandered thoughtfully back to his study, where his notes for his Sunday homily lay on his desk. He picked up one of the sheets of paper and laid it back down.

If he walked out of the rectory and scanned the sky from horizon to horizon, he would see an endless transparent blue where cumulus clouds floated their slow stately way as they had since early June with no indication that they might form themselves into darker shapes carrying the rain his parishioners prayed for. And yet his sense of stormy weather on its way had grown.

He shook his head. Pat Adams's guess about the reasons for his father's attack were perhaps as near to the mark as anyone could come. The disappointed and angry man, fueled with liquor supplied by a bootlegger or by one of the nameless, nearly invisible men who made the liquor runs down from Canada at night, in cars whose headlights no one spoke of. Frustrated by what he saw as his son's willful disobedience, had Ferrell lashed out in mindless rage—the most charitable view—and then what? Had he thought he'd killed Pat? Had he thrown Pat across his saddle and ridden down to Plum Creek to dump the body on another man's land?

The last words Pat had heard him speak: *You can crawl the rest of the way to your moccasin squaw.*

"Fighting words," Sister St. Paul said. "Yes, he meant to hurt. And yes, Mildred wears moccasins when she isn't in boots. And some would look askance of her wearing men's—and an Indian's— clothing. But anyone who knew old Thaddeus Harrington would know he'd kill a man who said a thing like that about a member of his family. So to say such a thing about Mildred . . ." she didn't finish.

Two days after he dumped Pat, Ferrell Adams had returned to the place he'd left him. Mildred's account of the rider who had searched along the trail and searched it again was, for Father McHugh, the most troubling part of the whole episode. Why? To make sure Pat was dead? To finish him off if he wasn't? Or possibly regretting what he'd done? The only clear part of Ferrell Adams's behavior was that he hadn't known Mildred Harrington would return late on horseback after delivering a child, find Pat, and somehow get him on her horse and take him home with her.

The larger question. So Ferrell Adams had come back to where he'd left Pat, and Pat wasn't there. What would Ferrell Adams think had become of him, and what would Ferrell do next?

Pat thought he might go after Mildred.

Father Hugh released an exasperated breath. If cowboys were going to show up at the convent door, looking for Mildred, he needed to warn the nuns, all of them. And then talk to the county prosecutor. And then, God willing, finish that— He caught himself in time. Finish that homily.

8

Old Alex LaFountain stopped by the convent that afternoon with a crate of garden produce for the nuns, and while Sister Boniface carried the crate down to the cellar to unpack the produce, Alex and Sister St. Paul caught each other up on what little news they had. Here they were, nearly into July, and still dry as a bone out Alex's way, and Alex had given up on rain. At least his chickens were laying, and he could carry creek water to his garden. He had shot a coyote. Sister St. Paul told him about the new young priest at St. Rose's.

"Heard you got yourselves a new priest," said Alex. "You got this one broke to lead yet, Sister?"

Alex laughed at his own joke and tipped his hat to her and climbed back in his wagon and slapped up his team. But Sister St. Paul was thinking about her conversation with Father McHugh about Patrick Adams.

"I like him," Father McHugh had said.

"I agree he's likeable."

"Does that mean you don't like him?"

"It means I have a healthy suspicion of handsome young men!"

Then she saw that handsome young man, Father McHugh, having trouble keeping his lips from twitching, and she added hastily, "I wasn't talking about you, Father!"

And he had laughed outright.

Sister St. Paul shook her head. Of all the priests she had— how had Alex LaFountain put it?—*halterbroken*, she had a feeling that halterbreaking Father McHugh would be no small undertaking.

All had been peaceful for so long, and now the cowboy. Father McHugh talked it over with Sister St. Paul and convinced her that although she had her doubts that anything would be done, they, or rather he, needed to talk to the county prosecutor. The issue being what it was, Father McHugh thought the county attorney might feel more comfortable hearing the story from him without Sister's presence.

Sister St. Paul had to shake her head. Men talking among themselves, women talking among themselves, often in codes and often, she suspected, about the same topics. But she knew Father McHugh was right. About the county attorney's comfort, at least. She still doubted the county attorney would hold an opinion different from the sheriff's all those years ago.

The Murray County courthouse took up an entire block of land at the south end of Main Street. Mown native grass around the building made what, with rain, might have been a lawn but now looked more like stubble, and shrubs had been started and kept watered around the foundations, along with a pair of young weeping willows planted on each side of the front walk. Marble steps led up to a double door flanked by carved marble pillars, imposing but sad in Father Hugh's eyes for the way the courthouse mirrored the hopes of the land rush of men and women looking for better lives in Montana than wherever they'd come from—Americans but also Scandinavians and Swiss and Croatians and Bohemians and Germans and Czechs. They got plenty of rain during the first years, Father Hugh had learned from his parishioners, and the price of wheat had risen during the war.

So—let's build schools! Churches! A fine courthouse with a jail behind it! Let's open banks! Plenty of banks!

We Protestants are leery of that Catholic priest, but we're sure as hell thankful for the sisters who staff the hospital.

Then, after the war ended, the flu epidemic swept through Murray County as it had elsewhere, and the price of wheat fell and the rains stopped falling and the land dried to cracked earth.

Mortgages were foreclosed on. Homesteaders packed whatever they still possessed and left clouds of dust behind them. A few, like Ferrell Adams and Thaddeus Harrington, who had come to Montana with money, did better and hung on. Some, like the Svobodas, dug in and doubled down.

Then the banks themselves began to fold, and no telling how much worse lay ahead.

The county attorney's office was on the second floor of the courthouse, and Father Hugh removed his hat and climbed still another flight of marble stairs through increasing heat and stale air and found the right door. The young woman he'd spoken with on the telephone looked up from her typewriter, "Mr. Clarke's expecting you, Father. You can go right in."

At least she had a fan to stir the air.

Framed diplomas on the walls of the office. Shelves of books. The county attorney himself behind his desk.

"Father!" said the county attorney. "George Clarke," he introduced himself, and reached across his desk to shake hands.

"Welcome to Murray County, such as it is these days. This heat just won't let up. I gotta get another fan in here. How long have you been living in Fort Maginnis now? Three months?"

He motioned Father Hugh to a chair and leaned back in his own chair, studying his visitor and probably wondering *now what?* Father Hugh thought.

"We've got Patrick Adams in the hospital," Father Hugh said. "He's been there close to six weeks now. With a broken leg and a blow to his head that he's lucky didn't fracture his skull."

"The hell! Sorry, Father. Have you talked to Ferrell? I assume Ferrell's been in to see him?"

"No. He hasn't."

Father Hugh had considered how best to tell his story. Sister St. Paul had told him about the county attorney. A man in his forties now. But born and raised here in Murray County. Very much a part of this country. Knows everyone, of course.

Tell it straight as he knew it from beginning to end, Father Hugh had decided. So he began with the good luck of Mildred Harrington's coming upon Pat and the story Pat told her of being thrown from a horse. How Mildred and Renny Archambault—"Renny works out there at the Harrington place," and George Clarke nodded impatiently, of course Clarke would know that—set and splinted Pat's leg and brought him to the hospital in Fort Maginnis in the back of a truck. How Renny and Mildred got to thinking about Pat's thrown-from-the-horse story and decided it didn't add up.

George Clarke stood up, pushed his chair away from his desk, walked to the window, and looked out as though expecting to see something interesting on the stubbled lawn below. A tallish, dark-haired man just starting to gray at the temples. A man who was certain of himself and wasn't certain now. He turned back to Father Hugh, glanced out the window again, returned to his desk.

"You ever see Patrick Adams on a horse, Father? No, wouldn't think you had. Put it this way. He knows how to ride. Hawthorns," he added, puzzling Father Hugh.

Clarke sat back down at his desk, but this time he didn't lean back. Something alert in his eyes. Alarm, even, Father Hugh thought. He went on.

"Sister St. Paul had her doubts too. Especially about the blow to Pat's head. And the way Pat was acting, like he wanted to rip himself loose from that hospital bed, broken leg or not. It took her a day or two, and she got a different story out of him."

Prosecutor's eyes and priest's eyes met briefly. No need to say more about Sister St. Paul's methods.

The letter from his father. A way of luring Pat home? Pat's return from Missoula . . .

Clarke nodded. "Heard Pat was back, what, a month, month and a half ago?"

The cowboys sent over east with the cattle. Pat asked to help with the fence repair. The crowbar attack from behind. Coming back to consciousness in the hawthorns near Svoboda's crossing.

Silence for a moment in the county attorney's office.

"Want a smoke?" Clarke offered Father Hugh a tailor-made and pushed an ashtray where they could share it.

Silence. The sound of women in heeled shoes walking past the prosecutor's door. Someone below the window calling, "I don't have time for that!"

"Ever feel the urge to pick up something and throw it through a wall?" said Clarke, and Father Hugh thought of Sister St. Paul and her paring knife.

"What do you make of that line, *Crawl the rest of the way to your moccasin squaw?*" he asked.

Clarke shook his head. "For one thing, it makes me think Ferrell knew Pat was alive when he dumped him. For another—"

"So you believe Pat's story?"

"Pat Adams never in his life has done anything to make me doubt his word. I still have friends at the law school in Missoula, and I know what they think of Pat." A pause. "What do you think of him, Father?"

"I haven't known him long as you have, but I like him."

Clarke's fingers clenched, and Father Hugh wondered if he really was going to see something thrown at the wall, perhaps that ashtray.

"Ferrell Adams and Thaddeus Harrington. Two old range bulls, one as mean as the other. Came to this country with enough money to set themselves above their neighbors. Only redeeming thing about Thad, he kinda liked Renny Archambault, for some reason. Trusted Renny. Hated everybody else he could call a breed or a bohunk. The only reason those kids turned out so well was their mothers and of course, in Mildred's case, Sister St. Paul. Thad had worked her mother to death by then."

Clarke stubbed out his cigarette. "They hated each other, of course. Then something happened—ten, fifteen years ago, I lose track of time—nobody knows what happened that made them both worse. Old Thad in particular turned reclusive. Wouldn't leave the ranch. Wouldn't allow Mildred off the ranch. How Sister St. Paul managed to pry that little girl loose from Thad, I'll never know."

"Well . . ." Father Hugh hesitated, but it wasn't like Sister St. Paul had told him the story through the confessional grille. Although, she had whispered most of it to him. "Actually, Mr. Clarke—"

"Name's George."

"Actually, George, I can enlighten you on that point."

And he did. And he saw George Clarke sit back in his chair, and he thought Clarke was not often a man at a loss for words.

George Clarke is old Murray County, but he's a decent man, Sister St. Paul had told Father Hugh.

Clarke's eyes returned from wherever they'd gone. He found words. "Wouldn't have thought it, even with those two old sons of bitches. But there it is. Do we charge Ferrell with assault and risk that story coming out?"

"Pat's afraid his father will go after Mildred Harrington. I think that's why he's so frantic at being tied down in a hospital bed."

Both men stood. "I guess bodily harm trumps the story coming out," said Clarke. "Tell Sister St. Paul to get Pat to speak out. Help us do something about it."

He walked Father Hugh to the door and said, "I'm about ready to drive out there and bring Mildred back to town myself."

Father Hugh thankfully finished his homily and folded the sheets into a sheaf. Then he walked over to the convent and asked Sister Boniface if she would visit the hospital with him, and Sister Boniface looked at Sister St. Paul, who gave her a minimal nod and went back to her own paperwork.

Sister Boniface, who never knew what to make of Father Hugh, walked with her hands folded in her sleeves and her chin lowered to make her veil hide as much of her face as she could. A result was that she couldn't look where she was going, and she caught the toe of her shoe in a broken patch of sidewalk and would have stumbled if Father Hugh hadn't caught her elbow. She chanced a look at him, but he just shook his head.

Down the corridor past the admissions desk, up the flight of stairs to the second floor, with Sister Boniface trying not to make eye contact with nursing nuns she knew. Father Hugh tapped on a door and opened it and walked into the room, with Sister Boniface shrinking behind him. When the young man in the hospital bed looked up, surprised, from a book he was reading, she shrank back farther.

"Pat, this is Sister . . ."

Father Hugh looked around for her, but she had backed up as far as the door.

". . . Sister Boniface," Father Hugh finished. "And Sister, I want you to walk over here by the bed."

Trembling, she obeyed. This was terrible. Not just Father McHugh with his eyes on her, but the young man in the bed, whose leg was sheathed in plaster and elevated.

"Sister Boniface, this is Patrick Adams, and I want you to tell him about the man you thought might be a cowboy who knocked at the door of the convent and asked if Mildred Harrington was there."

She took a deep breath and repeated what she had told Father Hugh, that she answered a knock at the door and there stood a cowboy who asked for Mildred and how she had lied—a quick glance at Father Hugh—and said she hadn't seen Mildred all summer.

"Why did you think he was a cowboy, Sister?" said the young man. He had a quiet, unthreatening voice, and she thought perhaps he was not given to saying strange things, as Father McHugh did, that turned out to be jokes she couldn't see the point of.

"Well, his face was really, really tanned, and he wore a big hat, out to here"—she measured a good six inches on either side of her coif with her hands—"and it was something about the way he walked, but I can't describe it."

"Do you remember what color his eyes were?"

"Blue, I think. And oh yes, he wore boots."

"Hm. Do you remember anything particular about his boots? Maybe when he walked away?"

Suddenly, Sister Boniface did remember. His boots were where her eyes had been for most of her short conversation with the cowboy. "Yes! The heels of his boots! I remember because I thought his bootheels might have to do with the way he walked. They were"—she made a sweeping, underhand motion—"They curved underneath him, more than any bootheels I ever saw."

Father Hugh looked at Patrick Adams, and Patrick Adams said, "Maybe."

"Do you want me to walk you back to the convent, Sister Boniface?"

"No! I'll be fine!" And Sister Boniface fled for the shelter of the convent and Sister St. Paul.

"I've never seen a nun so shy," said Father Hugh when the door closed behind Sister Boniface. "I think Sister St. Paul is trying to cure her of it. Sister Boniface is the one she always sends with messages for me."

"She was talking about undershot bootheels," Pat said. "A specially shaped bootheel," he explained when he saw Father Hugh didn't have a clue. "Some cowboys like em for the way they fit in their stirrups. And they do kinda affect the way a man looks when he walks in em, though just like Sister said, it's hard to describe. And most cowboys walk as little as possible."

"Every little piece helps, I guess. Too bad she didn't talk a little more with him."

"Although, I do know one blue-eyed cowboy who wears undershot boots. Which isn't saying it was him. He's a friend of mine."

They wrestled the question back and forth for some time. Supposing Sister Boniface's cowboy was Albert Vanaartsdalen, why was he looking for Mildred, and why was he asking for her at the convent?

"Anybody who knows Mil would know the convent is somewhere she'd go," Pat pointed out.

"Does this Albert what's-his-name know her?"

"Vanaartsdalen. Well, he knows her when he sees her. He probably knows the nuns raised her. I doubt he's ever actually talked to her. Not since we were kids, anyway."

And he told Father Hugh about the Plum Creek school and how he and Albert had been eighth graders when Mil started sixth grade there, "and eighth graders don't pay a lot of attention to sixth graders, especially when they're interested in another eighth grader, which Albert was at that time."

Father Hugh and Pat's conversation had run out. Pat had no idea whether Albert had gone on working for Ferrell after the posthole incident. Albert had been pretty fed up with Ferrell, he knew that. Maybe Renny knew.

Still Father Hugh didn't go. Finally, he said, looking at the hat that he was holding and not at Pat, "Sister St. Paul said you might want to talk to me?"

"Yeah."

Pat drew a breath and then another, and then he told Father Hugh about his and Mil's summer and their month of nights. What their month of nights came to.

"She was fourteen! And they hurt her. But what I did was the reason why they hurt her. And I can't make it not have happened, and I can't do anything for her."

"Have you talked to her?"

"Tried a few times. But she's as gun-shy as Sister Boniface. Maybe worse. If she sees me, she runs."

"You were how old?"

"Sixteen."

Long pause.

"If you were a Catholic," said Father Hugh, "I'd hear your confession, and then I'd give you a penance. And after you carried out your penance, I'd absolve you, and maybe you'd feel better."

When Pat couldn't answer, Father Hugh added, "God's ways. Consider this, Pat. Two other men than Ferrell Adams and Thad Harrington might have brought you and Mildred to town and found a justice and lied about your ages and made you marry her. And you'd have been a sixteen-year-old and a fourteen-year-old starting life on a ranch somewhere. No college or law school for you; no high school or nurses' training for Mildred. Just work and more work for you and for her."

Another pause.

"I'm not saying what you did wasn't wrong or what they did wasn't unspeakable. Just that what happened, happened. If it hadn't, something else would have happened."

More gently, "It doesn't always have to be bad for you, Pat. Or bad for Mildred."

Pat tore his eyes from the ceiling and met Father Hugh's.

"Father, if you gave me penance, supposing you could, what would it be?"

"Keep trying to talk to her. Find a way to tell her you're sorry."

Father Hugh stood, and he punched Pat's shoulder as Albert Vanaartsdalen would have done. And then he did leave, and Pat went back to his study of the ceiling.

9

Father Hugh walked back to the rectory, thinking of all the things people didn't talk about in this new state. This new part of the country. How little the men in his parish talked, and what they talked about. How's the weather out your way? Crops? Any rain? Nah, not us. You get any?

The women didn't talk much, at least to the men. Can I help you to more gravy, Father? he would be asked at a church supper. Are you ready for a piece of pie? If asked directly, one of the women would admit that, no, it hadn't rained out at Bohemian Corners either. He supposed the women said more among themselves.

Sister St. Paul, who held a curious status as a kind of genderless crossover by virtue of her veil and her authority, did move back and forth between the women and the men, and what they told her, she told Father Hugh.

And yet information somehow circulated around Murray County without words, as though it was inhaled and exhaled through the air. What everybody knew about everybody else. Maybe only a handful of people knew what two teenagers had done in the pine needles fourteen years ago or what had happened afterward—Ferrell, Sister St. Paul, Renny, the kids themselves, and now the county prosecutor, thanks to Father Hugh—but Father Hugh wouldn't lay money on it.

"We all knew Ferrell and Thad were ornery," Mrs. Svoboda had told Sister St. Paul, who told Father Hugh. Sister also explained to Father Hugh that *ornery* meant abusive. "The way Ferrell beat that boy," Sister went on. "Everybody knew, but what could they do?"

Because people in this new country not only didn't spill their guts, as they would put it. They also didn't interfere in another man's business.

The Plum Creek school sat on a low rise of prairie beside the county road, as close to equal distance between the homesteads in its district as its planners could figure out. The idea was for every child in Murray County, and for that matter in Montana, to have the opportunity to complete eight grades at a school within a walking or horseback-riding or buggy-driving distance. In 1910, when Pat started the eighth grade, the homesteaders were new to the country, and the land was being ploughed for the first time. Rain fell, crops were promising, and the school was full of children, forty or more of them crammed into a room of desks and a coal stove and a watercooler the teacher filled from a spring behind the school.

Pat and Albert and a girl named Elsie Wigg were the only eighth graders. By their age, most boys and lots of girls were needed at home and couldn't stay in school. Always too much work to be done. But the lower grades were crowded, although many of the smaller kids also stayed home when the snow fell and temperatures dropped—twenty, thirty degrees below zero, too cold for little kids to be riding horseback.

The early fall of 1910 was balmy, and Mr. Sloan, the teacher, opened the schoolroom windows and let the breezes carry in the scents of sage and ripening wheat while he moved from grade to grade, teaching lessons and hearing recitations and writing homework assignments on the blackboard. At recess, all the children ran out to play in the sagebrush for fifteen minutes, except Pat, who had his eye on the three shelves of library books that needed reading, and Albert, who had his eye on Elsie, and Elsie herself, and Mr. Sloan, who sat behind his desk keeping an eye on all three of them until it was time to ring the handbell and call everyone back into the schoolroom.

At noon, an hour to open lunch boxes, bolt whatever their mothers had sent with them, and race out again to play, or not, as with Albert, Elsie, and Pat. Lessons, recitations, assignments, afternoon recess, lessons, recitations, assignments, until school was dismissed at four. Pat remembered those days as placid and predictable and stretching toward the end of the school year in June or to infinity, whichever came first. He'd paid no attention to the little kids. Guessed he'd known which one Mildred Harrington was. The little sixth grader with the long brown braids.

One day, he was slow leaving school, because he had been arguing a point of grammar with Mr. Sloan, and everybody else had tightened their saddle cinches and climbed on their horses and started for home. He didn't care. Probably he was daydreaming about something as he left the school. He did a lot of daydreaming in those days. He untied whichever of his father's jughead horses he'd been riding that fall and tightened the saddle cinch and mounted and kicked the horse into a trot.

About half a mile from the school, he came to the first wire gate across the trail and saw that it was open with Mildred Harrington sitting beside it, crying.

"What's wrong, Mil?"

She looked up at him with wide hazel eyes full of tears and her brown hair full of sunlight, and all these years later, confined to a hospital bed, Pat could see her face and hear her voice wobble.

She'd ridden as far as the gate and dismounted to open it and led Banty through, and then she had trouble closing the gate. She didn't know why—she'd opened and closed it that very morning. The more she struggled, the worse she did, and Banty's bridle reins, which she'd hung over her shoulder and tucked under her arm, worked out from her arm as she fought with the gate, until they hung loose over her shoulder. And Banty, always a sly one, saw her chance and jerked her reins away from Mildred and started trotting toward home.

"I ran after her," Mildred told Pat, "and she kept trotting just ahead of me, faster than I could run. She knows how to cock her head to the side when she trots so she doesn't step on her bridle reins. And it's my fault, because I know that, and I know she's sly, and if I'd just tied her to a wire before I tried to shut the gate! And I lost my breath, and I knew I couldn't run all the way home, and I remembered I hadn't got the gate shut, so I came back, and I still can't shut it."

"I'll shut it for you," said Pat, and he rode through and dismounted—which horse? his father was always picking up unbroken or half-broken jugheads and setting Pat to riding them until they could be resold at a few dollars' profit—and tied the horse to a fence wire. Picked up the gatepost, gave it a jerk to straighten out its wires, set the bottom end of the post in its wire loop, put his shoulder to the post, and slipped its wire loop over the top.

"Stop crying," he said. "I'll take you home, Mil."

He mounted the jughead and slipped his boot out of his stirrup so Mil could get a foot into it, and he reached for her hand and swung her up behind him and felt her arms go around his waist to steady herself. The jughead snorted and sidestepped, and Pat growled at him and pulled him up short and spun him around a few times to distract him before turning down the fork of the trail that led, not to the Adams ranch, but to the Harrington ranch.

Mil's face with the sun gracing her hair. Mil riding double with him. And he'd lived to ride double with her one more time.

He'd ridden with her all the way to the Harrington ranch buildings, and there was Banty with her bridle reins tied to a corral pole.

"I'll get what for, now," she said as Pat swung her down.

"Tell you what, Mil," he said. "I'll wait for you at the gate tomorrow morning and open the gate and close it for you, and in the afternoon, if you do leave school ahead of me, you wait at the gate for me, and I'll open and close it."

"Thank you," she said in a small voice, and trudged off toward the cabin. Pat guessed her lunch box and books would still be tied to Banty's saddle. He saw Renny Archambault standing in the barn door and waved, and Renny waved back. Pat hoped Renny wouldn't let her father give her too hard a what for. He was going to get what for, too, riding home so late, but he had learned how to stand up and take it.

"Did she and I seem to you like special friends that year in school?" he once asked Albert Vanaartsdalen, and Albert said he didn't think so, although he hadn't particularly been watching them.

No. It had been a friendship formed during the half-mile ride between the school and the wire gate, and it had continued between the school and the wire gate until the school year ended. And then the friendship was cut off. He hadn't seen Mil again for three years and hadn't thought of her much. Too much else happening in his life. High school girls, for instance.

Keep trying to talk to her, Father Hugh had said, so you can tell her you're sorry.

Sure. But how, in hell, when she ran if she saw him?

Unaware of anyone calling him Sister Boniface's cowboy and worrying about his intentions, Albert Vanaartsdalen drove Pat Adams's truck up and down Main Street in Fort Maginnis and tried to think of what to do next. If they hadn't seen her at the convent, then where? Somebody, somebody must know something. Where Mildred was. What had become of Pat. Because Pat had vanished.

When Albert and Frank had left to drive Ferrell's cattle over east, Pat had been digging postholes for a stretch of fencing below the barn that the old man wanted built there for some reason. When Albert and Frank rode back from over east, Pat was gone and Ferrell was drunk.

Albert saw Pat's truck where Pat had parked it, in the lee of the shed. Albert looked inside the truck and saw its key in the ignition, which was where people in ranch country tended to leave their truck or car keys, and he hadn't known what to think.

No point in asking Ferrell. His personal business was the last thing Ferrell, drunk or sober, would talk about with one of his hands. The likeliest, Albert decided, was that Ferrell had pulled some stupid drunken stunt and Pat got fed up and went back to Missoula. But without his truck?

Then a postcard came in the mail for Ferrell from one of the ranchers over east. Ferrell better send them boys to move his cattle home, the rancher wrote, because they was plumb out of grass and starving. So Albert and Frank saddled up again and rode over east, a day and a half on horseback and another couple of days rounding up what cattle they thought had a chance of surviving the trip back. They shot the rest, and over three more days, they trailed the survivors back to the range they'd been trailed out of less than a month before.

Pat's truck, right where it had been when they left.

Pat was Albert's friend, damn it. Pat had vanished. Men didn't just vanish off the face of the earth for no reason.

One early evening while the light was still good, Albert listened at the kitchen door and eased it open. Heard soft snores from the front room. Listened a few minutes more and slipped through the door and up the stairs that led from the kitchen into a dim space that smelled of mice. His hair was prickling at the roots. He eased open a door and found a room full of junk. An old saddle on a sawhorse, some harnesses, clothes hanging on a rod and filthy with dust, a box of dishes somebody had started to unpack. Stacks of newspapers. An empty birdcage. Albert shook his head at the strange assortment.

The next door stood open. In the fading light from a dirty window in the eaves, he saw a made-up bed with a small suitcase lying across it. Uneasily, with a vision of Ferrell rousing from his stupor and trapping him here, Albert stole into the room on the toes of his boots. Don't creak, floorboards. Be nice.

The suitcase contained a few changes of underwear and some rolled-up socks and some handkerchiefs and a folded pair of Levi's. Albert turned to the rest of the room. A couple of shirts hanging on nails. Pat's good new Justin boots on the floor below the shirts. Of course Pat would have been wearing his beat-up work boots to build fence.

On a dresser, a comb and a toothbrush and a razor. A billfold that Albert recognized. He held the billfold toward the window and by its light found some official-looking cards having to do with the practice of law, as far as Albert could figure out, also a vehicle registration card and a card with Pat's name and his Missoula address written on it. Fifty dollars. And a small picture that looked as though it had been cut from a newspaper, of Mildred Harrington in a nurse's starched cap and collar.

Every hair on the back of his neck was standing up and screaming at him to get out of this room, to get out of this house, and Albert slipped Pat's billfold into his shirt pocket and stole downstairs and across the kitchen. He had his hand on the doorknob when he heard a snore and dared a look into the front room. The light was better down here, and Albert saw Ferrell sprawled back in his big armchair with his mouth open and his head lolling sideways. A cigarette still in his hand. An ashtray on the floor beside him, full of the butts of tailor-mades. Maybe the old bastard would get drunk enough to set the house on fire, and himself with it.

Possibilities. Over the next several days, Albert pondered them. He asked Frank what he thought, and Frank shook his head.

"I don't know, but I don't like it. I don't like it here, period. My dad's got a little spread up in Blaine County, and I don't spose the grass is any better there than here, but anything's better than working for a damned drunk who's so mean he's as liable to shoot somebody as look at him."

Albert thought hard. Pat. Riding one of the jugheads Ferrell still picked up and tried to sell for a profit. Pat could ride anything with hair, but freak things happened. The jughead kicking Pat in the head, for instance. Albert had heard Ferrell talk about a man he knew who died that way.

The jughead throwing Pat off—Albert couldn't quite picture that happening, but say it did—and Pat rolling unconscious or dead into some goddamn coulee or patch of underbrush where no one ever found him. Could happen, Albert supposed, and for some reason felt the prickles rise again on the back of his neck.

But surely even Ferrell would roust out the whole neighborhood to search if his son didn't come home from a horseback ride. If his son left behind his billfold and his personal effects and his truck with the key still in the ignition.

Albert didn't like where his speculations had led him.

10

"Sure do hate to see them cows like that," said Frank. "And hear em."

The cattle were starving and bawling, but there was no grass. Albert and Frank talked it over and agreed the only thing to do was round them up and truck them to the sales ring in Fort Maginnis before they purely starved. Would they even sell for enough to pay for the trucking? They would never make it on their own hoofs, but trucking them might be just better than shooting them all.

Albert and Frank flipped a coin, and Albert lost. He picked his time, late morning, when Ferrell had stoked himself with coffee and seemed rational, more or less. Sometimes he even saddled a horse and rode off on some purpose of his own. Albert caught him in the horse barn and tried to talk to him about the condition of the cattle and his and Frank's idea of trucking them to the sales ring. Ferrell just waved Albert off. When Albert said the only other option he and Frank could see was shooting them, Ferrell bellowed something about nobody shooting *his* goddamn cattle and rounded at Albert with his fists, and Albert retreated.

"Ferrell's cattle," he told Frank. "If he wants to let em starve . . ." he trailed off.

Frank nodded. "Hate to watch it, though. The old bastard."

"I'm starting to think he's worse'n that," Albert said, and he told Frank the direction his thoughts had taken him.

By lantern light in the half dugout, half shed Albert and Frank called the bunkhouse, Albert studied the little picture of Mildred Harrington he'd found in Pat's billfold. A pretty girl, he guessed, if a girl who never smiled. Her mouth in the picture was a straight line. Nice eyes, though.

Albert knew she'd turned out to be a damn good nurse and that people respected her for the work she did. Word was that anybody who sent for her—it didn't matter, day or night, summer or winter—could expect to see her riding up on horseback with her black bag. Albert wasn't sure he'd seen her more than once or twice, himself, since their Plum Creek school days. She'd never smiled, even back then.

Pat, though. Albert hadn't been paying attention, but even at the Plum Creek school, he now realized, there'd been something between Pat and Mildred. Well, she'd been just a little girl, hadn't she? A fifth grader, he thought. And ever since, there had been something between her and Pat, whatever *something* was.

Hard as the *something* was to understand. Elsie Wigg, now, the last Albert had seen of her was in the back seat of a Model T loaded with what the Wiggs still owned and the Wiggs themselves. Albert hadn't given Elsie a thought since then, until he found Mildred Harrington's picture in Pat's billfold and got to speculating about what kept Pat hanging on so long.

Surely Pat had had girls since Mildred?

"Well, the hell," Albert said out loud, and Frank looked around to see what Albert was cussing about and shrugged and went back to mending his bridle. Not like either of them had any real work to do, with cattle dying all around them.

The more he studied her unsmiling young face, the more Albert knew in his bones that Mildred Harrington had something to do with whatever had happened to Pat. All he could do was ask her, he guessed. In the morning, he saddled a horse and rode across the browning prairie and past the Svoboda place, where smoke curled from a stovepipe and wash hung on a line, and he saw that Stan Svoboda had gotten his hay in, what there was of it. Albert rode on through the sweltering heat and down into Svoboda's bottomland, where the grass was still good enough to keep the cattle grazing a while longer. He rode along the hawthorns that choked the banks of the creek, and he smelled the mud and water at the crossing and let his horse drink before he rode across.

Another hour's ride and Albert saw the roof of Mildred Harrington's cabin and the tops of the cottonwood trees that shaded it. He rode past the cabin toward the barn and corrals, and when the dogs erupted from the barn, bristling and barking at him, he saw Renny walking out of the barn and to his astonishment found himself in the sights of Renny's rifle.

"What the hell, Renny?"

Renny recognized him and lowered the rifle partway. "What do you want, Albert?"

"Is Mildred here?"

"She's not here."

Albert waited, but Renny said nothing else. He just stood there, holding his rifle at the half ready.

"Thanks anyway, I guess," said Albert, baffled, and he turned his horse and rode back the way he had come. It wasn't until he'd reached the creek and crossed it to the Svobodas' land that he felt the muscles between his shoulder blades relax. When a situation went as far as Renny Archambault running him off with a rifle, it had gone too far.

When he got back to the Adams ranch, he threw his clothes and good boots and his wallet and razor into a gunnysack and told Frank what he was going to do, and then he threw the gunnysack into the cab and his saddle into the back of Pat's truck and climbed in himself and turned the key in the ignition. Thankfully, the battery wasn't dead after its long sit. The motor turned over and started, and Albert drove off toward the county road. He didn't care whether Ferrell saw him drive off in Pat's truck or not.

"Serious bodily injury like that, I'd have expected the doctor to have reported it," George Clarke said.

"There was Pat's riding-accident story," Father Hugh pointed out. "And it was old Dr. Naylor at the hospital when Renny and Mildred brought Pat in."

"Old Doc Naylor."

"The sisters have themselves a new doctor up at the hospital now."

The new doctor who replaced Doc Naylor had moved all the way from St. Louis to work at the Hospital of the Good Samaritan. He was a short dark-haired man named Bart Riggio, who had been a trauma surgeon during the war and felt restless when he came home. Practicing in Montana struck him as adventurous, maybe even a cure for what ailed him. When he discovered the piano in the Catholic church, he asked Sister St. Paul if he could drop by and play it from time to time. She asked Father Hugh about it, and the nuns soon became accustomed to hearing the piano being played in the church at odd hours.

Dr. Riggio examined Patrick Adams and shook his head. The young man was losing muscle tone, and he looked slack faced, with eyes that moved back and forth and here and there.

"How've you been feeling?" he asked Pat.

"Damn fed up."

"We've got to get you out of this setup."

Pat's eyes shot to the doctor's face and stayed there.

"How long have you had him strung up like that?" Dr. Riggio asked Sister St. Paul. He'd dropped by the church to play the piano and seen that she was on her knees, so he waited until she rose. Now the doctor and Sister St. Paul sat together in one of the back pews.

"Without checking his charts . . ." she thought for a minute. "They brought him here in early June, and now July's almost done. Six weeks, probably, not the full two months for a break like his."

"Why wasn't he discharged to his family?"

"He wouldn't go home, so Dr. Naylor wouldn't discharge him."

"I think if you could look at him with fresh eyes, you'd see what I see. He's like an animal getting weaker in a cage, and he's got something, I don't know what, on his mind that isn't helping him. Way better for him if we put a walking brace on that leg and get him on his feet than keeping him on his back like that. Since he won't go home, is there somewhere else he can go?"

"I'll think of somewhere," said Sister St. Paul.

"Thank you, God," said Pat. The nursing sister had unhooked him from his pole and pulley and laid his leg and cast flat on the bed. Being able to raise himself a few inches off the mattress with his hands felt so damned good that he couldn't believe he'd endured the pole and tether as long as he had. He couldn't see what Dr. Riggio was doing with his big shears, because Father Hugh was standing by his bedside and blocking his view, but he could feel some pressure from the blades and hear a sound like distant cracking ice while he half-listened to Father Hugh, who seemed unusually talkative this afternoon.

Every few ice cracks, he could feel the blades being withdrawn and returning shortly to make a few more ice cracks. It seemed to Pat that cutting off his cast was taking a hell of a while. But then Dr. Riggio handed the shears to the nursing sister and returned to whatever he was doing behind Father Hugh's back. Pat felt the doctor's fingers on his leg, exploring between his leg and the cast, an actual human touch on his leg after weeks in the goddamn cast. After a major and prolonged ice crack, Pat felt Dr. Riggio lift his leg and lay it back on the mattress. Then he saw the cast, a ruptured length of dirty white plaster, being handed to the sister. It was also the moment Pat heard, really heard, what Father Hugh was saying. That one of his parishioners who knew Albert Vanaartsdalen had seen Albert in Fort Maginnis, driving a truck up and down Main Street.

Pat's leg felt strangely light, as though it wanted to levitate toward the ceiling. He wondered if he was light-headed as well.

The doctor reemerged from behind Father Hugh. "We'll see if we can get you fitted into this contraption. That's right, Sister, you can put that stocking on his leg now."

The "contraption" turned out to be a kind of padded felt shoe with high padded sides and iron ribs. Father Hugh cranked up the head of the bed so Pat could watch the doctor slide his foot and strangely shrunken leg into the shoe and buckle its adjustable straps.

"You'll want to keep it snug, but you can loosen the straps as you get your muscle tone back. And you don't have to sleep in it. Let's see you try to stand up."

The sensation of sitting up straight. Swinging, no, dragging his legs over the edge of the mattress and letting them dangle.

"How does that feel?"

"Feels wonderful."

"We're going to steady you."

Father Hugh on one side, Dr. Riggio on the other—uneven props, because Father Hugh was so tall and the doctor so short. Pat's arms over their shoulders, theirs around his waist. He slid off the bed and felt his bare foot and padded foot touch the tiles. He had never felt so unsteady.

"You can put some weight on your left foot as long as you're careful. Go ahead, take a step."

Both of his legs had forgotten what to do. But he willed the padded foot to lift, and it did. And he lowered it and let it take his weight and lifted his bare foot. He took five or six tottering steps between Father Hugh and Dr. Riggio to a chair and sat, exhausted.

The nursing sister clapped. "Hurrah!"

"Damn I'm weak."

"You'll get stronger. At your age—you're not quite thirty yet, are you? No, I didn't think so. Main thing is to keep up the exercise."

Whatever Father Hugh had been saying about Albert.

"You were talking quite a bit, for a while there," Pat said, and Father Hugh grinned.

"Yup. I was your designated distracter. Sister St. Paul told me to keep your attention off the cast cutting. And I'm going to bring my car around, and we're going to get you out of here. Sister St. Paul and I are going take you to Josie's. She and Evangeline are going to help get you on your feet."

Who were Josie and Evangeline? Pat wondered, before he remembered that Josie was Renny Archambault's aunt. Evangeline? Had to be another of Renny's relatives. God only knew how many relatives Renny had.

Two nursing sisters helped Pat to dress in the clothes he'd worn the day he'd been dumped in the hawthorns. The only clothes he had now, he guessed. The nuns had laundered and pressed them, and his Levi's still were slit up the side where Mil had used a skinning knife to open his pant leg and get his boot off, so the Levi's accommodated his new brace, boot, whatever they called it, just fine. And one of the white shirts he'd always favored.

Giggling, the two nursing sisters lifted Pat and set him in a wheelchair and wheeled him down the corridor to the lift. Pat wondered at the way he was entertaining so many women so much and hoped he never would again. But the sisters didn't trust him to walk so far, even with one of them supporting him on either side, and Pat had to admit he also didn't trust himself.

On the first floor, the sisters wheeled him out of the lift and past the admissions desk—a big smile and a wave from the nun at the desk, "Goodbye, Pat!"—and out to the curb where Father Hugh's car waited. One of the sisters opened the rear door while the other sister told him to put his weight on his right leg and steady himself on the car when she pulled the wheelchair away, and then he could sit on the seat of the car and swing his legs inside.

Swing his legs, hell. Turned out he had to lift them with his hands to get them in the car. Weak as a goddamn kitten.

"Sister St. Paul will have instructions for you to take care of your brace and your legs and to exercise," called one of the sisters. Then the sisters were standing on the sidewalk with the empty wheelchair, beaming at him and waving—"Goodbye, Pat!" "Goodbye, Pat!"

Sister St. Paul sitting beside him in the rear seat. Father Hugh up front, behind the wheel. Father Hugh put the car in gear and pulled out from the curb at a stately fifteen miles an hour.

11

Somebody, maybe a teacher at the Plum Creek school, once told Albert that if you gave a monkey a piano to pound on, sooner or later by pure accident the monkey would pound out a tune. Probably later than sooner, Albert always thought. The monkey might die of old age first.

But Albert, drive Pat's truck up and down Main Street while you try to decide what next to do, and sooner or later you'll happen to drive past the hospital just as two white-habited nuns push someone in a wheelchair to a waiting black automobile, and you'll happen to see that someone's face.

By the time Albert could drive to where he could turn the truck around and come back, the black automobile had pulled away with Pat, and the nuns were returning to the hospital with their wheelchair. Albert fell in behind the black automobile at what he deemed a discreet distance. He was, by God, going to tail it until he found out where Pat was being taken and—from what he'd seen of Pat's face—why Pat looked like he had been put through hell and a wringer.

It was about time, Albert thought, that he caught a break in this whole miserable monkey-pounding sorry situation.

Josie lived in the old part of town, along Spring Creek. Pat didn't think he'd ever been down here, although of course he knew from Renny how those first dozen Métis families had traveled down from Canada in the 1870s in their screeching wooden-wheeled Red River carts. A caravan of Red River carts, Renny said someone had described for him, sounded like a thousand fingernails scratching blackboards. Before there was a town of Fort Maginnis or even a white settlement, the Métis built cabins along the creek, including the cabin Father Hugh was pulling up in front of, and the Métis cleared underbrush and planted gardens and orchards. Several years later they built a school with the help of stonemasons who had come from Croatia to settle in Murray County, and eventually, with the help of the Croatians, they got the Hospital of the Good Samaritan built.

A tiny woman in a long black dress with a silver cross on a ribbon around her neck appeared at the cabin's screen door. Came running to meet them.

"Sister! Father!"

She had a face like a dried apple. White hair pinned back in a bun.

"Here your young man? You bring inside!"

Pat put his weight gingerly on his right leg and let Josie Archambault, surprisingly strong, steady him while he lifted his left leg out with his hands and shifted himself from the seat of the car to a seat on the fireman's chair Father Hugh and Sister St. Paul had formed by gripping their own and each other's wrists with their hands. They carried him up Josie's short graveled walk, with Josie hurrying ahead, chattering and opening doors for them. Pat thought of Ferrell's reaction if he could see his son being carried into a Métis cabin by a Catholic priest and a nun, and he had to laugh.

"Laugh! Good for you! Bring through here!"

A small room off the kitchen. Log walls and a narrow bed with a crucifix hanging over it. A chair. A kerosene lamp with a sparkling clean chimney. Nails in the walls for clothes. Sister St. Paul and Father Hugh lowered Pat to the bed, and he lifted his legs with his hands and lay back, suddenly worn out.

"Evvie will help. Help you walk. Help you with pan until you can walk to outback."

Evangeline was introduced to him. Josie's grandniece, which was hard to believe, because Evangeline had to be close to six feet tall and strongly built. Bobbed black hair, gold hoop earrings, lipstick.

"Evvie wash clothes for you—"

"I don't think he has any other clothes," said Father Hugh.

"Evvie shop for him if he have money—"

If he had money to buy clothes with, Pat thought. He'd come to this, with nothing but the clothes he stood up in. In point of fact, the clothes he couldn't stand up in.

"Um . . ." said a voice from the doorway, and everyone turned and saw a sun-browned, blue-eyed face under a Stetson. Shirt and Levi's, boots with undershot heels.

Father Hugh said, "Sister Boniface's cowboy!"

Pat said, "Albert!"

"Sister Boniface have cowboy?"

Albert Vanaartsdalen looked perplexed but determined. "This be any help to you?" he said, and he pulled a billfold out of his shirt pocket and tossed it to Pat.

Evangeline brought glasses and a jug of Josie's chokecherry wine, and Josie poured wine for everyone, including Sister St. Paul and Father Hugh, who sipped their wine with everyone else. Like they were celebrating something, Pat thought. Maybe for solving the mystery of Sister Boniface's cowboy. He sipped his own wine, and it was pretty good.

Albert, however, looked as baffled as though he'd walked into a roomful of lunatics. He was a man with one question on his mind.

"Pat," he said, "what the hell happened to you?"

What the hell had happened to him? Pat himself wondered after Sister St. Paul told him, and repeated to Josie and Evangeline, how to care for his leg and promised to be back tomorrow to check on him—oh yes she would—and departed with Father Hugh.

Albert wasn't going anywhere. He waited until Evangeline went to help Josie with supper, and then he sat down beside Pat and told him what he knew and what he didn't know. His and Frank's pointless cattle drive over east. Returning and finding no Pat. Pat's truck and Albert's worry. Driving back the starving cattle to purely starve. His prowl through the upper floor of the ranch house and what he found.

"I might be able to sneak back and fetch the rest of your clothes," he said.

"Not worth it. Though I wouldn't mind getting my Justin boots back," Pat said.

He would have time enough to worry about the Justins when he could walk in them. With the fifty dollars in his billfold that Albert had retrieved, he at least could buy a change of clothes and give Josie a little money for his board and still have enough to get himself back to Missoula if that was what he wanted to do.

Albert went on. "So I got to thinking what Mildred might know, and I rode down to the Harrington place, and—"

Renny telling him she wasn't there. Running him off at rifle point.

"The convent was the only place I could think to look. And I don't even know who this Sister Boniface is," he added, and Pat had to laugh.

But he didn't like any of what Albert was telling him. If Renny had taken Mil anywhere but the convent, it would have been here, to Josie. What Renny's rifle told Pat was that Mil probably was right there in her cabin. Probably she had watched Albert ride in.

Or not. And no way of knowing.

"Dunno whether Frank's still out there with Ferrell or whether he left."

Evangeline came in with coffee and a bowl of stew for Pat's supper. She looked at Albert, who glared at her.

"I ain't leaving him alone," Albert said.

Evangeline studied him for a moment, returned to the kitchen, and came back with coffee and a bowl of stew for Albert.

When Pat and Albert had finished supper, Evangeline brought a moccasin for Pat's right foot.

"Feel like walking some?"

"Sure."

Sitting up, lifting his legs over the side of the bed. One arm over Albert's shoulders, one over Evangeline's. Feeling the floor under his feet. A step, another step, another. Evangeline held the back door open for him with her free hand, and she and Albert eased Pat's way down the stoop. The difference in thickness between the moccasin on one foot and the padded boot on the other made him feel, with every step, like a hipshot horse, but every step also felt damned wonderful.

He had a goal now. Walking all the way to what Josie called her outback. Maybe in a day or two, walking there by himself. No more nursing nuns with pans, none of Evangeline and her pan. And that evening, he did walk to the little shed at the back of Josie's garden, although Albert and Evangeline supported him all the way, and Albert had to help him inside and wait and help him outside again.

That night, awake in the narrow bed, where he could hear the creek current through the window and see the moving shadows of cottonwood leaves and where he could turn from his back to his side if he felt like it, while Albert snored from the sugans Josie and Evangeline had spread for him on the floor when he refused to leave Pat, Pat leafed out his plan. One step at a time, one foot in front of the other. Once he could walk, once he'd roused his dormant muscles, he'd think what next to do.

He raised his right leg as he had the night he'd pulled the head of the hospital bed over on himself. Flexed it and lowered it, raised and flexed and lowered. After a while he tried raising and flexing his left leg, and he got the leg a few inches off the mattress and his knee a few inches closer to his chin. Did it again and again, until his weakened muscles got too tired and quit on him.

He clasped his hands behind his head and tried an army-style curl-up, which made the bed creak and Albert stir in his sleep, and he decided better to wait until morning. He settled himself on a pillow that wasn't a hospital pillow, pulled up the sheet and quilt that weren't hospital issued, and sent a message to Mildred the only way he had.

Mil, I'm thinking about you.

Eventually, he slept.

Mildred had seen Albert Vanaartsdalen ride in, and she saw him ride out. Knowing that Albert was cowboying for Ferrell Adams, she had kept out of sight. Renny would tell her the reason for Albert's visit if he knew or thought she needed to know, and as it turned out, Renny didn't.

The following afternoon, Mildred was picking green beans when she straightened her back and saw another horse and rider pounding past the barn and heading for her cabin. When the rider turned and spotted her in her garden, she saw that it was the ten-year-old Danvers boy—Billy, she thought his name was—bareback astride one of his father's workhorses and that he was crying.

"Miss Harrington! Miss Harrington! It's my mom, and she's bleeding! Can you come?"

Butcher knives. Hatchets. All the tools women used. "Bleeding where? Did she cut herself?"

The boy's face was a battlefield between tears and embarrassment. "From her *down there*."

"Get what you need," said Renny. He had run from the barn with his rifle when he saw the horse and rider galloping past him. "I'll saddle Smokey for you."

Mildred ran for the cabin. Boots instead of moccasins. Her hat. Her black bag. Carrying the black bag, she ran to meet Renny and Smokey halfway from the barn, and she tied the bag to the saddle strings and swung into the saddle.

"Thought of saddling Pink for you, she's so much faster than Smokey, but she's gettin so damn mean . . ."

But Mildred already was too far away to hear the rest of what Renny was saying. Thinking what she would need to do. Thinking it was about two miles to the Danvers homestead, no problem for Smokey at a gallop, though maybe a problem for Billy's workhorse, and so she kicked Smokey into his hard lope and felt him answer her.

A mile along her rutted dirt road, a two-track joined it on its way to the county road. Mildred turned Smokey up the two-track. Billy and his workhorse had fallen well behind her now, and she was riding through a barren country where cattle had grazed off every blade. Nothing growing between the two tracks. Some never-say-die thistles along both sides of the tracks. No shade in sight, nothing green from horizon to horizon, nothing moving but cloud shadows and Mildred on Smokey and the dust that rose and drifted behind them.

And then she could see the tops of cottonwood trees along Plum Creek where it widened just before it joined Spring Creek. Smokey was breathing well, and she was following the tracks where they cut through chokecherries and hawthorns and willows. She came to the Danvers crossing, where she spurred Smokey across. No drink of water right now, Smokey, no time, and anyway, you're breathing too hard now. Only another couple of hundred yards now. Billy and the workhorse were nowhere in sight.

She saw a thread of smoke rising from the chimney of the Danvers shack—at least Will Danvers had had the sense to start a fire and boil water. At the fence, she jumped down from Smokey, tied him to a post where he could heave his sides and rest, and took her black bag down from her saddle.

Inside the shack, Will Danvers knelt beside the bed. Melissa Danvers raised her head from her pillow to look when she heard Mildred come in and then let her head fall back. At the foot of the bed huddled two small girls.

A teakettle on the stove. Mildred poured water into a basin without asking and found soap and scrubbed up. No point in trying to save time by risking infection. She finished and saw nothing clean to dry her hands with, so she took a hand towel from her black bag and used that. Careful not to touch anything, not her own clothes, not even the basin to empty it, she went to Melissa Danvers's bedside.

"Can you lift her dress for me?" she asked Will.

He stared at her and swallowed and did as she asked, and she could see she was going to have a shock patient next. She only hoped Will could hold on for as long as she needed him.

Too much blood.

"Melissa," she said. "I'm going to get your bleeding stopped. I don't think I'll hurt you, but you'll feel me doing it. And you'll feel pressure."

Leaning over the woman, she started with the index and middle fingers of her right hand to enter Melissa's vagina and felt Melissa stiffen and try to close her legs. "It's all right, Melissa. You need to let me do this. Can you spread your legs a little for me?"

Her fingers through the vagina, finding the cervix and pressing it forward. Her left hand on Melissa's belly above her uterus, finding it, kneading it down toward the pelvis in order to start the contractions that would stop the flow of blood.

The things cattlemen learned to do. What Renny once had done for Mildred on the seat of a pickup cab.

Drive, you son of a bitch! Do you think I can do this and drive at the same time?

Drive where?

To Fort Maginnis, damn you! To the sisters!

Contractions. Mildred took a breath and breathed it out. Going to be all right. All she needed now was good luck. "Will," she said, "bring me a basin of clean water and another cloth from my bag."

When he didn't answer, she turned and saw that he had fainted.

Billy, however, was standing by the stove with a little sister wrapped around each leg. Mildred repeated her instructions, and Billy freed himself from his sisters and did as she asked, with only a frightened look at his mother.

She sponge-bathed Melissa Danvers and removed her blood-stained dress and made her a pad of rags and dressed her in a clean nightgown fetched by Billy, and then—bloodied sheet and bedding eased from under Melissa and replaced by a clean, if nearly threadbare, sheet and blanket, and with Melissa's pelvis elevated by a couple of pillows from the children's bed—she squatted down and got Will Danvers, conscious now but with a bleached face, to drink a cup of twice-heated coffee with plenty of sugar.

"She gonna be all right, Mildred?"

"I think so. But you ought to take her to Fort Maginnis, to the sisters."

"Ain't got the money for that."

Mildred knew the sisters would never turn anyone away, but she also knew there'd be no money for the gasoline to get Melissa to town. "I'll ride back tomorrow," she said. "And you can send Billy again, if you need me sooner."

"She's an awful good woman," he said, and Mildred saw his eyes travel to his wife in their bed.

Mildred gathered up the bloody sheets and clothing and put them to soak in a tub of cold water. She would wash them and hang them out when she came back tomorrow. Then she folded the towels she'd used into her bag and told Will Danvers to get the kids fed their suppers and Melissa fed hers and not to let her get up until Mildred came again. Help Melissa with a pan if she needed it. And keep himself warm. Not that that was a big problem. The shack was stifling in end-of-July heat.

Mildred thought about leaving them some aspirin and decided not to risk thinning Melissa Danvers's blood, and anyway Mildred had turned against aspirin. During the flu epidemic, she'd noticed how many of her patients she was giving Josie's tea for their pain were recovering and how many old Doc Naylor, with his aspirin bottle, was losing. No certain connection, of course, but still.

What she'd seen in the bucket beside Melissa's bed. Miscarriage or home abortion? She would never ask. Three children already, and the prospect of bringing another into this world?

12

Mildred made a mental note to bring a can of milk and some eggs when she visited Melissa tomorrow, and she tied her black bag to her saddle and mounted Smokey for the ride home. Smokey was rested now, but she was in no hurry. She let Smokey drink at the creek before she crossed it and followed the two tracks toward her own road.

Old Doc Naylor. She wondered how his treatment of Pat's leg was coming along. It had been a long time since she'd had news from town, but surely Doc had had Pat off his back and out of traction for a while now.

Last night she'd wakened in the dark with that strange sense of Pat in the room with her. Seemed as though he now came often by night. She told herself maybe it was his hat on her dresser, conjuring him, and she wondered why she kept it there.

She rode slowly, and her shadow and Smokey's were lengthening when she saw her barn and corrals ahead. Renny met her at the corral gate. "Mildred, you look plumb wrung out. I'll take Smokey and unsaddle and brush and grain him. You go sit and be quiet and let me come up and cook your supper for you."

The air was a little cooler now. Maybe a fine drift rising from the creek current. She saw her bucket of green beans in her garden where she'd left it, and she retrieved it and climbed the porch steps in the shade of cottonwoods. So familiar. Her home. She hung her bag on its nail and dropped down on the leather couch, and then she thought she must have slept, because the next she knew, Renny was rattling something in the kitchen and noticed her.

"Rode after the mail today," he said, and handed her a letter. "From Sister St. Paul."

....

George Clarke knew where Josie Archambault lived, and one afternoon, instead of driving straight home after leaving his office, he drove to the old Métis quarter along Spring Creek and parked by the chicken wire fence around Josie's log cabin. He got out of his car and opened Josie's gate and shut it carefully behind him when he noticed that a couple of hens had escaped their coop and were scratching in the dust under an apple tree.

Knocked on Josie's door.

Josie answered. She looked surprised. "Mist Clarke! Come in!"

Clarke stepped over her threshold while she smiled at him. Her eyes were watchful, though. He always was struck by how tiny she was. And he wondered how old she really was. Did Josie herself know?

"You drink coffee," she informed him, and disappeared into her kitchen, as supple on her feet as a girl.

Pat Adams was sitting at a table by a window. He looked up from a book he'd been reading, and when he saw it was Clarke who had come in, he stood of his own power and walked the few steps to meet him and shake hands.

"Patrick," Clarke said. "It's been a while."

"Yeah."

Clarke thought Pat looked pretty good, considering everything Father Hugh had said about his injuries. In Clarke's eyes, altered, because Pat had been out of the sun too long and lost his tan. Pain, of course, left marks other than scars. Otherwise, Pat looked like himself, blue eyes and fair hair and off-kilter nose. A white shirt open at the neck. Levi's slit up the left side seam to accommodate the brace. Posture a little off-kilter, also, because of the brace on one foot and the moccasin on the other.

Josie was back with his coffee. "Sit, Mist Clarke, sit!"

Pat pulled a chair up for him, and Clarke sat, wondering if he was Josie's only visitor who didn't rate a glass of her illegal choke-cherry wine. Well, probably the sheriff also was on Josie's list, and the Fort Maginnis city police, supposing they ever visited Josie. Clarke suspected that jugs of her wine regularly found their way to the Catholic church, where Father Hugh consecrated the wine for the nuns and the parishioners to drink thimblefuls at Mass.

"What are you reading?" he asked Pat, and tipped the cover of his book to see. Thomas Dimsdale's *Vigilantes of Montana*, a tattered old copy with its cover torn off.

"Evvie get library card!"

"Yeah," said Pat, "and what she brought me home the first time—after that, I wrote out a list for the librarian. Miss Clara Manning. Not that she ever has everything on my list, but some of it. And now that she's sent me over a stack or two, she kinda knows what I like, and she'll pick out a book for me. Like this *Vigilantes*."

"Must work do now!" Josie told Clarke, and vanished into the kitchen, although it looked to the prosecutor as though she'd spread out her beads and her waxed thread on the table across from Pat and had been beading a glove. Clarke had a flash of the tiny old Métis woman with her beading and the young lawyer reading his book about vigilante justice in the Montana Territory, enjoying their late afternoon in companionable silence.

"You look to be on the mend, Patrick."

"Yeah. That new doctor at the hospital got me out of my cast and tether, thank God, and fitted me with the brace. Father Hugh and Sister St. Paul brought me over here to Josie's, and Josie has been Josie. Evangeline—Evvie—has been my prop, literally. Waits on me hand and foot. She and Albert—you remember Albert Vanaartsdalen?"

"Albert's here too?"

"Has been since late July."

"For somebody who's been away from Murray County for so long, sounds like you've made some friends."

"Yeah. Beautiful friends."

But Clarke could tell that Pat was waiting for the real reason why this particular visitor was sitting across Josie's table from him.

"Patrick," he said. "I've been talking with some people. The sheriff for one. Your friend Father Hugh for another, and Father Hugh told me how you ended up in that cast—he didn't think he'd been told the story in confidence."

Pat's face went distant. Something written there, but white light from the window blurred it. And Clarke went on.

"We want to arrest Ferrell and charge him with assault with intent to do serious bodily injury. Maybe charge him with attempted murder even."

A silence.

"There's a risk in trying him. Father Hugh told me a little of an old story. My view, bodily harm trumps the old story being told. And it may not have to be told."

"You could get a conviction?"

"With your testimony. And we'd get Doc Naylor back to testify, and some of the nursing sisters." And Mildred Harrington's testimony, thought Clarke, although he didn't say it. He added, "And we'll lock up Ferrell where he can't get drunk and swing any more crowbars."

For some reason Clarke didn't understand—vindictiveness wasn't Patrick Adams—Pat's face came back to life.

"Yeah," Pat said. "And yeah, I guess Father Hugh is a friend of mine. Hell, what am I saying? He's as good a friend as I ever had, except for Albert, and I've known Albert all my life."

"Does 'yeah' mean yes, you'll testify?"

"Yeah."

"Good," said Clarke. "I'm relieved to hear it."

He knew something he'd said had tipped a balance for Pat, but he wasn't sure what. He pushed back his chair and then hesitated. "So. I hear you passed the bar? And you have a job offer in Missoula?"

"Yeah."

"It's a good firm. I know Ellenberg and Kramer pretty well. So I suppose that means you'll be leaving us as soon as your bone is all the way healed?"

For a minute, he didn't think Pat had been listening to him. Then Pat's eyes raised.

"No. I appreciate their offer, but I'm not going back to Missoula, if I have to go back to horse breaking. I'm going to stay in Fort Maginnis until I can make things right with my girl."

Clarke started to ask and stopped himself. Of course. After all these years.

"Mildred Harrington is a fine girl," he said, and got the full force of Pat's smile. "A fine woman, I should say, and you won't find anybody in the Plum Creek country who doesn't think so."

"Yeah. A pity she doesn't think so."

"Well. My wife will be wondering if I fell into Spring Creek. Tell Josie thanks for the coffee."

Pat walked with him to the door, and they shook hands, and Clarke held the handshake a moment. "Patrick, I don't know if you know Harry Fallon has been wanting to retire?"

"Your deputy prosecutor?"

"Only reason he hasn't, I haven't found a replacement. And now Harry's going to have to stay on through a Ferrell Adams trial. I can't hire somebody who's going to testify for me. But I wouldn't want to see a prime replacement prospect go to breaking horses."

Clarke broke the handshake and put his hat back on. "In the meantime, I hear they're short a file clerk in the county clerk's office. I'll put in a word, unless you think file clerking is too big a comedown from horse breaking."

"Appreciate it."

"Patrick," Clarke said, "your mother was a fine woman too."

Pat's mother had taught him to ride. She had been a tall woman, fair-haired and blue-eyed, and Pat thought he must have gotten his height and coloring from her people, although she spoke little of them. She had grown up in Wyoming and learned to ride properly, and she wore a serge divided skirt when she rode. Women did, then, if they could afford a divided skirt.

Mil, as a little girl, had worn a dress when she rode. Girls did. Mil was wearing a dress the day he found her crying by the wire gate she couldn't shut, and she wore a dress when she rode to meet him during their month of nights. The next time he saw her, after the calamity he'd brought down on both of them, she was wearing men's Levi's belted at the waist. Which was what she still wore. Moccasins on her feet when she wasn't wearing boots.

Pat's mother had had a couple of good saddle horses Pat thought she must have got Ferrell to freight up from Wyoming, maybe by rail. A dark bay gelding named Irony, a bright bay mare named Harmony. After her death, Pat speculated about a woman who named her horses Irony and Harmony, when horses usually got names like Star or Socks or Buck.

His mother had had her own tack, a bridle and a hand-tooled saddle, and she would saddle Harmony and lift Pat, from the time he could toddle, into her saddle with her and let him hold Harmony's reins. The feel of the horse's motion through the reins. The feel of the horse through the saddle. His mother's arms around him, his mother's warmth behind him in the saddle.

Then Ferrell, who had not been so surly when Pat was so small, bought Pat his own little saddle, and Pat's mother had shown him how to saddle Harmony by himself, by standing on a box to throw the saddle over Harmony's back. After that, Pat and his mother had ridden side by side for miles and hours on Harmony and Irony.

Pat had come back to the ranch from college his first summer and found Harmony and Irony gone and his mother distant.

Well, they would have been old horses by then. But he wondered what had become of his mother's saddle and what had changed his mother.

"Didn't you have a mare once, named Lucy? Short for Appalucy?" Pat asked Albert.

"Um—yeah, I used to ride Lucy to school. Remember? Big dark mare with a lotta white spots on her rump? None too speedy but a hell of a horse for endurance. My dad traded for her over in the Palouse country."

"Hm."

"Why'd you want to know?"

"Just thinking about horses' names."

Albert shook his head. The strange things Pat thought about.

Albert thought quite a bit about his own changes of circumstances. He'd found a job out at the stockyards, mostly shoveling manure and pitching straw for not much pay, but once in a while he got pulled in as a ringman during an auction, which was kinda interesting. Scrawny cattle driven in lots into the sales ring by the ringmen. The auctioneer's chant—it took some listening to understand what he was chanting about. Finally, the chant ending with "Sold—Swift!" or "Sold—Hormel!" and Albert and the other ringmen driving that scrawny lot out of the sales ring and driving in the next.

Also, Albert now was a Three Musketeer, a puzzling designation of Father Hugh's for himself, Albert, and Evangeline. "What does it mean?" Albert asked Evangeline, who laughed and shrugged.

"I don't know, either, but don't worry about it. Father's like that. You never know what he'll come up with."

As a Three Musketeer, Albert had the night shift, which was why he pulled his sugans in front of the door in Pat's room and why—his assignment from Father Hugh, to keep an eye out—he woke in the night and stole to a window where he could look out at the street. Evangeline had the afternoon shift, and Father Hugh had the morning shift, when Albert left for work at the stockyards, except on Sundays when Albert and Father Hugh swapped. Because Father Hugh's duties often were unscheduled and unexpected, he had drafted one of his catechism boys to substitute for him when necessary. If Josie wondered why she was seeing so much of Sammy St. Pierre loitering in front of her cabin and playing with his yo-yo, she didn't ask. Albert imagined that Josie also kept an eye out.

Now that Albert and Evangeline had gotten Pat back on his feet and walking by himself, they all felt easier. Still.

13

Caroline was Pat's mother's name. Carrie, Ferrell had called her. Pat remembered Caroline in tears, though he couldn't have said when the tears started or exactly when she stopped riding with him. Pat had been eleven or twelve when Ferrell started buying jugheads to haul home for Pat to top off and ride down until they were mannerly enough to take back to the sales ring in Fort Maginnis and sell for more than what Ferrell had paid for them and the feed that had gone into them.

"One thing I will say for the kid, he can ride," Pat heard Ferrell telling somebody. But Pat knew his mother hated the jugheads. And he knew she hated the beltings from Ferrell that Pat had learned to stand up and take with no change of expression on his face.

It wasn't the jugheads that caused his mother's tears, though, or the beltings. A something else preceded the jugheads and the beltings, a something that Pat had observed but didn't understand. Still didn't understand, although he speculated and wished he could ask Mil, who might have an answer for him, always supposing she would let him near enough to her to ask.

Every so often, maybe every year or so, something would be hidden from Pat. Nothing spoken. But his mother smiling and hopeful, and Ferrell in better moods. Then his mother in tears, and Ferrell gone surly. How often—between the age when Pat could notice and remember and his age when his mother's smiles stopped? Perhaps five, maybe six times before all smiles and better moods stopped. Pat thought the last sweet episode might have been about the time he started riding the jugheads, but if there was a connection, it eluded him.

It occurred to him that if he couldn't ask Mil, he could ask Sister St. Paul. He might be embarrassed by the question, but Sister St. Paul wouldn't be. The next time Sister St. Paul visited Josie and had Pat unbuckle his brace so she could see how his leg was doing, Pat did ask her.

And he saw Sister St. Paul and Josie exchange glances.

"And you were an only child, Pat. Her first child."

Josie nodded. "Sister, you remember Marie Crozier?"

"Oh, yes, I remember Marie. Pat, your guess—that your mother was miscarrying—is probably right. Maybe Ferrell knows for sure."

"Maybe."

"Sometimes a woman gives birth to a healthy child, but when she tries to bear another, she miscarries. And miscarries again, and miscarries again, every time she tries to bear another child. We don't know why. Why the first child is healthy when all the rest are lost. Something in the woman's blood perhaps. All we know now is that it happens—thankfully rarely—but it happens."

"Terrible thing for woman," said Josie.

"Terrible. Some used to believe it had to do with women riding horseback—"

"Phooey," said Josie. "Métis woman ride in carts. Still happen to Métis woman, not very often, but sometime."

And Pat saw Josie cross herself, and he saw Sister St. Paul cross herself, and he felt the force of the memories that flowed between the two women.

George Clarke left the judge's chambers with his signed arrest warrant and carried it down to the sheriff's office on the first floor of the courthouse.

"Guy Temple in his office?" he asked the deputy at the front desk, and the deputy nodded and waved him past.

Guy Temple looked more like a banker than anybody's idea of a Western sheriff. He wore his graying brown hair parted in the middle, and he kept his mustache trimmed. And in his office he wore an ordinary brown suit with a vest and a shirt and tie. The only giveaways were his cowboy boots and the steer's skull he'd hung over a photograph of himself shaking hands with the new Democratic governor of Montana, John Erickson.

"You handed me a doozie this time, George," he said, after he read the warrant.

"Yup."

Temple pulled out his pack of tailor-mades, offered one to Clarke, and lit one himself. They drew deeply and exhaled.

"Oughta quit these things. Think they're cutting into my wind. Ferrell, the old bastard. I knew he was mean. But I never thought he'd try to kill somebody, least of all that boy of his."

"Guess we never do, until they do."

"No." Another deep drag on his cigarette. "A damned mess of a one you got here, George. You happen to hear about a fight out at the Plum Creek post office?"

"No."

"One of the Frazier boys from over Beaver Creek? He'd ridden across to Plum Creek for some reason—they got their own post office at Beaver Creek. He said something about Mildred Harrington living out on her ranch alone with a breed, and Will Danvers had just come in for his mail, and Will turned around and never said a word and knocked the Frazier kid down."

Clarke shook his head.

"I'll tell you, George. To hear some of those old boys talk, you'd think they got here first and had to run the Indians off for trespassing on their land. And now they got the bohunks to worry about."

"I know. They just want to make it a white man's country again, one man told me. I had to wonder. Wouldn't think he meant the Swedes. Maybe he meant the Bohemians."

"Well, hell. I gotta think which of my boys to send out there and bring Ferrell back."

Clarke left Guy Temple talking to himself.

Temple decided his best bet was to send two of his deputies out to arrest Ferrell Adams on charges of assault with intent to do bodily harm and attempted murder. That way, one deputy could back up the other. He picked Dwight Johnson and Milton Bill, ex-doughboys who had seen action in France, and told them that he didn't think Ferrell would be stupid enough to resist arrest but maybe they better sign out a shotgun and take it with them.

"Tomorrow morning's soon enough. But bright and early."

Dwight and Milton looked at each other and did what they were told. Along with the shotgun, they signed out a Model T with *Murray County Sheriff's Department* stenciled on its doors, and they headed for the Adams ranch with Dwight driving and Milton staring out at the countryside. Neither Dwight nor Milton were ranch boys. Dwight was born and raised in Fort Maginnis, and Milton had moved down from Havre when the drought hit the Hi-Line at the end of the war and the banks started closing, including the bank where Milton had a job, and he thought prospects might be better farther south. For a while they were, and then they weren't. Milton, whose first and last names people tried to switch around on him, always said the damned drought had followed him down from Hill County to Murray County. Neither he nor Dwight could see why anybody was drawn to live out here in the endless rolling prairie and endless sagebrush when they had a town to live in.

After an hour and a half of dust and heat, they rolled into the Adams ranch yard. All peaceful. A stocking-legged sorrel horse stood in a corral, switching flies in his sleep. They saw that Ferrell must be home because his truck was parked by an overgrowth of chokecherry brush near the house, where a dog had crawled out from under the front steps to look his visitors over.

"Well—"

Dwight and Milton climbed out of the Model T, Dwight carrying the arrest warrant, and walked up to the house. No point in causing Adams's alarm by taking the shotgun with them, they had decided. A curious flagstone path led to the front steps and the door. The dog sniffed their legs and wagged politely. Dwight knocked on the door.

They waited. Dwight knocked again, and they waited again.

"Ferrell Adams?" called Dwight. "You in there?"

Silence.

"Ferrell Adams? We got a warrant for your arrest."

"It's an attempted murder charge, Ferrell, and you'll be a damn sight better off to come outa there and come with us."

That was when the door opened a crack and somebody, Ferrell Adams they supposed, whistled the dog inside and slammed the door again. Milton, trying the knob a second later, found it locked.

Ker-rack! The unmistakable sound of a rifle fired inside the house, and the deputies, trained in combat, flattened themselves on either side of the door.

Silence.

Make a run for the Model T and try to retrieve the shotgun when there's a man with a rifle behind them?

They both unholstered their revolvers—maybe circle around the house from two directions and try to get the drop on him?

The sound of breaking glass above them made up their minds for them. To stay put.

Ker-rack! And the Model T jumped as if startled.

"Jesus Christ, the bastard's hit the gas tank!"

Ker-rack! Ker-rack!

And Dwight and Milton could only watch as that dirty cocksucking bastard Ferrell Adams shot out the tires of the Model T from a window above their heads.

Silence. Dwight and Milton looked at each other. Was he reloading? Then, still flattened on their sides of the door, Milton looked to the left, and Dwight looked to the right. And it was Dwight who noticed some disturbance of underbrush next to the house and saw the burly figure running with his rifle and jumping into his truck and starting his engine.

The truck leaped into gear and roared off. Milton spun around and fired his revolver after it, and Dwight ran to the Model T and grabbed the shotgun and fired both barrels at the truck. But it never slowed, and soon all the deputies saw was the dust it raised.

"How the hell are we getting back to town?"

Dwight put his thumb on the hole in the Model T's gas tank, and the spurt of gasoline slowed and stopped. "Think we could find a way to plug this hole and make it back on the rims?"

"Think Sheriff Temple will send somebody looking for us, we don't come back with Adams?"

"Maybe. You rather wait for him here or partway down the road?"

Ranch boys might have thought to catch the stocking-legged sorrel horse and see if he was gentle enough to saddle and ride double back to town, but Dwight and Milton decided to stay put, where at least they would have water and shade while they waited, and maybe even find some grub.

Back at Josie's house, the deployment of the Three Musketeers was a little thin on the ground. Albert had left for work at the stockyards, and Evangeline was down the street where a cousin was helping her lay out a dress pattern and cut out a dress for herself. Father Hugh, the morning-shift Three Musketeer, saw a parishioner hurrying toward him and thought, oh no, and called to Sammy St. Pierre to walk across the street with his yo-yo and cover for him.

When a truck pulled up in front of Josie's house with a load of firewood, Sammy looked up from practicing Around the World with his yo-yo and recognized the driver as his uncle Renny. He watched Miss Harrington get out of the truck and walk up to his auntie Josie's house while Renny turned his truck to drive down the bumpy stretch along Josie's fence. Sammy guessed that Renny planned to toss his firewood from his truck into Josie's backyard to stack in her woodpile, and he would have gone to help Renny if he hadn't been covering for Father Hugh. Instead, he switched to Time Warp with his yo-yo and practiced that while he looked up and down the street.

Several minutes passed, although, asked later, Sammy had no idea how long he practiced Time Warp before another truck pulled up in front of his auntie Josie's house. Sammy didn't know the big burly man who climbed out of that truck, but he didn't like the look of him. Sammy switched to Walking the Dog until he got on the other side of the man's truck, and then he ran like hell. First for Evangeline, who was the nearest Three Musketeer. Then he ran like hell up the street to where Father Hugh was meeting his parishioner. At last! Some excitement to make all his yo-yo practice worthwhile.

14

"I gotta load of firewood for Josie," Renny had said at breakfast. "You want to ride to town with me and visit with Josie while I unload it?"

Mildred did. Maybe she also could drop by the convent and talk to Sister St. Paul, who had written that the new doctor had cut the cast off Pat's leg and fitted him with a walking brace and discharged him. Sister St. Paul also wrote that she had visited Pat and examined his leg and had seen that the brace was doing its work. Pat's muscle tone was returning, and his leg had filled out until he could loosen the buckles on the brace a notch. And he was walking easily by himself.

But Sister St. Paul hadn't written *where* Pat was walking by himself.

Renny drove up their teetering road and turned toward Fort Maginnis on the county road and drove some more, thinking his thoughts while Mildred thought hers. Bright sunlight falling through the windshield, windows rolled all the way down, a rush of wind the truck stirred up, and the scent of sage and the dust rolling up behind them. Dusty prairie, dusty sage, empty fields and pastures. Before they knew it, it would be time to bring the cattle in from summer pasture and separate cows and calves and sort out the replacement heifers from the calves they'd truck to the auction ring in Fort Maginnis.

Pat had come to her again last night. She had wakened, without knowing why, and listened to night sounds. A cottonwood limb creaking over the cabin roof. One of Renny's dogs growling under his breath, maybe at coyotes again. She sat up in bed and made out the outlines of her dresser and lamp table in the dark. The foot of her bed, where Pat materialized. Pat in his white shirt and Levi's. Pat's eyes met hers. His lips moved, and she thought he spoke to her, though she could not hear his words. Her arms reached for him without her asking them to, and Pat dissolved.

She knew some women became strange when their bloods and moons stopped, but she was years away from that time. More likely, it was her weeks without talking to anyone except Renny or Smokey. She knew Sister St. Paul didn't like it.

She remembered a time in high school when Sister Boniface, then Mary Fitzgerald, had been reading a book about the lives of saints and was telling Sister St. Paul about an anchoress in the Middle Ages who had wonderful visions, and Sister St. Paul wondered aloud if the poor anchoress hadn't been alone too long. Mary had been shocked, but Sister St. Paul, sometimes uncomfortably for others, kept her feet firmly grounded under her.

The hour passed, and they reached Fort Maginnis. Renny drove through the old part of town and stopped his truck by Josie's cabin to let Mildred out before he pulled around and drove down by the creek to throw the firewood out of the truck and into Josie's backyard where he could stack it.

Dusty cottonwood leaves overhead. A dusty apple tree in Josie's front yard, twin to the apple tree in her backyard. A boy, maybe eight years old, played with a yo-yo in front of Josie's fence. Mildred opened the familiar gate and closed it behind her and walked up Josie's graveled path. She knocked on Josie's door and, without waiting for Josie to answer her knock, opened the door and let herself in and found herself face-to-face with Pat.

Later she guessed he'd come to answer the door, Josie being out back supervising Renny. In the moment, he seemed to have materialized, by daylight this time, in Josie's front room. He looked down at Mildred, his mouth slightly open in his surprise, and she looked up at him and supposed her mouth also had fallen open.

In slow motion Pat's hand reached for hers, and her hand reached to meet his. Warmth of touch.

"Mil."

He led her a few steps into the room, and she knew he was going to kiss her. And what then, if the door hadn't burst open behind them?

Pat pulling her back by her wrist. Standing in front of her.

Ferrell Adams had come so close that Mildred could see the sweat pouring down his face, and she could smell his stink of sweat and his years of wearing the same grimy shirts and overalls and the grime embedded in his face and hands and, overlying the sweat and grime, the odor of something sharper, an odor like Renny's hooch. She was smelling his rage, she thought. This was how rage smelled.

Ferrell Adams smiled, a smile eerily like Pat's except for his broken teeth.

"I'm going to kick that goddamn brace out from under you," he told Pat, "and then I'm going to break you in half. And then you can watch while I give your moccasin squaw what she's asking for."

She felt Pat gathering himself for what was coming, and she looked wildly for a weapon, any weapon. She knew Josie kept a hatchet in the kitchen, and where was Josie? Out in her backyard, stacking wood with Renny. And then she heard another voice.

"Maybe you'd like to try breaking me in half?"

Ferrell spun to face his new adversary. It was Father Hugh in the open doorway, bouncing on the balls of his feet. The slim young priest confronting the old bull, Ferrell. Ferrell bellowed and charged Father Hugh, and the springs in Father Hugh's feet lifted him and set him down to Ferrell's left. Ferrell turned, trying to keep Father Hugh in his sights, and Father Hugh feinted with his right fist, confusing Ferrell. Then Father Hugh's left jab connected with Ferrell's chin, and Ferrell dropped of his own unbalance so heavily to the floor that chairs jumped and came back down and Josie's rocker started rocking by itself.

Ferrell tried to sit up, failed, and fell back again.

"Mildred," said Father Hugh, "do you know how to drive? Will you take my car and drive over to Water Street and bring back a policeman or two? I'll stay here, just in case Ferrell gets any more ideas."

"Mildred not have a do that, Father," said Josie from the kitchen door. She was brandishing a cast iron skillet. "He try anything, Evvie will sit on him, and I will bash him."

Evangeline, glowing with excitement and dancing on the balls of her feet herself, had followed Father Hugh into Josie's house.

"Don't worry, Father," said Renny over Josie's shoulder. "Josie, she'll bash him a good one if she needs to, and I'll fetch the cops."

Father Hugh rubbed the knuckles of his left hand, smiling and clearly pleased with himself.

"Kinda glad I got to do that," he said, "although I'll have to hunt up Father Pritchard to hear my confession. Mildred, you be sure to tell Sister what happened. I don't know that she believes me."

Mildred was past telling anything to anyone. She felt herself sway. Pat caught her and picked her up and carried her in his arms to Josie's room and laid her on Josie's bed, and he held her hand until Josie and Evangeline came with cloths and water in a basin and some of Josie's concoctions and chased him away. And then she must have slept.

She awoke to a lower sun through Josie's bedroom window and thought Josie must have given her something to make her sleep. She sat up to the sounds of vigorous voices, an argument going on in Josie's front room, and she stood and felt all right. Fainting! When had she ever fainted?

"Renny, she stay here, like before. She sleep in my bed with me—"

"We'll take care of her, Uncle Renny!" That was Evangeline.

"Nah," said Renny, "I'm taking her back to the ranch. That's where she'll want to be."

"Sister St. Paul—" began Father Hugh.

"Sister St. Paul's so concerned, you can drive her out to the ranch tomorrow and let her see for herself."

A pause.

"Pat Adams, you're a goddamn lightning rod, and I ain't lettin you pull down no more lightning on her."

Pat turned and saw her in the doorway. They all saw her. Mildred's stray thought was that Ferrell was gone, so the Fort Maginnis police must have come for him while she slept. And had they taken him to the hospital first or straight to jail? Pat stood close to her, hiding her from their audience, and she didn't know how he got to her. Stray thought, he walked easily—his leg must be nearly healed. No more thoughts. She closed her eyes and wondered if there ever would be a time when she didn't see Ferrell over Pat's shoulder. When she opened her eyes, Pat kissed her on her forehead, and Renny drew her away, Renny's bear of an arm as loving as Pat's, but not Pat's.

Goodbye was goodbye, she reminded herself.

....

Bereft, Pat watched her go. *Damn. For a minute back there . . .* and realized he'd said it aloud, because Father Hugh said, "Believe me, we weren't shillly-shallying, Pat. You should have seen Sammy run. That boy's going to make a sprinter."

Evangeline giggled—"You shoulda seen Father run!"

". . . for a minute back there, I thought I was all right again with Mil."

Then they realized their mistake. Josie was hugging him around the waist, Josie hardly higher than Pat's waist herself, and Evangeline, almost as tall as Pat, was hugging his shoulders. And he felt disconcerted, women's sympathy for him being worse to take than women's entertainment with him, but he also felt thankful for their comfort. And Father Hugh, smiling gravely at Pat.

"Renny the problem, pas de Renny. I talk Renny. Take me day or one, maybe. Might you have drive me, Father."

"I'll be proud to."

Then Albert came in from his stockyards job, and a babble of voices rose to catch him up on their afternoon. Now that they had a new target to vent their excitement on, Pat thought he would just sit quietly in a corner for a while.

"We drink wine now!" Josie announced. And they did.

...

"I'd love to box like that," said Pat the next day, "and not have had to stand around in this damned brace and watch you bring him down."

"I'll tell you what, Pat," said Father Hugh, "I have a boys' catechism class, and after class I've been teaching the boys to box. You come to catechism class after you get that brace off, and I'll teach you to box too."

"Yeah," said Pat, "I'll do that. And Father Hugh, I'll be looking forward to seeing you on horseback one of these first days."

Father Hugh didn't answer, and Sister St. Paul had to turn away and hide her face at the expression on his face. Good one, Patrick, she thought. She had come to love Father Hugh over the past few months, but it didn't do him one bit of harm to get back a little of what he gave out. She controlled her face and turned in time to see Father Hugh punch Pat on his shoulder and Pat punch him back.

Pity the poor teacher if those two had gotten together, say, in the seventh grade.

It did look to Sister St. Paul as though Pat had pulled himself together after yesterday's excitement, which she'd pieced together from a selection of narratives: Father Hugh's, Evangeline's, Josie's—with Josie's description so heated that she was speaking as much in the French-Cree patois, Michif, as in English.

A lot for Pat to pull himself together after. She shook her head. He was Montana tough, she guessed. As rooted as sagebrush and as resilient.

...

It took Guy Temple awhile longer to piece a narrative together. First, he had to wait and wait some more for his deputies to arrest

Ferrell Adams and bring him back to town with them. When the time came that Dwight and Milton should have arrived and they didn't, Temple paced his office for a while and went out and looked over the parking lot in back of the jail, hoping to see Dwight and Milton drive in. Instead he saw a Fort Maginnis police car pull into a parking slot and two uniformed cops jump out and run in his direction.

The cops were so excited that they talked on top of one another to get their stories out, and at first, Temple could only gather that the whole Fort Maginnis police force was on the boil. But then, "We got him! We got him! Well, *we* didn't; Father McHugh did, but—"

"Father McHugh? The Catholic priest? He did what?"

"He knocked him cold!"

"Knocked *who* cold?"

"Ferrell Adams!"

Guy Temple sat down heavily behind his desk and regarded the two worked-up cops until his silence and the expression on his face finally registered with them, and they quit jabbering and looked back at him.

"You boys sit down right there," he said, and they sat.

"Now. Start at the beginning. One of you at a time."

First arrival at the police station was one of the St. Pierre kids, probably about eight years old—

"I know the St. Pierres. Go on."

—yelling that something bad was going to happen at his aunt Josie Archambault's house—

Was *going* to happen? The desk sergeant hadn't known what to make of that, but next came Renny Archambault himself, driving up in his old truck with the news that Ferrell Adams had been knocked cold by Father McHugh and was stretched out, even now, on Josie's floor. So they—the two uniforms now sitting in Guy Temple's office—followed Renny back to his aunt's house, and sure enough, there was Ferrell, conscious by this time and mad as hell but unable to retaliate or even get up, because Renny's niece Evangeline—

"Big Evangeline, you know her, Sheriff?"

"Yes, yes!"

"—was sitting on his stomach while Josie stood over him with a skillet." The cop suddenly began to laugh. "You shoulda seen it, Sheriff."

Guy Temple kinda wished he had. "Where's Ferrell now?"

"We got him in the city jail. We went to handcuff him"—both cops were laughing now—"and when he put up a fight, Josie gave him a smack with her skillet, backhand, and settled him down. We took him up to the hospital to have the sisters look at his skull, and that head sister said she thought he'd be all right, only not to let him go to sleep for a while, so we brought him down to the jail and locked him in a cell. And we got a boy with a big tin can and a spoon to beat it with if Ferrell shows signs of going to sleep. A course, he's stinking drunk."

"And oh yeah," said the other cop, "did we tell you Father McHugh was still there? And also Ferrell's son?"

"Patrick Adams," said Temple heavily. He might have known which direction this story was going to take.

"We got Patrick Adams and Father McHugh coming in tomorrow to make their statements—"

"Yes, yes," said Temple. "You boys get right on that. And Ferrell may as well stay where you've got him. A pity Josie didn't hit him harder with her skillet and spare George Clarke a trial. And now I got a couple of deputies to find."

15

Guy Temple decided he'd better see for himself what was going on at the Adams ranch. He nabbed Sandy Duncan as a driver and told him, as he'd told Dwight and Milton, to sign out a shotgun and a car from the sheriff's department and make sure the car was fueled, and he strapped on his belt and holster with his revolver under his suit coat. A little too much caution, maybe, but something sure as hell happened out there today.

Sandy Duncan drove for an hour and a half, and the sun was sinking when he and the sheriff pulled into the ranch yard. They looked around. Cattle bawling somewhere, bawling and bawling. The stocking-legged sorrel in the corral, the—yes, the sheriff's department's Model T sitting at a tilted angle in an island of dark, reeking fluid that had soaked into the dust. The sheriff looked closer and saw that the tires on the side of the Model T turned to the house were shot out and flat.

He turned his attention to the house. The broken second-floor window. Sitting on the steps under the broken window, Dwight and Milton looking disconsolate.

"You dumb sons of bitches," Temple said. "Has that horse been watered?"

They looked at each other and then stared at him, and he could tell the horse hadn't crossed their minds. Dwight started to get up, but Temple waved him back. "I'll water him."

He walked back to the corral to a sporadic chorus of bawling cattle and found a piece of rope to use for a halter and led the sorrel through the gate to the water tank, which was almost dry, so he raised the pump handle with his free hand and pumped until Sandy Duncan saw what he was doing and came to pump for him.

The horse drank deeply, and Temple turned him back into his corral. He didn't like to leave any animal within the smell of water and unable to get to it, but he thought the sorrel was probably better off in the corral than turned loose to roam. He would tell Pat Adams about the horse when he saw him.

Back at the house, he started to open the door, but Dwight said, "You don't want to go in there, Sheriff. There's a dead dog in there, and he's starting to purely stink."

The hell with it, Temple thought. Let Pat Adams deal with the dog. No sign of a crime out here, anyway, unless he counted the dog and, of course, the shot-up Model T.

"All right, boys," he said, "let's go." And Milton said, "Where?" And Dwight said, "With you?"

"Unless you want to wait and try to catch a better ride."

Pat and Albert took Pat's truck out to the ranch. Albert drove, and Pat mostly looked out the window. Familiar county road, familiar turnoff. Bare empty hills.

"God," Pat said, and Albert glanced at him.

The question was whether it was worth the taxes to hang on to the ranch. A little rain, not enough, had fallen several weeks ago, and no knowing whether there would be winter snows and spring rains to start the grass growing. Pat put that question aside as one he couldn't answer yet and watched as the road changed from gravel to dirt and rose to cross the high prairie. Tough-rooted sagebrush hanging on. Endless blue bowl of sky, white cotton clouds floating out of reach. The shadows of clouds. A sameness that the truck seemed hardly to move through.

A first sign of life. A jackrabbit startled from a clump of sagebrush, and Pat remembered one of Renny Archambault's remarks: *This country's getting so damn dry, even the jackrabbits have to pack their lunches with em.*

Then Albert was driving into the familiar ranch yard. Barn and corrals and sheds, bunkhouse and big house, strange for their familiarity.

When they got out of the truck, they heard cattle bawling and, closer at hand, a horse that whinnied from one of the corrals. Pat and Albert looked at each other. Ferrell, going off on his murderous errand. Leaving his saddle horse shut in a corral without water.

"Guess that's the first thing," said Pat, although he knew Guy Temple had watered the sorrel yesterday afternoon.

Albert pumped water into the tank by the barn while Pat caught the horse, knotted the rope around his head and nose for a halter, and led him out of the corral. Smelling water, the horse picked up his pace and plunged his nose into the tank and drank deeply again while Pat and Albert watched.

"Jeez," said Albert.

"Used to be," Pat began, felt something swelling in his throat, and started over. "He was a good cattleman once. A good stockman. He never would have done this to a horse."

"I know that."

"Never let his cattle starve rather than selling them or shooting them."

They let the horse drink his fill, and then they turned him back in to the corral and grained him and walked across the road to the house.

"Albert, what I'll ask you to do," said Pat, "is saddle him—what's his name? Socks?"

"Socks."

"Ride out and see what cattle still are alive—some must be, to hear em—and try to get some kind of count. And come back and tell me. Then I'll take Socks and the rifle, and you take the truck and drive it around to the neighbors and tell em the beef, such as it is, is theirs for the skinning and butchering. When I see the first trucks and wagons on the road, I'll start shooting cattle."

"Jesus, Pat, I can do that."

"You and Frank already had to do too much of that."

Pat watched Albert walk back to the corral to saddle Socks, and then he turned and walked up his mother's flagstone path to the kitchen. Opened the door on a horrific stench—what in the hell had Ferrell left dead in here?

Ferrell's dog. Shot in the head. Temple hadn't said anything about that.

So that was another first thing. Find a shovel, dig a hole in what had been his mother's garden, grown now to weeds that had dried to stalks.

It felt kinda good, though, that in the face of everything, he could stand on his padded brace and drive down the blade of the shovel with his moccasined foot, even if it was to dig a grave. He carried the shovel back to the kitchen and used it to half lift, half slide the dead dog onto a tablecloth he found in a drawer. Then he carried dog and shovel back to the garden, where he buried the dog in his tablecloth shroud.

He supposed the kitchen ought to be scrubbed with boiling water and bleach, but that could be a sixth or maybe a tenth thing. He wandered through his mother's living room. Sheet-covered furniture. Dust. Boot tracks through the dust—those would be Ferrell's.

A door that had been repaired after Pat kicked it off its hinges fourteen years ago. A room Ferrell called his study. Ferrell's rolltop desk, which had replaced a flat-topped desk that fourteen years ago had been axed to splinters by Pat. Pat warned himself to keep his mind on what he needed to do today. He supposed he would find ranch records in Ferrell's rolltop desk. Bank records. Sorting through them was maybe a third or fourth thing after the judge issued the court order that Pat had requested this morning. Shouldn't think there'd be any question, George Clarke had said, and Pat didn't think so, either.

Nothing to smile about, and yet. And yet. Being appointed Ferrell's guardian.

The key to the gun case had been on Ferrell's key chain, which the police had relieved him of and given to Pat. Pat unlocked the case and saw the empty brackets for the thirty-aught-six Remington that had hung in the back window of Ferrell's truck. Maybe the Remington was still in the truck, or maybe the police had it. He took down the two-fifty Savage, which was plenty of rifle for his purpose, and found the cartridges for it and shut the case.

No sign yet of Albert. Pat set the rifle down and climbed the stairs off the stinking kitchen and followed the corridor by the dim light of dirty windows. Opened the door to the room where he'd slept when he came back to the ranch last June. His suitcase open on the bed, a couple of his shirts hanging on nails, his Justin boots where he'd left them.

Where he had realized that Ferrell had nothing he wanted to say to Pat. That Ferrell's letter had been a ruse to lure Pat to the ranch and turn him back into Ferrell's horsebreaker.

Pat found a hammer and nailed boards over the window Ferrell had broken. Then he folded his shirts and added them to his clothes in the suitcase, laid his Justins on top of them, and buckled the suitcase. He started back down the corridor, and then he stopped and opened the door to what Ferrell had called his junk room.

Saw the crazy, crowded assortment that Albert had seen. Saw what Albert had seen and not noted. The hand-tooled old saddle on its sawhorse. The name carved on the back of the cantle. *Caroline.*

Ferrell had had her so browbeaten, toward the end, that she didn't dare even to write to Pat. And yet she'd had the spine to insist that Pat went to high school. Insist that he went to college in Missoula.

Pat could only shake his head. And then he saw, through the filthy web-shrouded window in the gable, Albert returning on Socks, and he lifted his mother's saddle to his shoulder and carried the saddle and his suitcase downstairs and, with the rifle under his arm, returned to his truck and threw the suitcase in the back and his mother's saddle after it, upside down as a saddle should be when not on a horse or a sawhorse or hanging by its horn from a rope.

Albert rode up and dismounted, and Pat saw that he'd been riding Ferrell's saddle, with the saddle scabbard. He took Socks's reins from Albert and sheathed the Savage in the scabbard and came back around Socks to mount. Paused. He knew Albert was watching in case he needed help.

He could do it. He always had taken most of his weight in his arms. He looped the reins around Socks's neck and tried the toe of his padded boot in the stirrup and found it would fit. Saddle horn in both hands, ready to take his weight. A spring in his right leg. Rising on his left leg in the stirrup, swinging his right leg up and over. Brace on one foot, moccasin on the other. No hat. What a cowboy.

When he turned in the saddle, he saw Albert walking to the truck as though Pat Adams mounting a saddle horse was the most ordinary sight in the world.

Pat rode as far as he could see across the high prairie and still watch the road. When he saw the first team and wagon trotting up the road, he drew the Savage from its scabbard and loaded it and turned Socks to do what he had to do.

....

When it was over and while the men were butchering, Stan Svoboda said he would see to it the hides were spread to dry. Might be a dime or two in them.

"What do you think?" Albert asked Pat. "Turn Socks out where he can at least find water?"

"That or ride him back to town. Put him up at the stockyards."

Albert gave Socks an appraising look-over. "You or me?"

"I'll do it." A long night ride suddenly was just what Pat wanted. "See you in town," he said.

Albert was counting and calculating. "You ain't back in town by ten, I'll come looking."

"Deal."

Albert climbed in Pat's truck and drove off, and Pat waited until the dust had settled behind him and then swung back on Socks and headed in the direction of Fort Maginnis at an easy trot.

I'm thinking about you, Mil. I'm riding horseback and wishing I was riding double.

16

Ranch work was down to minimal now. Mildred and Renny decided to ship cattle early and brought in the cattle from the summer pasture, which was pretty well bare now, and separated the cows and calves—horrendous bawling, cow for calf and calf for cow—and picked out yearling replacement heifers to hold back and culled the older cows for the sales ring. They turned the remaining cows and the two-year-old replacement heifers into the winter pasture with the bulls, the grass hopefully good enough to pull them through. Renny put the stock rack on his truck and backed it up to the log-built loading chute, and Mildred helped him drive cattle up the chute and into the truck for the jouncing ride to the sales ring, another glut of cattle for a glutted market. It would have taken Renny several trips, but Renny had a cousin—of course!—with a truck and a stock rack but no cattle who would help haul theirs and who waited until Renny's dust settled before he headed for the sales ring.

Then the peace and quiet of no bawling cattle and the winter wait until spring calving. Mildred picked two buckets of ripe chokecherries and stored them in the hay to keep until Renny could take them to Josie.

"Whaddya think?" said Evangeline, the day after Pat shot Ferrell's cattle. "You gonna keep working at the stockyards?"

"I guess for a while," said Albert.

They were sitting on Josie's back stoop in the late afternoon, sipping chokecherry wine and enjoying the last of the fall sunshine. Willow leaves turned to yellow and cottonwood leaves to gold. The sounds of the creek and the sounds of hens scratching dust in their yard and discussing their hen lives with each other in low contented clucks. Not many days left like this. But still a little while before Evangeline needed to get up and start supper.

"What did Pat say?"

"That he's no rancher. He's going to go to work for the prosecutor after the trial."

They watched a robin wing down to a branch of Josie's apple tree. The robin cocked his head at the hens in case they scratched up a worm, gave up, and winged off.

"Work at the stockyards is gonna peter out, anyway, after the fall sales. Pat talked to me about moving out to the ranch and keeping an eye on the ranch buildings. And what I can find to do. Fixing fence, like that."

"I thought cowboys never fixed fence. I thought they wouldn't get off their horses to do it."

"Ha. Movie cowboys, maybe. Like they never take their hats off? Ha. Anyway, we'd wait and see if we get any snow this winter and if we get any rain in the spring. See what hope there is of starting over, buying a few head of heifers, like. Which I'd manage. Maybe get Frank back to help me."

"You think you'd like to do that?" said Evangeline. "Living out there, year-round? Alone?"

"I think so," said Albert, "except for the alone part."

He looked at Evangeline, sitting beside him in the sun with most of her wine gone. Her bobbed black hair. The way the gold hoops in her ears danced when she laughed. Their hours together as they'd helped Pat to walk, getting him farther down the street every day. The day Pat said to let him try it alone, and he'd walked ahead of them, ten steps, and turned and smiled his goddamn Pat smile. Then he lurched, and Albert and Evangeline ran to catch him before he fell.

Evangeline, his fellow Three Musketeer.

A big girl, almost as tall as Albert himself. Albert had come to kinda like a big girl. What a cowboy would get off his horse for.

"Evangeline, you ever think you'd like living on a ranch?"

Evangeline giggled, maybe a little tipsy on chokecherry wine. "Albert, you ever think of turning Catholic?"

Albert gazed up at the clear blue above Josie's apple tree and the willows and cottonwoods along the creek. A few more yellowing leaves drifted down to the current. What with getting the last week behind him and now Evangeline ahead for him, Albert felt pretty damned good.

"You'd think it'd have to rain sometime in this goddamn country," he said.

Albert hadn't said anything to Pat. Maybe embarrassed to tell him, Pat thought. No, it was George Clarke who told Pat the news he'd heard.

It took Pat a minute for it to sink in. "Albert is receiving Catholic instruction from Father Hugh?"

"Yup."

"I'll be go to hell."

"Evangeline is a good girl."

"She is that," said Pat thoughtfully. He knew the Vanaartsdalens wouldn't like it.

When he saw Albert that evening, he said, "So do I get to stand up with you, or do you have to have a Catholic?"

Albert stood and looked at Pat with a blank face while Evangeline giggled.

Finally, Albert shook his head. "I dunno the answer to that. Have to ask Father Hugh. One thing you could do for me, Pat. Can you explain to me what a Three Musketeer is?"

"A what?"

"It's what Father Hugh calls him and us," Evangeline explained.

A three musketeer—Pat finally got it. "He means *The* Three Musketeers," and he explained to Albert and Evangeline about the old novel in which three French soldiers, riflemen Pat guessed they'd be called in English, roamed the countryside having adventures.

"And they had a motto," he concluded. "One for all, and all for one."

Albert and Evangeline nodded. Seemed to fit them.

"The damnedest things you know, Pat. And Father Hugh's as bad as you are."

"Too bad there weren't four musketeers, Pat," said Evangeline. "That way, you could be one."

"Actually, there were," Pat told her, "but the fourth one was only kinda, sorta a musketeer. Hung out with them, though."

"You could be kinda, sorta."

"Yeah," said Pat. He was trying to remember how D'Artagnan's love life had worked out for him. Not good, Pat thought, but he'd read the novel too long ago.

Poor Sister Boniface. Now she had to listen to people talking about Evangeline Archambault marrying Sister Boniface's cowboy. The last straw was when Father McHugh grinned at her after mass and, in the full hearing of a dozen people, said, "Sister Boniface! I hear you're going to give the groom away!"

Inwardly Sister Boniface cringed, but she had just listened to another lecture from Sister St. Paul on how to deal with Father McHugh. She drew herself up and faced him, although, being short, she had to tip her head back to do it. "Father McHugh," she said, "I have my dignity. And I truly believe, Father McHugh, that you go too far with my dignity!"

He stared down at her, wordless for once, and then he started to laugh. And laugh. "Good for you, Sister Boniface!" he finally managed to gasp. "Good for you!"

She turned and marched back to the convent to finish peeling potatoes for Sunday dinner. Laughter was contagious, she'd been told, and she'd almost caught it.

The judge granted Pat's request for a court order—no surprise there, as Pat and George Clarke had surmised. And the court order duly was registered, and Pat now was Ferrell's guardian, pending the outcome of Ferrell's trial, and thereby the manager of Ferrell's affairs and property. So he fueled his truck for the drive back to the ranch.

Albert had to work at the stockyards, at one of the final sales that Saturday, and Josie and Evangeline rode with Pat to drop off Albert before they headed for the ranch. Josie brought a box of sandwiches and a big pot of coffee to reheat. When Evangeline asked him what kind of cleaning supplies his mother might have left at the house, Pat had no idea, so she brought along a basket of assorted soaps and polishes, brushes and rags. Evangeline's mother and one of her sisters might come out later and help her and Josie clean house if they could catch a ride.

Pat parked the truck at the yard fence and went to help Josie down from the high seat, which was no problem for Evangeline. Then he opened the kitchen door, and the three of them looked in.

"Pee-yew!"

The dead dog had left his mark on the kitchen floor. Pat wondered if they'd ever get rid of the smell and the stains on the floorboards. He thought the boards might have to be sanded down.

"You like cuppa my coffee soon, Pat? We got start fire anyway, heat water."

"Sure," he said. "Thanks, Josie." And he saw that Evangeline was wiping out a cup for him with one of her rags and Josie was setting a match to kindling in the stove.

He wandered through the dust in the front room, leaving his tracks on top of Ferrell's, and opened the door to Ferrell's study. Wondered again about some of the words his parents used. *Study.* He guessed Father Hugh probably had one. Didn't know anyone else who would. Attorneys had offices.

Gun cabinet as he had left it. The police had found the Remington in Ferrell's truck when they towed it, and they told Pat he eventually would get the truck and rifle back, maybe after the trial. He still had the Savage in its scabbard on Ferrell's saddle.

The rolltop desk, the dirty windows. Pat sat at the desk on Ferrell's swivel chair, unlocked the roll top, and raised it.

Pigeonholes stuffed with papers. Papers in stacks on the desk itself, stacks and piles of papers.

Pat thought for a minute, and then he pulled an old feed bucket from under the desk. Ferrell apparently had been using the bucket as a spittoon, and Pat would use it for trash. He decided the best way to begin was top and front, on the premise that those would likely be the most recent receipts or records. From the amount of paper in the desk, he thought he might be looking at the story of the ranch from the time Ferrell first filed on it for a homestead.

Be a help to find Ferrell's checkbook. Did Ferrell usually carry it with him? Pat couldn't remember. He pulled out the middle drawer of the desk, the narrow one, and found more papers and the checkbook.

Apparently Josie and Evangeline had gotten the fire burning in the stove and the coffee reheated, along with their scrub water, because by midmorning Evangeline brought him a cup with a saucer under it—who would have supposed? And when she smiled at him, he thought how happy she looked to be scrubbing a house she was going to live in with Albert. "Thanks," he said.

And Evangeline said, "You're not getting too tired, Pat?"

"No, no. I drew the easy straw. You and Josie are doing the hard work."

He touched her hand, and she giggled and went back to work. Through open doors and windows he could hear her voice and Josie's, a patter between them that wasn't all in English. He leaned back in Ferrell's swivel chair and stretched out his legs and drank coffee, and then he took Prince Albert and papers from his shirt pocket and rolled a cigarette and lit it.

What he had learned. If Ferrell's checkbook was accurate and if Pat could believe a couple of recent bank statements Ferrell had not bothered to open—and why not believe them?—Ferrell had plenty of money to buy hay for his cattle instead of letting them starve. Rotten, overpriced hay, maybe, freighted in by rail from the Midwest, but hay. But he hadn't.

Pat guessed one next thing was a visit to Ferrell's bank, now that he had his guardianship papers.

By noon Josie and Evangeline had scrubbed the kitchen, ceiling to floor, and it smelled of bleach instead of decayed dog. Pat could see the faintest of stains where the dog had lain, since he knew where to look for them, but he doubted he'd would have seen them if he hadn't known.

They had scrubbed the oak table down to the grain. Evangeline unpacked sandwiches while Josie poured hot coffee, and Pat discovered he was hungry as hell. Paperwork wore him out worse than horse-breaking. He ate sandwiches of bread and butter and mustard and sliced pork from a can and drank coffee in pleasant silence with the two women, and then he poured himself another cup of coffee and carried it out to the back porch and rolled a cigarette and looked out over the weeds that had been his mother's garden and the fresh mound where he'd buried the dog

"He was a decent old dog," Albert had said, when he heard about it. "Who the hell knows?"

Pat dragged on his cigarette and looked up as Evangeline joined him on the porch steps.

"Want the makings?" he asked her.

"Sure."

He passed her his Prince Albert and papers and watched as she expertly rolled herself a cigarette. She might be a big girl, but she had long expressive fingers like Renny's.

Pat and Evangeline sat in the shade of the porch roof and smoked and looked out over sun-bleached fence posts and sagging barbed wire and dead weeds and sagebrush behind the weeds. A lotta work to be done.

After a while Evangeline said, "Hope I can plough a garden and plant it next spring."

"Yeah. My mother always planted a garden there."

"Pat?"

"Yeah?"

"Being I'm gonna be your kinda, sorta sister, musketeer sister anyway, can I ask you something?"

Pat turned to look at Evangeline. Her round brown face, her eyes as wide and dark as Josie's. He thought she probably was Mildred's age.

"Albert and I got to talking, and he didn't know. Pat, you ever have a girl except Mildred?"

Pat drew on his cigarette and exhaled and looked out over sagebrush and saw what lay beyond it. "One time," he said.

Evangeline said nothing.

"She was a French girl. I called her Veeve, but her name was Genevieve." Zhen-*ah*-vee-*ev*.

"What happened to her?"

"I don't know," Pat said. "No idea. My outfit was called out, and I left her all the chocolate I had and all the rations I could scrounge. And I just hope to hell she made it. You don't know what it was like over there, Ev."

"Just the newsreels at the Roxy."

Veeve. What she'd given him. What she'd taught him. And they hadn't even had a month of nights—more like a few days of snatched hours.

What he should do was ask Father Hugh to pray for Veeve.

"Would you have stayed with her, Pat, if you coulda?"

Something fluttered across a corner of the porch, a dragonfly living out its days until frost. Pat watched it out of sight.

"I don't know the answer to that, Ev. I thought a lot of her."

He turned to her. Evangeline's wide black eyes. Her laughing mouth that looked so serious now.

"Only thing I do know, Ev. All I want in this world is having Mil again."

Evangeline nodded. She finished her cigarette and stubbed it out and stood. "Josie's going to think I quit on her."

17

Pat went back to his papers while Evangeline and Josie moved their field of operations from the kitchen to the downstairs bedroom, which he guessed was going to be Albert's and Evangeline's bedroom now. Wondered what the women would uncover there, where Ferrell had gone on sleeping after Pat's mother's death. Probably slept there the night before his shoot-out with the sheriff's deputies.

The women interrupted Pat now and then with questions. "Pat, furniture! Cost lots money! What do?"

He looked up—what do, indeed. "The furniture belongs to the house," he finally told them, and they looked at each other.

Next, "We found curtains in a box. What should we—"

"God, I don't know! Wash em and hang em up if you want to."

Now a rising patter of women's voices from the bedroom. Excitement? Awe? And here came Evangeline and Josie, and when he saw what Josie was carrying, he stacked papers on papers and cleared space on his desk for Josie to set down his mother's jewelry box.

"Pat," she breathed. "We look quick and close it."

Mahogany box, inset with ivory patterns on its lid. Pat felt his mother's hands on his as he raised the lid on the scent of his mother's perfume rising from the velvet lining. "God," Pat said, and lifted out a rope of his mother's pearls.

And elaborate pearl earrings that, unlike Evangeline's hoops that went through the lobes of her ears, fastened with little screws on their backs. When he laid them on his desk, Josie picked one up. Dangled the pearls in her brown hand.

"Protestant woman not pierce," she explained.

"Whatever," Pat said, hardly hearing her. He lifted out a silver locket on a chain he didn't remember his mother wearing and a silver watch on a chain that he did, and he wound the little watch and saw its hands move.

Two rings in the velvet slot for rings. His mother had been buried in her wedding ring, and Pat didn't remember these. Yeah, maybe he did. The faceted deep-blue stone in the silver ring—not silver but white gold, he thought—the stone was a sapphire. He must have asked, and his mother must have explained, because he knew it was a Yogo sapphire.

He laid the ring beside the pearls and took out the gold ring set with a big faceted ruby in a circle of diamond chips, and he heard Evangeline's drawn breath.

Albert hadn't given her a ring. Didn't have the cash for it, Pat supposed. "Want to try it on?"

He saw that Evangeline sure did want to! She slipped the ruby ring on her ring finger, and it fit. The ruby shone and the diamond chips sparkled to be in sunlight again, and Evangeline stood by Pat's desk for a long minute, admiring her hand with the ring on her finger while Josie admired it with her. Reluctantly she slipped off the ring and handed it back to Pat.

"Oh, hell, Ev," he said. "I'd give it to you, except"—he had to laugh at the expression on her face—"I think instead I'll give it to somebody you'd probably rather gave it to you than me."

"Even if we are kinda, sorta," he added, and dropped the ruby ring into his shirt pocket. Then he dropped the sapphire ring into his pocket with the ruby ring. He knew neither of the women missed what he'd done with the second ring, but neither said anything. They went back to their cleaning, and Pat to his paper trail, reflecting that he never had seen Mil wearing jewelry. Not ever.

⋯⋯

Late afternoon. Pat leaned back in the swivel chair and stretched his legs. Dug out the pocket watch he'd been carrying since he went to work at the county clerk's office and saw it was almost six o'clock. Rubbed his eyes, scoured his face with his hands, and hoped he wouldn't need glasses before he was done. Take him at least another Saturday, he thought, to reach the bottom.

He should take a weekend to drive to Missoula and pack up his clothes and books and pay his landlady what he owed her. Nobody had said anything about Pat's wearing shirts and Levi's to work in the county clerk's office, he was out of sight in the shelves of files most of the time, anyway, but sooner or later he'd have to wear a suit and tie.

What he needed most was to think about what he now knew. Where Ferrell's money came from.

Ah-oh, he was stiff from following the paper trail all day. He supposed he should take his mother's jewelry box back to town with him, and he got up with the box under his arm and went to see if Evangeline and Josie had done enough cleaning to satisfy them for now. In the front room, he saw an enormous bundle of laundry tied up in a sheet to take home, and in the downstairs bedroom, a stripped bed. Evangeline and Josie sat at the kitchen table, talking in low voices about something that mattered, because they stopped talking when Pat came in with the jewelry box under one arm and the bundle of laundry over his shoulder.

"Ready to go back to town?"

And they nodded.

Mondays tended to be a little slow in the convent and the rectory after the excitement and ceremony of Sundays, and Father Hugh deemed that Monday a good one to drive Sister St. Paul and Josie out to the Plum Creek country to talk to Renny. Sister St. Paul agreed. At Sunday mass they let Josie know their plans, and on Monday morning they set out in Father Hugh's automobile.

All quiet in the Métis settlement, thank the Lord, where Father Hugh and Sister St. Paul picked up Josie. Pat at work, Albert at work, Evangeline suddenly with a lot of sewing to get done—

she was treadling away at the sewing machine she'd borrowed from her cousin and barely looked up to wave when they told her goodbye.

"Is that a new ring she's wearing?" Father Hugh asked.

And Josie smiled and said cryptically, "Nother ring in pocket."

Dust and dust. Even more dust when Father Hugh turned from the graveled road to the dirt trail Mildred and Renny called their road, which did its mountain goat teeter down the bluff, Sister St. Paul clutching one rear-seat door handle and Josie the other, as if they thought they could jump out and save themselves if Father Hugh tipped them over the edge. He shook his head when he caught a glimpse of them in his rearview mirror.

At the Harrington ranch, he drove past the barn and corrals and Renny's shack and parked in front of the cabin. Held one rear door for Sister St. Paul, the other for Josie. They climbed the steps to the porch and knocked on the cabin door. Father Hugh thought Sister St. Paul and Josie planned to rake Mildred over the coals, or whatever it was they were going to do to her, before they started on Renny's coals.

Mildred answered the door dressed for a day of late fall ranch work in men's shirt and Levi's and boots. Her hair braided back. She looked surprised to see them and wondered what she had on hand to feed them for dinner, but she invited them in and poured coffee all around and asked if they'd gotten any rain in town over the weekend. After several minutes of listening to polite chatter, Father Hugh realized that the coal raking or whatever—the black arts crossed his mind, and he had to rebuke himself—the *whatever* couldn't start while he was present, so he excused himself and carried his coffee out to the porch and shook a tailor-made out of his pack and lit it.

He wished he'd thought to bring Mildred some food for her unexpected crowd, and then he remembered that Sister St. Paul had carried a basket with her.

He sat on the porch steps and smoked and let his thoughts wander. How far he was from Fort Maginnis, how far from

Boston, in the midst of people whose lives he never could have imagined—customs that had puzzled him and many he still didn't comprehend—people who spoke a language he knew was English but often couldn't understand. Only gradually he became aware of some kind of ruckus going on at the corrals.

Horses. A pink horse in a corral, bumping against the corral poles and trying to get out. A big orange-colored horse outside the corral, rearing and trying to get in. Renny astride a reluctant gray horse, cursing and lashing the orange horse with a whip to drive him away from the pink horse. Even Father Hugh could see that the gray horse wanted nothing to do with the orange horse, and Renny lashed him and cursed him, too.

Finally the orange horse broke away from the lash and galloped up the road toward the cabin, with Renny lashing the gray horse to make him chase the orange horse and cursing until he ran out of English obscenities and switched to something that wasn't exactly French. Father Hugh thought the noise must have interrupted the coal raking in the cabin, because he heard the door open behind him and turned from watching Renny's combat with the horses to see Mildred look out. Mildred ducked back inside and appeared again, wearing leather gloves and carrying a coil of rope—a *lariat*, Father Hugh later would be told.

Father Hugh turned back in time to see the orange horse make a snaky turn in the road—*he swapped ends*, it would be explained later to Father Hugh—evade Renny and the gray horse, and make for the corral and the pink horse again.

Mildred, standing by the road now, was shaking out her rope in a way that formed a noose on one end—*she built her a loop*, Father Hugh would be told—and yelled, "Run him past me one time, Renny!"

Renny heard her and saw her and gave her a nod and a half salute and went to work with his whip, until finally the orange horse bolted again and tore up the road toward Mildred. Renny's dogs were growling and bristling beside Mildred, ready to defend her. Mildred paid no attention to the dogs. She swung her noose—*her loop, Father!*—twice, three times over her head, and Father Hugh, hardly able to breathe, saw the girl he'd last seen fainting in Pat Adams's arms throw her noose—*loop!*—in such a way that it carried itself through the air and raised itself to encircle the orange horse's front feet just midstride. He saw Mildred set herself, her bootheels digging deep in road dirt, and throw her weight backward just as the orange horse hit his end of the rope and came crashing down.

"Sit on his head for me, Father!" she shouted over her shoulder.

"Do *what?*"

"Sit on his head!"

Father Hugh left the porch and gingerly circled the thrashing horse. The lunging, kicking horse, raising his head and trying to regain his feet, which Mildred kept jerking out from under him.

"That's right, Father—get him by his ear next time I jerk him down. Get a knee on his head and hold it down. No, he can't reach you with his hind leg, even though it looks like he can. *Sit on his goddamn head for me, Father, so he can't get up!*"

That was how Father Hugh, fully agile in hand and foot once he understood his instructions, found himself holding a horse by his ear and kneeling on the horse's head and flinching every time the horse's frantic hind hoof reached for Father Hugh's head and came, Father Hugh thought, within an inch of him until the hoof drove instead between the horse's own front legs and stuck there on the rope.

Renny rode up on his frightened gray horse and dismounted, carrying a short length of rope—*his piggin string, Father!*—which, in movements too quick and deft for Father Hugh to follow, he used to bind all four of the horse's feet together—*he hogtied him, Father!* Renny loosened Mildred's rope from the horse's front feet, and she pulled it free and coiled it up again.

"Oughta take out my jackknife and end that colt's love life for him, here and now," said Renny. He looked at Mildred and grinned and sang to her in a rusty voice, *Oh, she built her a loop, a right tight loop, and she spread it good and true*, and gave her a bear hug.

"You can get off his head now, Father," Mildred said.

Father Hugh rose and brushed what he could of orange horsehair from his black pants and saw, on the cabin porch, an audience of Sister St. Paul and Josie. *Sit on his goddamn head for me, Father, so he can't get up!* He knew Sister and Josie had heard it, and he thought about how fast the story of Father Hugh being told to sit on a horse's head was going to travel around Fort Maginnis, and he had to laugh.

Montana women! They might not talk much, at least not to men, but what they did! Josie with her skillet; Sister St. Paul with her paring knife, not to speak of her ways and means; and now Mildred with her rope. He had to wonder what a force they'd be if they joined up with each other, and he realized some of them already had.

They must have finished with Mildred's coal raking, because Sister and Josie were walking down the road to Renny's shack with their heads together.

Sister St. Paul unpacked her basket and set out a ham and a skillet of fried potatoes for Mildred to heat on her range and a pan of light rolls someone had brought to the convent last night and several oranges and a chocolate cake. Mildred sliced beets from her garden and boiled them lightly while the potatoes reheated, and she set out butter for the rolls. Everyone filled plates and sat at the kitchen table and feasted, and Renny sang another couple of lines of his song: *He roped the devil round his pinted horns, and he took his dallies, too!*

Dallies, thought Father Hugh, after *taking dallies* had been explained to him, along with a short discourse on the advantages and disadvantages of dallies over tied ropes. Such words. *Tackleberry*, that was another one. He thought he'd ask Pat, or Albert, what it meant, rather than anybody at this dinner party.

How difficult Father Hugh had thought it would be to make friends in this strange new country, where people spoke in such strange ways when they spoke at all. Now he thought that Pat and Albert had become as good a pair of friends as he'd ever had. Not that he, as a priest, had ever been as forthcoming about himself as Pat and Albert had been with him, but it occurred to him that if he ever felt a need to talk to another man, to confess, say, in personal, not ritual, terms, it would be to Pat or Albert. And they might be embarrassed, but they could handle it.

He shook himself out of his thoughts and back to the cabin porch and complimented Sister St. Paul on Sister Boniface's chocolate cake. Renny offered him an inch of hooch in a glass, and Father Hugh accepted. And then everyone laughed and began to explain to him what he'd seen happening in the middle of the road.

So the pink horse in the corral was a strawberry roan mare named Pink; the gray horse was a gelding named Smokey; and Smokey was afraid of the orange horse because geldings always were afraid of stallions. The orange horse—*sorrel*, Father—was a mean renegade stud colt—*stallion*, Father—belonging to one of them Fraziers over on Beaver Creek, a worthless bunch who let their stallion run at large. Later, out of earshot of the women, Renny would ask Father Hugh if he'd heard what Will Danvers did to one of them Fraziers in the Plum Creek post office, and Father Hugh hadn't but soon was enlightened.

Anyway—threads of their story picked up—Renny couldn't ride Pink to chase the stud, because Pink was a mare and, well, because the stud was a stud. And Smokey, as a gelding, was so damn scared—sorry, Father—scared of the stud that it was all Renny could do to get him near enough to lash away the stud. Renny had driven the stud away, but the stud kept coming back, until finally Mildred saw what was happening and came out with her lariat.

Nobody had been in any danger, Father! A horse can't get back on his feet with somebody sitting on his head. And a horse's hind hoof can't reach somebody sitting on his head, even though the horse tries.

"Weren't you worried about Mildred, Renny?" Father Hugh asked. He was athlete enough, himself, to know that he'd witnessed a remarkable feat of timing, even if he didn't understand how Mildred had done it.

Renny shook his head. "Nah. Knew she could do it. She's a good hand." After a moment and a sip of hooch, he added in a lower tone, "I'm always worried about her, Father."

Everyone sipped hooch. The air was warm but with a touch that told them summer was gone. Conversation turned to the scant rain of a few weeks ago that had set grass to sprouting and then went away. Would snow fall this winter? Would rain fall in the spring?

Then Josie asked, "What you do stud, Renny, now you hogtie him?"

Renny shook his head. Good question. "I'd like to tie onto him with a team of horses and drag him home hogtied. See how much hair and hide he has left when I get him there."

He considered the hooch in his glass, swirled it, and went on. "Be within the law if I shot him and dumped him in a coulee somewhere and let him rot. A man can't by law let his stud run at large and not expect somebody to get fed up and plug him."

Renny sipped hooch. "Or use my jackknife on him and turn him loose to bleed out. Or use my jackknife and sear him and end the—" Renny glanced around at the company he was in and changed gears. "And end his love life for him and turn him loose to limp home. Probly that's what I'll do. You got makings with you, Father?"

"Better than that." Father Hugh offered Renny his pack of tailor-mades and took one himself, and they settled comfortably down on the porch steps, and Father Hugh guessed that whatever coals of Renny's that needed raking had been raked.

By midafternoon the sorrel stud still lay hogtied in the middle of the road, occasionally raising his head and dropping it again.

Father Hugh thought that whatever Renny decided to do to the stud with his jackknife, he wasn't going to do it until his company left for home. Sister St. Paul and Josie helped Mildred wash her dinner dishes, and they packed Sister's basket with the clean skillet and some of the oranges to enjoy with Father Hugh on the drive home, but they left Mildred and Renny the rest of the ham and the cake and the rolls.

Hugs for Mildred. A handshake between Father Hugh and Renny. Nothing left now but the miles of dirt road and graveled road between the ranch and Fort Maginnis. And first he would have to maneuver his automobile around the hogtied horse in the road, Father Hugh remembered.

18

"Sister, when you first came to Montana, did people take such pleasure in what you didn't know?" Father Hugh asked.

"I think they've always enjoyed teasing somebody they can call a tenderfoot," Sister St. Paul said. "I don't know that I ever received quite as much teasing as you do. My habit may help. Also, I was a farm girl, and horses have to be hitched to wagons and ploughs on French farms, and sometimes they're saddled and ridden."

Tenderfoot. Another new word.

"Maybe you should go to more cinemas, Father," Sister St. Paul suggested. "The kind with cowboys in them."

When he told Albert what she had suggested, Father Hugh got a look from Albert of pure scorn. "You won't get no real help there, Father!"

Albert, when the story about the pink horse reached him, had to laugh. *Sit on his goddamn head, Father!*

"But you were safe, Father," he said. "Maybe in more danger from Mildred, if you didn't do what she told you, than you were from that stud horse. A horse can't get up and he can't kick you if you're sittin on his head."

Apparently, everybody knew that.

But not quite true, Pat told him later. "A horse struggles long enough, he'll throw you off his head, and then watch out."

Pat was pretty sure he could drive his truck wearing a brace and a moccasin as far as Missoula and back. He'd had no difficulty driving out to the ranch with Josie and Evangeline. Albert had fussed over Pat's driving all that way to Missoula alone, and they skirmished some. But Albert needed to work a final sale out at the auction ring on Saturday, and Pat said he'd be all right and was more worried about leaving Albert with no transportation. Albert finally said, no, what he'd do was saddle Socks and ride him back and forth between the stockyards and the Métis settlement. He'd water Socks in the creek and grain him and keep him in Josie's shed overnight—hell, the neighbors wouldn't complain over a horse in the shed for one night.

So early Saturday morning Pat drove Albert the three miles out to the stockyards to retrieve Socks, and then he headed for Missoula. It wasn't a bad drive, only about three hundred miles on graveled roads, some of them fairly well maintained. Call it eight, maybe nine or ten hours. He reached Missoula before dark and drove to his ex-landlady's house and listened to her happy greetings and accepted her offer of supper and a spare cot for the night.

Sunday morning he carried his boxes of books and clothes out of his ex-landlady's storage and loaded them in his truck and paid her what he owed her and hugged her goodbye. Once he thought they'd be home from church, he drove to Ted Kramer's house. Ted wasn't home, but he did find Clyde Ellenberg at home. Of course he'd written to both men, but he wanted to tell Clyde, at least, in person, how much he'd appreciated their offer of a job and how sorry he was to have to turn it down. Family reasons, he said, knowing the news of Ferrell's arrest and upcoming trial would reach Clyde soon, if it hadn't already. Clyde said he and Ted were sorry, too, but things happened. He told Pat that George Clarke was a good man, and he shook Pat's hand and wished him well.

That was that. Pat headed back to Fort Maginnis, feeling cut loose and in horizontal free fall. More worn out than he thought he'd be, and running late after his visit with Clyde Ellenberg. He stopped twice to refuel and take a leak along the highway and once for a cup of coffee, and it was way past dark when he finally pulled up at Josie Archambault's fence, where the lights in Josie's windows looked damned good to him and where Josie and Evangeline and Albert were waiting up with supper for him.

"You want to unload your books tonight?" Albert asked him.

"Nah, they'll be all right where they are. If I thought it would make it rain on them, I might leave em there all winter. No, what I'll do is drive over to the rectory tomorrow before work. Father Hugh says I can store em there. And if you want to ride Socks out to the stockyards tonight, I'll meet you out there and bring you back."

"Deal."

Albert left to saddle Socks and get a head start, and Pat dropped down in one of Josie's chairs. Josie laid down her beadwork.

"You tired out," she informed him. "You need bed. Not work in morning?"

"Gotta work. But yeah," he said. "I'll bring Albert home and go to bed."

"Eat soup. Albert not mind wait."

He managed a spoonful, although food had stopped tasting good to him. Then he went out to his truck and started it and turned his headlights back on and drove the three miles to the stockyards, and there was Albert, waiting for him by the horse barn.

Albert got a look at him in the cab light. "Want me to drive back to Josie's?"

"Wouldn't fight you over it."

They swapped places, and Albert drove to Josie's. When they got out of the truck, Pat sensed Albert at his shoulder to steady him if he needed it. Then Josie was bullying him to drink more soup, and he did drink a spoonful or two. And Josie and Evangeline hugged him good night and kissed him on the cheek, and Pat stumbled through the kitchen to his bed. Didn't know when he'd felt so drained, or why. Not since he first tried to stand and walk after the doctor took his cast off.

Threw off his clothes and brace, collapsed in bed. Left the lamp for Albert to blow out. Heard Albert arranging his sugans.

Albert, sleeping on the floor of Pat's room all summer and into the fall. Had to do something about that. Think of something in the morning.

Mil, I'm thinking about you. But not for long tonight.

....

"Patrick Adams, will you never learn not to overdo?" Sister St. Paul scolded when she saw him.

....

In the meantime, Pat overslept on Monday morning and had to throw his clothes on and shave before he could drive to the courthouse for work, with his luggage and books still in his truck.

"Hell, I'll drive you to work and then unload your clothes with Josie and your books at the rectory," Albert said. "If Father Hugh is there, he'll give me a hand." Albert's job at the stockyards had petered out after the fall sales, as he had anticipated.

So Pat wasn't much late for work, although he still had to wear a white shirt and Levi's slit up the left leg for his brace. Albert dropped him off at the courthouse, and when he passed George Clarke's second-floor office, he heard George and Harry Fallon in excited discussion and thought the county clerk's office could wait for him a little longer and looked in.

"We've got a trial date for Ferrell," George Clarke told Pat. "Monday, November 30. We'll hope we can wind it up before Christmas."

"Only gives you a month," Pat said. He'd been wondering which would come first, Ferrell's trial or Albert's wedding. Looked like the trial was going to be nosed out by the wedding, which was set for mid-November when Albert's instruction sessions with Father Hugh were to end.

Pat hadn't attended Ferrell's arraignment, and he would only attend his trial to testify.

"So, hard luck, Harry," said Clarke. "Another month to go."

"Aah," said Harry, "I've lasted this long. I'll last a little longer."

The two men enjoyed an easy relationship. Maybe someday for himself, Pat thought, and continued to the county clerk's office and his filing.

When he dropped by the prosecutor's office at noon, George and Harry were talking about Elmer Cole, who was Pat's doing, because at his arraignment Ferrell pleaded a defiant not guilty and demanded to serve as his own counsel, a demand the judge denied.

Well, Ferrell wasn't indigent, was he, so Pat talked to Elmer—a good lawyer, levelheaded, George said—and wrote him a check for a retainer. Elmer rolled his eyes at George Clarke's deputy prosecutor-elect having to testify at his own father's trial, commiserated a little with Pat, took the check, and shook his hand.

"What'll I do if Ferrell fires me?" Elmer asked.

"Talk to the judge, I guess. Maybe he can convince him that if you don't represent him, somebody else will. Or maybe they'll sober Ferrell up in jail, and he'll be more reasonable."

"What a mess."

Turned out, Ferrell already had fired Elmer a couple of times for urging him to consider a plea deal.

Pat needed to stay out of it. But, "Take you to lunch, George?"

Clarke looked at him, raised an eyebrow, and said, "Sure."

They found a corner of a lunch counter at a place called the Home Plate, a few blocks from the courthouse with a Pittsburgh Pirates banner hanging on its front door, and found stools more or less out of earshot of other customers, where Pat could tell Clarke about the old bank statements and the paper trails of inheritances he'd found in Ferrell's desk. The will, signed and witnessed in Lander, Wyoming, of a man Pat had realized was his grandfather.

"Wonder if Ferrell made a will."

"Didn't find one, if he did."

"Did your mother leave a will?"

"Not that I know of. Woulda been Ferrell's business, anyway. His wife."

Clarke nodded and looked with little enthusiasm at the hamburger and scoop of potato salad he'd been served. "Might be a record of one having been probated. Pat, I don't see where any of this is a problem for you. At his age, he'll be a damned old man if he does get out of prison. Those cattle—" he shook his head. Pat had told him about his afternoon of slaughter. "Only thing you could do, Pat. Don't know what would bring a man to that point. He used to be a good stockman."

"Yeah."

"What are your plans, Pat? Personally, I mean."

"I'm no rancher. I want to hire a manager. Wait and see if we get rains in the spring; maybe restock. If it doesn't rain, decide what to do then. And hope to be working for you after the trial."

"Hoped you'd say that. Your plans for Ferrell's ranch sound reasonable. You know of a manager you could put on the place? You don't plan to live out there yourself?"

"No. But a manager, yeah. Albert Vanaartsdalen."

"Albert's a good boy. I hear he's getting married in a couple weeks?"

Pat grinned. "He sure is."

Clarke nodded. Hesitated. "You doing any good with your girl?"

He knew Clarke would have heard, through the courthouse gossip vine, all about the scene that had unfolded in Josie's house that day.

"No. Not giving up, though."

A brief scuffle over the tab. Pat picked it up and paid, and they walked back to the courthouse together.

At five Albert was waiting for Pat in the courthouse parking lot. Yup, he'd gotten Pat's books unloaded and the boxes stacked in a back bedroom at the rectory. Last he'd seen, Father Hugh had been looking through the boxes as if he could use a book to read. Josie had shaken out Pat's clothes and told Albert to try on one of Pat's suits, the blue one, which had been a tad wide in the shoulders and an inch too long in the legs.

"Josie says she can alter it, if that's all right with you, and then alter it back for you."

"Don't you want to buy a new suit?"

"When would I wear a suit after the wedding?" Albert thought his thoughts for a few blocks. "Unless you were to get married sometime, Pat," and he punched his shoulder.

Albert pulled the truck up in front of Josie's fence, but he didn't get out right away, and neither did Pat. The early November dusk was settling over the street and the drifts of cottonwood leaves. Filigree of bare cottonwood limbs against a rising half-moon.

"You and Evangeline planning to move out to the ranch right after the wedding?" Pat said.

"Hopin to. She and her mom and Josie want to put in another good scrubbing day, I know that. They sure do look forward to scrubbing, for some reason."

"Seem to. Guess I can drive em out on Saturday. Or you can. Or both of us can, if they round up a big enough scrubbing crew. I've been thinking—" he glanced at Albert's shadowed profile. "If I can pry Ferrell's truck out of the police impoundment, you and Evangeline could use it. I don't know what kind of shape Ferrell left it in, but at least it was running."

Albert nodded. "That'd work. Wondered myself how we'd get to town once in a while."

They climbed out of the truck and walked together to Josie's front door in the deepening dusk, Pat telling himself he had to find the balance between doing enough and doing too much. Evangeline's ring was one thing. And the loan of the truck. But a suit, for instance. He knew he could have bought Albert a suit. And didn't.

19

One afternoon, after Albert's instruction session, Father Hugh asked him how his parents felt about his conversion, and Albert shook his head.

"None too happy," he said. "We're Presbyterians. I mean, my folks are, and I used to be. And Evangeline being, as they'd say, a breed girl, my mother cried about that. Said she couldn't have us in her house. But I still hope they'll come to the wedding."

The two young men were standing on the rectory steps in late September sunshine, and Albert felt like lingering, for some reason.

"Father Hugh," he said, "how'd you decide to be a priest?"

A silence. A rustle of dry leaves on the young oaks someone had planted in front of the rectory. Father Hugh with his hands in his pockets, Albert with his thumbs hooked in his belt loops.

"It wasn't me who decided," Father Hugh said finally, and he told Albert about receiving a call from God, which in his case had come in the middle of a boxing ring. Albert listened and remembered a warm afternoon drinking chokecherry wine on Josie's back stoop.

"Kinda like looking at someone you know and seeing what you hadn't seen before?" Albert said.

"Yeah, I think so," said Father Hugh. "Must be. Sometimes it's a struggle."

Albert thought about that. Had to be tough, he thought, particularly the celibacy part. What he and Evangeline were doing behind Josie's back was getting pretty intense and harder for him to stop when he needed to.

"Hope you win the struggle," he said. "It's gettin so we depend on you around here, Father Hugh."

....

Sister St. Paul, walking up from the convent, saw the two young men on the rectory steps and wondered what they were talking so intently about. Well. Albert and Father Hugh. There's hope yet for this world, she thought.

A few weeks ago she had Pat unbuckle his brace so she could run her fingers over his break, and then she had him put some weight on that leg and checked again for any unevenness. Finding none, she told him he could go back to wearing boots again—"But none of your acrobatics!" she warned him.

"*Acrobatics*, Sister? When have I done those?"

....

The next Saturday, the first Saturday in November, with time closing in on everyone and Evangeline with her dress unfinished but itching to get back to her housecleaning, Pat drove her and Josie out to the ranch with Albert—"Hell, I might as well come along and get a chance to look over the barn and sheds, see what Ferrell left out there"—shivering in a mackinaw in the back of the truck until he froze out and tapped on the rear window for Pat to stop and let him into the cab, where he held Josie on his lap the rest of the way.

At the ranch yard, Pat could hardly park the truck before Josie and Evangeline were out of the cab and retrieving their cleaning assortment and a big bag of clean laundry—bedsheets and towels, Pat supposed—and the box of sandwiches and the coffee.

"They sure do seem to love it," Albert remarked, and Pat nodded and wondered if Mil loved housecleaning, although Josie and Evangeline's fervor for it didn't seem to fit Mil. Then he and Albert shared a cigarette and looked up at the changing clouds and thought the same thought. No snow yet.

Albert left for his ramble through the outbuildings, and Pat went inside to pick up his paper trail where he'd left off. He thought he could finish by afternoon and pack up the papers so the women could pitch into the study, which they clearly could hardly wait to do, because every time Pat looked up, he saw one or the other assessing his progress.

·········

Josie stopped working long enough to heat her coffee and open her sandwiches and call Albert in from the barn and Pat out from his study, and by the time they'd finished their noon meal, Evangeline's mother and sister had arrived, dropped off by one of the Croziers, who said he had to drive over east to look at a team of horses and would be back. Pat returned to his remaining papers and listened to women's voices and women's feet doing a sightseeing tour through the house, he guessed. He reached the bottom of his papers and divided them into three stacks—a stack to keep, a stack to store, and a stack for the burn barrel.

He stood up and stretched and thought, damn, it felt good to be wearing Justins again instead of a brace and a moccasin. Acrobatics. He remembered Sister St. Paul's warning and wondered what she pictured him doing.

The day had darkened, and Pat heard thunder. God, let it rain. Rain in November seemed unlikely, though. Then he wandered through a transformed living room: curtains hanging at clean windows and a polished floor; every rung and curlicue on the chairs wiped of dust; and judging by the odor, the leather couch cleaned with saddle soap. He glanced into the downstairs bedroom—clean windows and curtains, bed made up, and furniture polished—shook his head, and saw the women drinking coffee around the kitchen table, all their heads together, while they waited for him to finish in the study.

Their chatter stopped, and four pairs of eyes watched Pat walk across the kitchen and start up the stairs. And then he heard Evangeline whisper something to Josie and their chatter resume.

He opened the door to Ferrell's junk room, where he thought he remembered an apple crate he could use to store papers, and then found himself daydreaming at the web-shrouded gable window that looked south over the high prairie as far as the break in the hills that eventually would become the bluffs over Plum Creek. A blackening sky, lightning dancing over the horizon.

That was when he saw lightning strike the high prairie to the south in two places, and rising plumes of smoke, and he was down the stairs at a run.

Met Albert at a run from the barn with shovels and sacks.

The light wind was blowing out of the north. The women and the ranch buildings were in no danger unless the wind changed, they agreed, and they ran to Pat's truck.

Starving cattle had picked the range as clean as though by geese, but a little rain had fallen a few weeks back, and the grass perked up enough to provide some ground cover before turning brown again with the first hard frost. Weather moved in and clouds rumbled and lightning danced on the horizon and struck the high prairie in two spots. When the plumes of smoke rose where no smoke should rise, every man in the Plum Creek country ran for shovels and gunnysacks and buckets, and every woman started boiling water for coffee and slicing bread for sandwiches.

Knowing they had Plum Creek between them and the road up to the high prairie, Renny brought in the Belgians and hitched them to the wagon. He tied Pink and Smokey to the back of the wagon and threw their saddles in back with the shovels and buckets and sacks. Mildred came running with her black bag, of course, and climbed up on the wagon seat beside him as he whipped up the Belgians as fast as he thought they could travel and still have wind enough to reach the smoke.

Neighbors closer to the flames than Renny and Mildred already were setting backfires. Just enough contrary wind to keep the backfires shifting, and the men had to beat out their fires with shovels and gunnysacks and reset them. Still, they were getting a pretty good fire break burned off, Renny saw.

Better luck than the crew on the other fire, a half mile away to the north. He could see men running in front of the flames and beating them with sacks, while the natural drafts created by the two fires pulled their flames toward each other and around the unlucky bastard's sheds and corrals and homestead shack that lay between them.

Renny's idea was to leave Mildred well behind the fire break with the heaving Belgians and the wagon, where she could set up her aid station. He'd just untied Pink from the wagon, thinking to saddle her—old bitch, even after that run behind the wagon she wasn't out of breath—and take a shovel and sacks and try to ride around the fire to help the shorthanded crew to the north, when something apparently happened, because everybody started jumping and shouting.

Somebody yelled in his ear. "Let me have your horse, Renny!"

"Jesus, Pat! I ain't even saddled her yet—"

But Pink's reins were jerked out of his hand.

"Pat, she'll bite the hell out of you! She's tried enough times with me—"

Pat had torn off his shirt and was tying it around Pink's head as a blindfold, and Pink was letting him do it. With a handful of mane and one quick swing, Pat was astride Pink, bareback, and Pat and Pink were outa there in a thunder of Pink's hoofs.

Renny saw what was causing all the excitement. At the door of the shack, a hundred yards away, stood a woman holding a baby. The flames from the burning grass were low, but not low enough for a man to run through or dare to drive a truck with tires and gas tank through.

Pink, the fast old mare, still the fastest horse in Murray County. The mean old mare, letting Pat Adams ride her bareback through hoof-deep burning grass and flaming weeds.

"Who's the crazy son of a bitch with no shirt on?"

"Patrick Adams."

"Jesus. Look at him go."

They all watched. What else could they do? Pat and Pink ran ahead of the flames now, with Pink devouring the hundred yards with her great slashing Hambletonian strides and Pat riding as though he were part of her. They saw him rein in Pink at the door of the shack, not quite to a halt, more of a four-hoofed dance in place. The young woman handed up her baby to Pat, and Pat tucked the baby in the crook of his arm and, with his other hand, reached for the young woman's hand and swung her up behind him on the dancing Pink, and Renny thought his heart would stop. Pink, who'd never carried double in her life, Pink with the white blindfold tied over her eyes. Well, nobody ever said Pat Adams didn't know how to handle a horse. But Jesus Christ, Pat, you crazy son of a bitch.

They saw Pat wheel Pink around. Shirtless. Bundle of baby in one arm. Pink's reins in his free hand. The woman's arms clasped around him. Pat paused, deciding his best angle, and then he leaned forward and gave Pink her head. She leaped and came down in her slashing strides toward the flames that burned toward her, and again she was racing hoof-deep through fire.

"God almighty, look! The bastard's laughing!"

How long had he watched? Afterward Renny tried to figure. All his life? Less than a minute? The horse and the rider with the baby in the crook of his arm and the young woman with her arms wrapped around the rider's waist and hanging on for dear life. Low flames, rising black smoke. Renny knew he'd never forget the sight. Nobody on the high prairie that afternoon would ever forget the sight.

Almost before the watchers could draw their next breaths, Pink had slashed across the flames and over the backfire line to blackened ground, and Pat had reined her down to a rear and a dance. White teeth flashing in Pat's smoke-blackened face, and Pat still laughing, the crazy bastard, from whatever exhilaration was coursing through his blood.

Collective letting out of breath.

"Guess this means his leg musta healed," said a farmer.

"Yup. Guess what we can use around here every once in a while is a cowboy."

Pat let the young woman slide to the ground. Renny yelled at her to get away from Pink, but all she wanted was her baby. As Pat handed down the howling baby, she snatched it from him and began to howl, herself, and Mildred somehow was beside her, wrapping a wagon blanket around the woman and baby and leading them away.

Pat slid off Pink. He untied her blindfold and took it off and handed her reins to Renny.

"Hell of a horse," Pat said. He slapped Pink on the flank. "You might use some of Mil's ointment on her hocks, Renny."

A hell of a horse she was. Renny took Pink's reins to lead her back, and she bared her teeth and tried to bite him.

They never stood a chance with the sheds and corral and the shack, and all were lost, but the men fought and fought on and encircled the fire. And then they leaned on their shovels and watched it burn out. Then a cheer went up as a woman drove up with a team of horses and a wagon with urns of coffee and packets of sandwiches, and the men fell on the food and coffee. Everybody was laughing and slapping each other's backs, and more women came with food and coffee. And a woman who knew her took the young woman and the baby away in the wagon. She and her husband were squatters, somebody said, with nowhere to live but that abandoned homestead shack. Nobody knew where her husband might be.

Or where Pat had gone, for that matter. The last Renny had seen, Albert Vanaartsdalen had been tearing off his own coat and wrapping it around Pat.

"Guess that's what Sister meant by acrobatics," Albert had said.

Whatever that meant, Renny wondered.

Renny tied Pink to the back of his wagon and judged that the Belgians had got their wind back for a slow pace home. Mildred had applied ointment to burns and bandaged several scrapes and one deep cut from a shovel swung in the wrong direction, and it looked like she was ready to go home. Her face was as still as though it had been sculpted, and she spoke not a single word all the way home. Or for some days after, not that Renny heard.

But more thunder rumbled, and rain fell before Renny and Mildred reached her cabin, where Renny let Mildred off and saw her run for her door through the rain. Rain in November. He drove the team down to the barn and got the saddles under cover and took care of the tired horses. Renny didn't know if he'd ever felt better about unharnessing horses in the rain. It looked to him as if the rain would turn to snow by morning, though.

20

"You shoulda seen it, Father Hugh."

"I wish I had." Father Hugh shook his head. "I can*not* imagine."

Albert was still seeing Pat's ride in his mind's eye. "You won't tell Sister St. Paul, will you?"

"No. No, I certainly won't tell her, not I."

Father Hugh could just imagine Sister's reaction to Pat's—*acrobatics* was a good word—and Father Hugh had enough mischief in him to relish his secret knowledge. He didn't doubt that Sister would resort to torture, if she had to, to get it out of him. If she ever had an inkling of it.

Father Hugh should have known better after living in Murray County for nearly six months, but he badly misjudged the speed at which information in Murray County was inhaled and exhaled through the air. Word of Pat's ride breathed down from the high prairie and reached the convent soon enough.

"Patrick Adams!"

Pat had been drinking coffee in the rectory kitchen and discussing Albert's wedding plans with Father Hugh and Albert when Sister St. Paul walked in on them. He stood to face what was coming, while Father Hugh and Albert backed away and watched and listened as Sister St. Paul gave Pat what for.

Afterward, Father Hugh and Albert agreed they were kinda glad they'd been there. Not everybody got to see Pat Adams backed up against a kitchen wall in the rectory. Also, the experience had been informative in its own way. Neither Father Hugh nor Albert had dreamed Sister St. Paul knew some of the words she used. Sister

Boniface, who had accompanied Sister St. Paul to the rectory with eggs for the housekeeper, Mrs. O'Shea, had never heard those words and didn't know their meanings, although from where she cowered behind the stove, she guessed Sister St. Paul's intent.

Sister St. Paul seemed to have run out of epithets. Pat looked a little dazed.

"Sister," Pat said meekly, "would you rather I'd left em to burn?"

Sister St. Paul looked at Pat, and Pat looked at Sister St. Paul. In that moment, Father Hugh thought he'd never seen anyone with an expression on his face more innocent than Pat's.

Sister St. Paul made a sound—couldn't have been a sob, could it? Well, yes, it could. And then what Father Hugh and Albert saw was even more unbelievable than Pat's what for they'd just watched: Sister St. Paul sobbing in Pat Adams's arms.

It didn't last long. Hardly long enough for Father Hugh and Albert to be sure they hadn't both seen the same figments of their imaginations. Sister St. Paul sniffed and swirled away, they supposed to pray, and Father Hugh and Albert looked at Pat because they didn't dare look at each other. But at least now they were free to laugh, and they did look at each other. Father Hugh said, "Backed up against the wall," which sent Albert doubled over laughing, and Albert said, "Backed up against the wall," which sent Father Hugh off.

Then Sister Boniface crept out from behind the stove, and the young men turned and saw her and laughed some more. And Sister Boniface suddenly realized that laughter really was contagious and that she had caught it. After all, what could Sister Boniface do, what could the young men do, but laugh, when such a terrible thing could have happened on the high prairie but hadn't?

Father Hugh, at least, realized that what might have happened and hadn't was why Sister St. Paul had been so angry with Pat and why she had cried. But for now, Pat could only shake his head as Father Hugh and Albert and Sister Boniface laughed at him.

"Some friends," he said. "I'd a thought one of you would have my back."

"Not I," said Father Hugh, laughing.

"Not me either," said Albert, and laughed some more.

"Anyway, it wasn't like you needed either of us," said Father Hugh.

"I'm sure they love you, Pat," said Sister Boniface, and then she ran to catch up with Sister St. Paul.

Pat walked past the county prosecutor's office on Monday morning and was greeted by big grins and clapping from Harry Fallon and George Clarke and Clarke's receptionist, Betsy Anglaterra. They beckoned him in.

"Wish I'd seen it," said Harry Fallon, and Pat thought, oh God, the Pat-Adams-backed-up-against-a-wall-in-the-rectory-kitchen story had traveled all the way from the convent to the prosecutor's office.

Then Clarke said, "I always knew you could ride, Pat, but that must have been something to behold," and Pat realized they were talking, not about the what for Sister St. Paul had given him, but about his ride.

"Is the horse doing all right?" Betsy asked.

"Oh, yeah. She might have picked up a few blisters on her hocks. Nothing Renny can't take care of. But I tell you, Betsy, Harry, George, she sure was pickin em up and puttin em down."

Everybody laughed, and then they all went back to work.

Josie hand-altered Pat's blue suit for Albert and pressed it for him, and then she brushed and pressed Pat's dark-gray suit for Pat, muttering to herself that with the weight Pat was losing, she might have to alter his suit, too. She laundered two of Pat's white shirts and starched and pressed them, one for Pat and one for Albert. She rummaged through Pat's box of clothes and found a necktie for Pat and one for Albert—

"Hell no, I'm not gonna spend money on a necktie! When else am I ever gonna wear a necktie?"

Out of Pat's earshot, he told Josie, "Pat ever got married, I guess I might buy one."

Josie said, as she had to Father Hugh, "Nother ring in pocket," and unlike Father Hugh, Albert thought he caught her meaning.

Yup. That had been one pretty good day for Albert. First Pat pulling that ring with the red stone out of his shirt pocket and dropping it in Albert's shirt pocket—"Think I know who'd like to have it off you." Then Evangeline's face when Albert got her alone and took the ring out of his pocket and showed it to her. Evangeline held out her hand, and he slipped the ring on her finger, and—yeah.

Josie hung their suits and shirts in her bedroom and told Pat and Albert to polish their own boots. "Won't hurt you buy good pair socks," she told Albert, and he did.

So they were as ready as they could be. Now, if Evangeline just got her dress finished in time. Evangeline treadled grimly away at her cousin's sewing machine, and nobody liked to interrupt her.

"You coming to town with me for the wedding tomorrow?" asked Renny.

"No."

Mildred had washed their supper dishes and was drying them. Renny had taken to sleeping at his shack again after that first hard frost, but he and Mildred had fallen into the habit of meals together at the cabin. Now, when she didn't hear his footsteps on his way to the door, she turned and saw him behind her, looking down at her.

Dark-eyed Renny. His dark face showing his age. Hairy-armed and grizzle-bearded Renny, like an old bear. Wool shirt, pants held up by suspenders.

"Because you don't want to see Pat," he said.

How to explain to him. She didn't know where to begin.

"Mildred," Renny said, "I was wrong about some of the things I thought, and I've changed my thinking some. And you're gonna make yourself sick if you keep on like this. And you seen his face. You're makin him sick over it. Josie says he's stopped eating."

You're making yourself sick, Sister St. Paul had warned Mildred, and Josie had nodded. Two women who loved her, but she couldn't explain to them either.

"You know how Josie's gonna feel if you don't come with me? You know how Evangeline's gonna feel?"

"Ever since . . ." she began, and faltered. "Ever since I found him that night and got him on Smokey . . ."

Renny was waiting for her to go on, and she didn't know how. "I think I was all right till then. I'd, I thought, gotten over all of it, but since then . . ." She was sobbing outright now, "I've kissed him goodbye twice since then, and I can't do that again, Renny. I can't."

"Baby," Renny said. "Honey. You don't have to do it again."

Crying like a baby was right. What she was doing to herself. Yes, doing it to herself. So stiffen up, she told herself. Cowboy up.

"You don't have to kiss him goodbye. You do have to go to Evangeline's wedding. You got nice clothes, don't you?"

"Yes."

"You change your clothes after we do the chores tomorrow morning, and I'll get cleaned up too," Renny said. And over his shoulder as he went out the door, he added, "A course, you could always try kissin him hello."

Rain was falling again, rain that would likely turn to snow by morning. Renny bowed his head against the rain, while his dogs fell in behind him for the walk down to the shack in the dark. He guessed he'd have to start carrying his lantern up to the cabin and back, it was getting dark so early now.

Ah, hell. A girl who could front-foot a marauding stud colt and bring him down—Renny still had to laugh, *sit on his goddamn head, Father!*—now tearing herself apart over that long-ago atrocity.

He had to say that Josie's lecture, mostly in Michif, had turned Renny's thinking around, some, about Pat Adams. *The sweetness of the flesh* had been one of Josie's topics, and *how it hurts*, another, and *as I know you know, René Archambault.*

Yup.

Sister St. Paul had listened to Josie's Michif and nodded from time to time, although Renny was pretty sure she didn't understand the patois, and just as well, considering Josie's topics. Occasionally Sister St. Paul pursed her lips. Once, she lifted an eyebrow when she heard Josie speak a name.

Perry's name. Pierre LeFrombois, dead these twenty years and more and buried in the Catholic cemetery in Fort Maginnis.

Renny reached the shack and lit his lantern and hung it on its hook. He thought a little hooch tonight would go down well, though he knew it wouldn't hurt him to haul a washtub inside and heat water and take a bath, what with tomorrow being Evangeline's wedding day. Finally, he took the bath and splashed around for a while in the washtub and then dried himself and pulled on clean long johns and threw out his bathwater.

He poured himself a little hooch and listened to the rain on the shack's tin roof and watched the fire in the stove flicker and die down and remembered when Thaddeus Harrington had ridden into this country on a good horse and filed his homestead on the prime bottom land along Plum Creek. Thad had planned his barns and corrals and cabin, and then he'd hired hands, mostly young men from the Métis settlement in and around Fort Maginnis. René Archambault, for one. And René's second cousin Pierre LeFrombois, whom everybody called Perry. Thad set the young men, boys really, grubbing underbrush from along the creek and cutting cottonwoods to cure for barn and cabin logs and cutting and snaking firs down from the mountains to cure for corral poles.

Everybody, including Thad, lived in tents that first summer and cooked over campfires and drank from the creek until they got a well dug. By first snowfall they'd built the shack Renny still lived in, and most of the Métis boys went home for the winter, except for Renny and Perry, who'd decided to try their luck with a trapline.

The next summer, the Métis boys came back and cut and stacked hay on the meadows they'd cleared the year before, and they fenced pasture for Thad's cattle. They built the barn and Thad's cabin from cottonwood logs, and they hauled river rock for Thad's big fireplace. At snowfall, when Thad moved up to the cabin and the Métis boys went home again, Renny and Perry, who'd had good luck with their trapline last winter, decided to run it again. They had the shack to themselves now, which must have been when, sometime that winter, snow deep around the shack—damned if Renny knew how it happened, some things beyond telling—Renny and Perry discovered the sweetness of the flesh.

They hadn't known a damn thing about the world, but they knew enough to keep quiet and careful about what they were doing.

How it hurts. Yup. Renny knew all too well. Thad had married Mildred's mother by then, and Mildred was maybe three. Mildred had turned twenty-eight this summer, so it was twenty-five years ago. Thad had bought that mean bay gelding, mostly thoroughbred, with a thoroughbred's long legs, and kept him haltered and tied in an open stall. Perry, probably thinking he was well out of reach of those long hind legs, walked behind the gelding to pick up a feed bucket, and the gelding's leg shot out and connected with Perry's head. Renny, pitching hay at the other end of the barn, saw it happen.

He pulled Perry out of the gelding's striking distance and yelled for Thad, and he and Thad lifted Perry into the back of Thad's truck, with Renny in the back with Perry, trying to shield Perry's face from the sun and his head from the worst of the jolts as Thad drove to Fort Maginnis as fast as he dared on a road more treacherous, even, than it was now. Renny had known, long before they reached the sisters at Good Samaritan, there would be nothing they could do for Perry.

That was that. Father Quinn performed Perry's funeral service, and they buried him in the Catholic cemetery in Fort Maginnis. And Thad went home and shot the gelding. One or two things could be said for Thad.

Yup, Josie. Renny knew how it felt. He'd felt so bad that he'd confessed to Father Quinn, and Father Quinn had been so horrified that Renny—Renny never wanted to see a priest that horrified again. Didn't know how Father Hugh would react to such a confession, and he damned well wasn't going to find out.

Renny sipped his hooch and thought his thoughts.

Sister St. Paul hadn't spoken during Josie's lecture in Michif that lilted and bubbled and spilled over and overflowed some more. When Josie had said everything she needed to say to Renny, Sister St. Paul said, "Renny, Patrick Adams told me that he would do anything if he could make what happened to Mildred not have happened. He said he would do anything to keep her from being hurt again."

Renny had looked directly into her eyes for a long minute. "Do you believe him, Sister?"

"Of course I believe him."

Renny finished his hooch. The fire had died down; the shack was cooling. Tomorrow was tomorrow. At least it was raining. It did seem to him, though, that the world sometimes doubled around and circled back on itself. Seemed to swap ends, so to speak. Desperate drives to the sisters in Fort Maginnis, for instance. He thought Mildred must be feeling something circling back on her.

21

Mildred unbraided her hair and washed it and combed it out to dry in the warmth of the stove while she bathed in the galvanized tub with her knees under her chin and the sheet pinned around her neck. By the time her bathwater had cooled, her hair had dried enough to rebraid and tie with a bit of string.

Flannel nightgown. Bathwater flung over the end of the porch on the stalks of last summer's hollyhocks, where no one was likely to slip and fall if the water froze before it could sink into the stalks and the earth.

She set the lamp on the table by her bed and fetched her moccasins where she could easily reach them in the morning, when the fire in the stove would long have gone out and the floor grown icy. Blew out the lamp, pulled the bed quilts high around her. Looked at the ceiling in the dark and saw Pat riding through flames.

She had been standing in the wagon, unpacking her black bag, when she heard the shouts and straightened and turned in time to see Pat Adams vault bareback on Renny's mare, Pink. Her first thought was of the anchoress's visions. She couldn't be seeing what she was seeing. The great slashing mare, the shirtless rider—an illustration from a high school book about mythology—*centaur* was the word, the horse-man. Racing, rearing, four-hoofed dancing in place. The baby now in the arm of the horse-man, the horse-man swinging the woman up behind him with her skirt rucked.

Rearing, turning, hesitating, and then the great slashing strides, hoof high through flames, devoured the distance between Mildred and the horse-man. His laughter. Her sensation of her body being thrown back by force, exhausted, helpless, her own body not her own.

Of course not. Mildred came back from wherever she'd been. She was standing in the wagon where she'd been standing all along, looking over the heads of the men, and she heard the howling woman—hysteria?—and snatched up the wagon blanket and ran to her.

Alone in the dark, sheltering under quilts in her cold cabin, she remembered being rendered helpless long ago. No. Never again. Maybe—she lay awake for some time.

Her wrist gripped by her father. Being jerked along by her father, half dragged to his truck. Thrown bodily into the cab. Then Renny was there, running from somewhere. It was night; she was seeing the indistinct figures of Renny and her father arguing. The metal walls of the cab dulled the words Renny and her father flung back and forth but did not dull their rage. Then her father was in the cab with her, cursing and jerking the truck into gear. Renny—afterward, she knew Renny must have vaulted into the back of the moving truck.

Headlights cutting into the night. Moving shapes along the road, pairs of eyes, cattle waking at the sound of the truck. Her father driving and cursing her, cursing Pat—"Little bitch, gettin bred with that damned Adams brat—by God make him do the right thing"—driving for what seemed forever toward her doom, whatever it would be, and then in no time at all reaching her doom.

The Adamses' ranch yard. Massive shape of the house. Her father jerking her along by her wrist again, pounding on the door until a light shone through a window and the door opened on a man wearing nothing but pants with suspenders and carrying a lamp. Afterward she supposed he had gone to bed and been wakened by her father's pounding. A man nearly as big as her father. Bearded. Hairy chested. Bare feet. Ferrell Adams, a name later branded on her first sight of him.

Words thrown by her father at Ferrell Adams, words thrown back by Ferrell, words making no more sense to her than the bawling of cattle at branding time. Words of rage, rage at her, rage at Pat, but by now she was too empty to feel afraid. She wasn't a girl named Mildred but a thing jerked around by its wrist.

"No, by God, he won't marry her—kid's not worth powder and shot to blow him to hell, can't get his nose out of his book, but—his life's not going to be ruined for him, his name ruined over a slut of a girl who can't keep her . . ."

Ferrell had her by her wrist now. Jerking her through the door. A glimpse by lamplight of a frightened woman in a wrapper, a woman with fair hair and eyes like Pat's.

"And you just tend to your knittin, Mama!" He spat the word again, "*Mama!*" and the woman vanished.

Through a long room, into a smaller room. By lamplight, a flat-topped desk and a chair and a gun cabinet.

"This way you can keep it quiet and hold your head partway up. You gonna help me, or you'd rather I butcher her?"

Her father had her wrists now, and he and Ferrell were stretching the thing they'd been jerking across the desk on her back, her head hanging over one side of the desk and her knees over the other. She kicked, a headless chicken's kicking, when Ferrell lifted up her dress and pulled down her underpants. And there was crashing, kicking, against the door, Ferrell turning to look, her father looking, and she raised her head enough to see Pat, Pat kicking down a door to get to her.

Ferrell laying down a length of wire, advancing on Pat. Ferrell's massive fist striking Pat's face, Pat staggering back and launching himself at Ferrell again and receiving Ferrell's second blow. Blood spurting down Pat's face. Her father now holding Pat at bay while Ferrell returned to his wire.

Ferrell slapping her across one cheek and then the other to make her lie still. Pulling her legs apart. Ferrell's fingers in her *down there* and a pointless screaming from her, a headless chicken's screaming. Something rigid in her *down there*, something probing, striking a blue lightning of pain inside her. Headless chicken's screaming.

Renny in the room, Renny's hand on Ferrell's shoulder, wresting Ferrell back, slamming him back, Renny lifting her from the top of the desk and carrying her through the door off its hinges, through the long room, and through an outer door also off its hinges, a door she later knew had been kicked in by Renny to get to her.

Renny laying her on the seat of the cab, Renny kneeling by her. Renny's fingers in her *down there*, Renny's other hand on her belly, and she was too gone now to care.

"Drive, you son of a bitch!"

"Drive where?"

"To the sisters, you damned fool! You want her to bleed to death?"

Pat's bloody face. His nose had been broken. Mildred thought he'd likely gritted his teeth and straightened it himself, as best he could. His nose was a little off-kilter now, with a knot to tell where it had been broken.

She knew she wouldn't sleep now. She struck a match and lit her lamp. Slipped on her moccasins and wrapped a quilt around her shoulders and went to start a fire in the fireplace. She got the kindling blazing and topped with a log, and she huddled on the leather couch in her quilt and watched the fire.

So this was where the horse-man had carried her. Not slashing through flames, but to reliving the worst moments of her life.

So much she hadn't known. The names for the parts of her body or for the parts of Pat's body. She had seen how the bull freshened the cow, but she couldn't have described it aloud or had the words to tell anyone, even Sister St. Paul, what Ferrell and her father had done to her, except that they had hurt her and made her bleed. Maybe Renny told Sister St. Paul whatever she hadn't been able to see or surmise for herself. Or he told Josie, and Josie told Sister St. Paul.

But then the nuns took her in hand and sent her to high school and trained her in their diploma program for nurses, which gave her a voice to speak the names of parts, the names of actions. Sister St. Paul's word, *penetration*. To be penetrated, which to this very moment in the middle of the November night, she never had been, except by Ferrell's wire and Ferrell's fingers. She still called her menses by Josie's words, bloods and moons, although only to herself.

The mons veneris, the vulva, the vagina. The clitoris, which her midwifery textbook described as *the seat of the voluptuous sensations experienced by the female during copulation.*

Copulation. She now knew the word for what the bull did to the cow to freshen her.

Voluptuous sensations. Maybe the cow had them, because the cow never objected to the bull's copulation with her, but Mildred never had felt them. Sensations, yes, making them both want more when she and Pat discovered the sweetness of each other's flesh during their month of nights.

Well. Middle of the night mind rambling. Maybe she should stop sleeping in her father's bed, new sheets and pillows and bedding or not. Or sleeping in the same room with Pat's hat. Maybe she should start climbing up to the loft at night, where she used to sleep.

And now she had to go to Evangeline's wedding.

....

Their chores in the morning were few. Mildred and Renny, working in the pleasure of fresh snowfall. Hay pitched for the horses, grain poured. Hay pitched for the cow and her calf, which Renny had turned in with the cow. The cow was almost dry, anyway, and would freshen again in the spring. Water tanks pumped full. The chickens, kept shut up now, water pumped and poured in their tin troughs. Their feed poured in tin troughs. Lamps blown out and readied to be relit. Last thing, fires carefully doused in the stoves in the cabin and in the shack.

Mildred retrieved her buckets of chokecherries from the depths of the haymow to take to Josie, and she wrapped her wedding present for Evangeline, a pair of pillowcases she had embroidered last winter, in tissue. In the back of her closet she found her good navy shoes with heels, which she seldom wore, and she dressed in clean underthings and a garter belt and a slip. She put on silk stockings, one by one, and attached them to her garters. A blue wool dress dotted in white that she seldom wore, a small felt hat. Coat and gloves.

Renny looked her over and nodded. "You look nice, honey."

Renny, whose idea of cleaning up for Evangeline's wedding was brushing and combing his hair and beard, cleaning his fingernails, and wearing new Levi's with suspenders and a brown jacket that looked as if it once had been part of a suit and wouldn't meet to button around him. His boots polished. He hadn't done much in the way of wrapping his wedding present, just white paper tied with string that had traveled out to the ranch around some store purchase or other and carefully saved, but Mildred knew he'd tooled a headstall for a bridle for Albert. Renny gave Mildred a hand up in her unfamiliar shoes to the high cab seat, and they were off.

Evangeline and Albert's wedding was scheduled for late morning, in the Catholic church, of course, with a reception following in the parish hall next door. Mildred and Renny were a little early. They climbed the steps of the church, which had been swept clean of snow, and Mildred left her tissue-wrapped pillowcases with a note on a table in the entryway placed there for that purpose. She followed Renny as he touched the font of holy water and crossed himself and genuflected at a rear pew. Mildred knew all the proper ritual gestures, of course, but she hadn't walked through that door. Just hadn't, just didn't. Wouldn't.

Someone was playing the piano at the front of the church, music unfamiliar to Mildred and lovely. Not a priest, but a short dark-haired man in an ordinary white shirt collar and a necktie and suit was lifting sounds from the keys with his fingers, sounds that rose and seemed to caress the stained glass windows on either side of the church and fall in love with them, and Mildred, who knew little about music, sensed the order underlying what the man was playing. A beauty in the order.

The man played and played, and more people came into the church to bless themselves and genuflect and sit in pews or kneel for a few moments in prayer. Mildred knew a little more about the order underlying what they were doing than the order created by the pianist, but she felt the peace in both and longed for it. Then Josie was genuflecting and slipping into the pew beside Mildred and looking up and smiling at her. Mildred had Renny sitting on one side and Josie on the other, and where could she find more peace and still have to long for it?

The pianist switched to more exultant music, and a stir swept through the assembled wedding guests. Father Hugh, formal in white vestments, stood at the foot of the altar. Also at the foot of the altar, a woman in a dark-red dress, one of Evangeline's sisters, Mildred thought. And Albert, hatless and looking frightened and unfamiliar in his suit. And Pat wearing a dark suit that fit him too loosely. When had he lost so much weight?

Had Pat seen her? She knew he had, he always saw her, but his eyes were on Albert now. And Father Hugh was raising his arms, and the wedding guests were rising to their feet, Mildred rising to her feet, and everyone looking back over their shoulders, where Evangeline's father was escorting a smiling Evangeline, looking like a large full-blown rose in her ruffled pink satin, through the doors of the church and up the aisle to Albert.

Father Hugh, inviting the wedding guests to be seated. Father Hugh, smiling at Evangeline and Albert and Pat, while Mildred, knowing nothing of the Three Musketeers and a kinda, sorta fourth one, sensed their bond and felt envious. And Sister Boniface, seated in a front pew with the other nuns, braced herself for a wicked glance from Father Hugh when he asked who gave this woman in marriage and Evangeline's father said he did and sat down, and then Sister Boniface did get a wicked glance from Father Hugh that asked, Are you going to give the groom away, Sister? Sister Boniface bravely lifted her chin and smiled at Father Hugh, while Mildred, not as brave, watched from her strange limbo in the midst of peace and order even as she rose and knelt and rose and sat with everyone else.

Father Hugh knelt at the foot of the altar with Evangeline and Albert and Evangeline's sister and Pat and began to perform the sacrament of marriage in the Latin that Mildred no longer followed easily.

Adiutorium nostrum in nomine Domini.

Qui fecit caelum et terram . . .

And Mildred spared a thought for Albert Vanaartsdalen's Presbyterian parents, who had swallowed their disapproval and brought themselves to see him married and now would be asking themselves why the priest's back was turned to the wedding guests, why they could not see the faces of the bride and groom or the faces of their attendants. What incomprehensible language was the priest speaking, and why was he taking so long?

Propter hoc dimittet homo patrem et matrem, et adhaerebit uxori suae, et erunt duo in carne una. Itaque iam non sunt duo, sed una caro. Quod ergo Deus coniunit, homo non separet.

Finally, Albert, tentatively and then with enthusiasm, took Evangeline in his arms and kissed her, and Father Hugh presented Mr. and Mrs. Albert Vanaartsdalen to the assembled guests.

An exultant thunder from the piano—Renny, the old Métis fiddler, later would remark that whoever that piano player was, he sure could make one piano sound like twenty pianos—and Albert was walking back down the aisle with his beaming Evangeline on his arm, and Father Hugh walking behind them, and Pat with Evangeline's sister on his arm, to wait in the foyer to receive the wedding guests with much hugging and kissing and handshaking and slapping of backs in the chill November air. Then it was time for Josie and Mildred and Renny to rise from their rear pew and join the receiving line, which, led by the nuns from the front pews, now flowed down the church steps and along the sidewalk and into the parish hall.

Keep walking, Mildred told herself. Follow Renny and Josie. The receiving line slowed. Josie was hugging Pat, Renny was shaking Pat's hand, and then while Josie and Renny moved on to Father Hugh and Albert and Evangeline, Mildred raised her eyes and met Pat's.

Pat's face, pale and foreign to her without its deep color from sun and weather. His dark suit that fit too loosely.

"Mil."

People behind her, waiting to get out of the church, and Mildred nodded and was able to walk on and receive Father Hugh's greeting and shake Albert's hand and embrace Evangeline.

Renny waited for her on the sidewalk. He had retrieved his coat and held hers for her. Josie was somewhere, chattering with relatives. Mildred saw Albert's father and mother looking uncomfortable after enduring the strange and elaborate rites that had joined Albert to Evangeline Archambault, not to mention sitting in church with people they thought of as breeds and probably hoping they could slip away unnoticed from the reception in the parish hall.

"Do we have to go to the parish hall?" she asked Renny.

"Yes."

22

Another pretty good day so far, thought Albert. His mother and father had come to see him be married to Evangeline, and although they were nowhere to be seen in the parish hall, Albert thought there was hope they might feel better in time about Evangeline. Albert himself had been congratulated and wished well so many times he lost count, and Renny Archambault had shaken his hand and visited with him for a few minutes—had Albert and Pat gotten any rain and snow out at the ranch? Renny had asked, and Albert said yes, and they felt a little more hopeful for spring, and had Renny and Mildred gotten any moisture down on Plum Creek?—without any mention of the day Renny ran Albert off at rifle point. That was a day, Albert hoped, that maybe he and Renny could put behind them and forget about. Right now, it was almost time for him and Evangeline to cut their wedding cake, and pretty soon after that, he'd be taking her out to the ranch with him and getting her out of them damned pink ruffles and—yeah.

....

"You coming out to the ranch with us tonight, Father Hugh, for the shivaree?" Pat asked him.

"What's a shivaree?"

From across the room Sister St. Paul noted Father Hugh and Pat Adams with their heads together and knew exactly what was being planned.

....

Mildred accepted a glass cup of overly sweet lemonade and sipped and looked around for somewhere to set it down. She saw, as Sister St. Paul had, Father Hugh and Pat with their heads together and, like Sister St. Paul, knew exactly what they were hatching between them.

She felt again the stab of envy she had felt at the sight of Pat and Father Hugh and Albert and Evangeline, now Evangeline Vanaartsdalen, standing together at the foot of the altar while Father Hugh joined Albert and Evangeline in marriage. Somehow, over the past summer and fall, while Mildred lived out at her ranch, talking to no one but Renny and sometimes her neighbors when they asked for her help with their babies or their broken bones or their coughs, Pat and Father Hugh and Albert and Evangeline had become friends. While Mildred—stop! No feeling sorry for herself. Cowboy up, she told herself, and wondered how soon she could persuade Renny to take her home.

She looked up.

Pat. Standing in front of her in the unfamiliarity of his dark suit and shirt and necktie. His fair hair rumpled as though from the mischief he'd been plotting, but with a strain in his face that hadn't always been there. Pat's blue eyes she didn't want to raise her eyes to meet.

"Mil."

Say something. "I thought you were going back to Missoula."

"Changed my mind."

The horse-man stirred from her dark edges, and she willed him not to wake.

"Mil, will you please talk to me? Will you let me talk to you?"

"You lied to me," she said. "How you broke your leg."

"Yeah. I did. But I'll never lie to you again, Mil. And I'll promise never to try to touch you again if that's what you want. If you'll let me talk to you."

"How can I know what I want!"

Horrified at what she'd just admitted, Mildred did raise her eyes to Pat's and saw his—what? His stunned expression, which was changing rapidly to—that was the precise moment a young cowboy from the Box Elder country blundered up and punched

Pat on the shoulder. "I hear there's big doins at the ranch tonight, Pat!" and Mildred set her cup of lemonade on a windowsill and saw her chance and fled.

Father Hugh had been watching Pat and Mildred from not far away. He saw the damage done by the cowboy from the Box Elder country, who blundered off with no notion of what he'd wreaked, and Father Hugh threaded his way through happy wedding guests to Pat.

Pat looked as though he was adding complicated columns of numbers in his head and coming up with different totals. Then he seemed to come back from wherever he had been doing his addition.

"I can't very well chase her around the parish hall," he said.

"No," Father Hugh agreed.

They could not see Mildred through the throng in the room, but they could see Renny, taller by a head than most of those present, looking down and speaking forcibly to someone much shorter than himself.

"I'd talk to her if I thought it would do any good," Father Hugh said. He wanted to ask Pat how he was. Like everyone else, Father Hugh had hoped that, with Ferrell behind bars and Pat back on his feet again, some of the strain in Pat's face would ease.

"Although," said Pat, and Father Hugh waited.

"I told her I'd promise never to try to touch her again, if that was what she wanted . . ."

Pat's columns of numbers seemed to be tumbling down and having to be restacked and retotaled.

"And she said, *How can I know what I want?*"

Father Hugh thought it over. "She didn't say she wanted you never to touch her again?"

"No. She did not say that."

Albert and Evangeline, untroubled by the nuances of language, built a good fire in the stove in the living room of the Adams ranch house, stacked plenty of wood in the woodbox for morning, and went to bed. The early nightfall of November hid the sight of what they did there, even from themselves, but not what they heard and felt and sometimes smelled and tasted. Now they were on the verge of sleeping, at least for a while, when they were startled into sitting up in bed by a racket that, as Albert complained later, was enough to bring that damn dog of Ferrell's crawling out of the grave you dug for him, Pat!

Blaring horns from cars and trucks parked in a circle around the house. Nearer to Albert's and Evangeline's window, torches were carried and pans beaten with spoons. Somebody was squeezing a Klaxon and making it squawk, and somebody else had brought his goddamn bugle and was blowing *Charge* on it, *Charge* over and over again.

Albert and Evangeline sat up in bed and looked at each other by the light of torches outside their window. Then Evangeline realized that what she could see, the torchbearers also could see, and she screamed and pulled the sheet over her, as Albert sat on the edge of the bed and looked around for wherever he'd dropped his pants. He reflected that, at least with snow on the ground, the damn fools with their torches were unlikely to start another grass fire. And he knew, with absolute certainty, who was behind his and Evangeline's shivaree.

He didn't know if Father Hugh played a bugle, but he wouldn't put it past him.

And I'll get you one day, Pat Adams, he vowed.

"Hell," he said, and pulled on his pants. "Now we gotta invite em in."

He tramped through the house in his bare feet, thinking the best he could do was hold them off long enough for Evangeline to get dressed. He opened the front door to all the young men and many young women who laughed and beat their pans and blew their horns at him, and he saw they had brought their own refreshments.

Mildred and Renny drove back to the ranch in silence after the what for Renny had given Mildred in the parish hall.

Makin yourself sick! Makin him sick! Tell him hello, or tell him goodbye and get the hell outa my life, one, and get it over with. You can talk, can't you? Still got a voice?

It was nearly dark by the time they reached their barns and corrals. Mildred stole a look at Renny's bearded profile and saw, beyond his profile and through the cab window, the unlighted window of the shack, and something surfaced for her, not exactly from the dark edges, but close.

"Renny," she said, when he'd driven up to her cabin, "weren't there two of you once?"

Two faces at the window of the shack, she had meant to say.

"You remember Perry?" said Renny. "You were pretty little."

"All I remember is seeing him look out that window. And you were looking out the window too."

"Two of me, I guess you could say. Pierre was his name, but everybody called him Perry. He was one of the LeFrombois boys."

Mildred waited. But no.

"You need any help starting your fire?" Renny said after a moment, and when she said, no, she'd be fine, he came around and helped her down from the high cab, on account of her heeled shoes, and waited until he saw that she'd lit her lamp, before he turned the truck around and drove back to the shack.

"You care to ride out to the ranch with me this Saturday, Father Hugh, and watch Albert buck his bronc out?"

Buck his bronc out. Father Hugh guessed he'd like to watch Albert doing whatever that was. And he wondered if Pat and Albert didn't speak a patois of their own, not unlike the Michif that Renny and Josie sometimes spoke, except that Pat's and Albert's was mostly in some kind of English.

On Saturday Pat drove and Father Hugh studied the snowbound prairie until they reached the ranch yard and parked by a house that was large by ranch standards. They got out of the truck, and Father Hugh carried one of the boxes of supplies Pat had brought out for Albert and Evangeline, and Pat carried the other box of supplies, and Evangeline welcomed both men with smiles and bouncing earrings and told them just to set their boxes on the kitchen table and that they'd find Albert out at the horse corral.

"It feels damn strange," Pat remarked, as he and Father Hugh walked together to one of the corrals, "to walk into that house that used to be Ferrell's, and you cannot imagine, Father Hugh, the shape Ferrell left it in. Now it's very much Evangeline's house, and I think she lets Albert live in it with her as long as he's being good."

Up here on the high prairie, the wind had scoured off much of the snow, except where snow had drifted around the roots of sagebrush and into fence corners. Pristine blue sky, bright sunlight, cold. Father Hugh turned up the collar of his overcoat to cover his ears, and Pat grinned. He had tied a silk scarf under his Stetson.

"Cold, all right. Wouldn't think Albert will want to ride long. He'll probably top his bronc off, and we can watch the show, and then we can come back and drink Evangeline's coffee."

Top his bronc off.

Father Hugh sat on a top corral pole, shivering, and wondered why corral poles always were attached to the insides of corral posts instead of the outsides, which would have seemed more attractive to him. Pat in his sheepskin coat and silk scarf and Stetson leaned against the corral fence beside Father Hugh, and they both watched Albert, carrying a lariat, walk toward an off-white horse with black flecks in his coat—"He's a flea-bitten gray," Pat explained—that backed away from Albert, clearly wanting nothing to do with him.

In a movement too quick for Father Hugh to follow, Albert swung his lariat and caught the flea-bitten gray, not around his front feet, as Father Hugh had seen Mildred rope the marauding stallion, but around his neck. The gray horse tried to back away and then, hesitant step after hesitant step, approached Albert as Albert drew him in with his rope.

"Albert's got him halterbroken," Pat explained, clarifying another mysterious use of *halterbroken* that Father Hugh once had overheard.

They watched as Albert bridled the gray horse and swung a saddle on his back—"Albert's probably been sacking him out for the last week," said Pat—and in another lightning movement—"Don't kick me, you bastard," said Albert—retrieve a wide strap from the other side of the gray's belly and secure it to the underside of the saddle with rapid lashings of another, narrower strap.

Albert led the gray a few steps by the bridle reins.

"Look at the hump in his back," said Pat, laughing, and Albert looked over his shoulder at Pat and grinned.

"Pat, you just wish you were doing this. Don't you?"

"Oh yeah," said Pat.

Father Hugh looked from Pat's enjoyment to Albert's boot toe in the stirrup, hand on saddle horn, quick swing—

"Powder River, let er buck!" yelled Pat, and Father Hugh really did not levitate from the top corral pole and land in France, but he felt as though he had.

Powder River, let er buck. The battle cry of the Montana and Wyoming boys in the Meuse-Argonne when they went over the top.

Meanwhile, the gray horse was doing everything a horse could do to get rid of Albert—"He sure did come undone," Pat explained later—looking as though he was trying to stand on his head and kick with his hind legs in between leaps and jumps, while Albert, with the bridle reins in one hand and his hat held high over his head with his other hand, didn't even try to slow the horse but raked him with spurs from his shoulders to his flanks. Once, the horse threw his right side into the corral fence, trying to crush Albert between himself and the fence, and Albert swung his leg out of the way and swore and kept spurring. And Father Hugh reflected on his new understanding of the construction of corrals.

"Why doesn't Albert hang on?"

"Father Hugh, you really think Albert would pull leather?"

The gray horse gave up. He stood, sweating and shivering, in the middle of the corral with Albert astride him. When Albert touched his sides with spurs, he took a step forward, then another, until Albert was riding him around the corral, first at a walk and then at a trot and then back to a walk to cool him off.

"Guess he'll do," said Albert, when he came back from the barn, where he'd unsaddled the gray horse and haltered him and tied him where he wouldn't get too cold after all his exercise and pitched him some hay.

"Looks like it. Maybe by next Saturday?"

"Like it real well if you could do that, Pat."

The three young men walked back to the house to drink her coffee with Evangeline at her kitchen table. Pat took out his makings, and all four rolled cigarettes and smoked.

"General Pershing's Wild West Division," said Father Hugh, and saw Albert and Pat exchange glances.

"Yeah," said Pat.

"Lucky, both of you."

"Three hundred sixty-second infantry," said Albert. "That's where most of us Montana boys ended up. Pat and me never bumped into each other, though. Different outfits and a little too much goin on just then, like Powder River, let er buck."

"You were there, Father Hugh?" asked Pat. "Gesnes and through October?"

"I was. But somewhere safe. Somewhat safer, anyway."

"Father, you should see what Albert and Pat brought home on their little ribbons," Evangeline said. "Not that they'd show you. Or tell you what they did to get em. I had to sneak to see Albert's. And he never has told me."

"You need to cut out that damn sneakin," said Albert. He took Evangeline's left hand and held it, and she looked first at Albert with a mix of tenderness and mischief and then at Pat.

Albert and Evangeline asked Father Hugh and Pat to stay for supper with them, but Father Hugh said he really needed to get back to the rectory, also thinking that Albert and Evangeline were still very new newlyweds. And he had a feeling Pat thought the same.

"Did Pat look to you like he's lost weight?"

"I thought so," said Evangeline.

23

On the drive home, Pat explained to Father Hugh some of his and Albert's patois, like *pulling leather*, which was grabbing the saddle horn and was disgraceful, or *sacking out*, which was flapping a gunnysack at and all over the horse to make him try to run and fall and wear himself out. "Could be kinda hard on the horse," Pat said. "Renny said, when Mildred was breaking Smokey—"

"*Mildred* does what I just watched Albert do?"

Pat grinned—"I think she goes about it a little slower. And I don't think Renny lets her ride the rough string."

Whatever that was.

Anyway, Albert would have sacked out the gray colt every day for the past week and halterbroken him, to get him ready for his first saddling, which Albert waited to do while Pat was around.

"He'll saddle him again tomorrow and buck him out and ride him around the corral, and he'll do that every day until next Saturday. Evangeline'll come out and watch through the corral poles, just in case."

Father Hugh thought about *just in case*. "Does Evangeline know how to drive the truck?"

"Yeah. I woulda come down on this bronc-stompin of Albert's a little harder if I thought she couldn't. And I wish Albert had picked warmer weather for his bronc-stompin, but he needed a second saddle horse."

"What happens next Saturday?"

"Albert will ride that gray colt outside the corral for the first time, which is why he wants me to ride Socks with him while he rides the colt."

"Just in case, I suppose," said Father Hugh, and Pat nodded.

Powder River, let er buck. Father Hugh thought about the Wild West Division and the Wyoming and Montana boys in October of 1918 and the casualties they'd taken, nearly a thousand Montana boys dead at Gesnes alone. But the Montana boys had fought on, through October and into early November, and brought the war to an end.

The things on ribbons that Evangeline had sneaked behind Albert's back to see, of course, were medals. Father Hugh knew, as Evangeline did, that they'd never hear from Pat or Albert what they had done to earn them. And he supposed that, after Gesnes, a little bronc-stompin didn't seem like that much of a scrap to them.

Montana boys. And what happened when one of them came up against a Montana girl? Father Hugh shook his head. I'm praying for you, Pat.

"Sure do wish I knew what Ferrell did with the rest of his saddle horses," said Pat.

Pat Adams took the morning off work from the clerk of court's office on Monday to testify at Ferrell's trial. He dressed in the same dark-gray suit he'd worn to stand up with Albert, which Josie had pressed and hung up for him after the wedding. Damn, he had to think of some way to keep Josie from having to wait on him. He chopped her kindling and started her fires and fed her chickens when he could get ahead of her, but maybe he could hire one of the Métis girls to come in and at least do the laundry and the heavy cleaning for her. Guessed he'd ask Evangeline what she thought, next time he saw her.

He drank the coffee Josie brought him, and he tried to eat a little of her porridge and gave up. It seemed to him that nothing had wanted to go down him since sometime before Albert's wedding. Then he swapped his suit coat for his sheepskin coat and carried his suit coat over his arm, and he kissed Josie goodbye and was off. Last day of November, and damn, it was cold.

The courtroom and the judge's chambers took up one end of the second floor of the courthouse. The county prosecutor's office was closed when he passed it, and he supposed George Clarke and Harry Fallon were already in the courtroom. In the county clerk's office, he swapped coats again and hung his hat and his sheepskin coat on a hook.

"Good luck, Pat," from one of the clerks.

"Good luck, Pat."

The courtroom doors were closed, so Pat sat on the bench outside the doors and rested his forearms on his thighs and studied the tiles on the corridor floor and wished he could roll a cigarette and smoke it. Wished they'd goddamn call him in, so he could get it over with.

Then the bailiff stuck his head out and nodded to Pat, and Pat was walking through the courtroom doors and seeing, over the backs of spectators' heads, the American flag and the Montana state flag behind Judge Browning on his bench, the stenographer at her desk, and George Clarke by the witness stand. Winter light falling through high windows.

Sounds of his own bootheels walking up the aisle, climbing the stand to the witness box, where he held up his hand and swore to tell the truth and was told to sit down, and he did.

Harry Fallon at the prosecutor's table. Elmer Cole sitting beside Ferrell at the defense table.

Pat had told himself to look nowhere but at George Clarke or at the jurors in their box, and yet he saw that Ferrell was sprawled in his chair with his legs stretched under the defense table, just as Ferrell always sprawled, and also that they'd cleaned him up in the jail and combed his hair and beard and decked him out in a suit and tie Elmer's secretary probably had gone out and bought for Ferrell with a check Pat gave her.

Ferrell had been silent on why he had ridden back and forth along the chokecherries the day after he had thrown Pat there and left him, and he would say nothing of what he had done with his other saddle horses. But when Elmer asked Ferrell how he knew where to find Pat, the day Ferrell had burst through Josie Archambault's door, Ferrell smiled his wide broken-toothed smile and said he'd always known where that squaw of Pat's hung out.

"Pat, will you tell us about the events that unfolded on"—George Clarke made a show of looking at his notes—"the fifth of June, of this year?"

And Pat turned to the jurors in their box and told them about Ferrell's sending the cowboys to drive the cattle over east and asking Pat to help him build fence and everything he could remember from that point to the time when he woke in the hawthorns near Svoboda's crossing, heard a horse and rider passing, and crawled out and recognized Mildred Harrington.

"What happened then, Pat?"

"Mil—Miss Harrington—got me on her horse and took me home with her, and she set the bone in my leg and splinted it. And the next morning, she and Renny Archambault loaded me in the back of their truck and brought me to town and left me with the sisters at Good Samaritan."

He didn't know what the jurors might be thinking of his story, but they certainly weren't missing a word of it, some even leaning forward in their chairs, one or two mouths open.

"And then, Pat?"

He shrugged. "Nothing much. The sisters and Doc Naylor patched me some more, and my leg healed. And since then, I've been boarding with Josie Archambault and working in the clerk of the court's office, here in the courthouse."

George Clarke strolled a few feet across the courtroom, looking pensive, and strolled back.

"Pat, the fifth of June, the day your father asked you to help him build fence, was not the last day you saw your father. Is that right?"

"Yes."

"When did you next see him?"

"In July, I don't remember the exact day—"

"July 19 sound about right?"

"Yes."

"Where did you see him?"

"At Josie Archambault's house."

"Was he angry?"

Elmer Cole said automatically, "Leading the witness," and the judge nodded. George Clarke looked irritated, probably with Pat for making him drag the story out of him, and said, "What did you observe your father's mood to be?"

"I thought he was drunk. And angry."

"Why did you think he was angry, Pat?"

"What he said."

Seeing the expression on George Clarke's face, Pat took a deep breath and held it and let it out. Feeling as though he could float on the weight of silence in the courtroom, he closed his eyes and said, "My—*Ferrell*—said he was going to kick my bad leg out from under me and break me in half, and then he was going to make me watch while he gave my moccasin squaw what she'd been asking for."

Silence in the courtroom.

When he opened his eyes, he saw that George Clarke was watching him and looking concerned. Judge Browning said something over Pat's head to George, who said, "Do you need to take a break, Pat?"

God no. Get it over with. "I'm fine."

"Did your father do the things he said he was going to do?"

"No." At George's expression, Pat hastily went on. "Because Father Hugh McHugh came in just then and kept him from doing them."

"Pat, the woman your father referred to as your moccasin squaw. Do you know to whom he was referring?"

"Yes." Get it over with, he told himself. "To Miss Harrington."

Another gasp from somewhere, and Judge Browning gave his bench a vicious whack with his gavel and snarled something over

Pat's head about having order in *his* court, and Pat had to draw his mind back from wondering how much punishment the judge's bench had to take in the course of a trial.

"Pat, your story about your father's attacking you with a crowbar is not the story you initially told to Miss Harrington or to the nursing sisters. Why is that?"

He knew George Clarke and Harry Fallon had decided to tackle the issue of his two stories straight on. Don't know how weak a link in the narrative the two stories make in my case, George had said, but I don't like a weak link in an otherwise strong case.

"I believed that—*Ferrell*—thought he'd killed me. And I was afraid he would try to hurt Miss Harrington when he found out she'd helped me, so I told her, and I told the sisters and Doc Naylor, I'd been thrown off a horse and broken my leg. I—wasn't thinking clearly for a day or two. When I did clear my head, I told Sister St. Paul what really happened."

"Which version is the truth, Pat?"

"The one I told under oath this morning."

Another potential question from Elmer that George Clarke had decided to tackle straight on.

"Why did your father disapprove so strongly of your friendship with Miss Harrington?"

Pat was prepared. "I think he would have disapproved of any woman I cared about, unless he got to pick her out, maybe," and from the edge of his vision, he saw Ferrell straighten in his chair and glare at Pat and snarl something at Elmer Cole, who stood and called, "Objection," to the judge. George Clarke called something, sharply, which Pat was beyond hearing, because he'd just gotten an awful inkling of what Ferrell might have told Elmer to ask Mil, and he saw Elmer's defense strategy unroll itself.

The two attorneys, Clarke and Cole, batted arguments back and forth for a while, and finally the judge said, "Overruled." And Clarke said to Cole, "Your witness."

Elmer Cole strolled over to the witness box, and Elmer wasn't interested in Josie Archambault's skillet or how Father McHugh happened to drop by Josie's house on July 19 of that year or even how Mildred Harrington happened to be at Josie's house that day to be called a moccasin squaw.

"Mr. Adams, how would you describe your relationship with your father?"

"Poor."

"And why is that, Mr. Adams?"

"We've disagreed on many things."

"Could you give us some examples?"

"He disliked my reading books as much as I did, when he expected me to be breaking horses for him."

"And did you? Break horses?"

"Yes. Some."

"I understand you enlisted in the army in 1917, Mr. Adams. Did your father approve?"

"No. He wanted me to apply for a deferment for an agricultural occupation."

"Did he approve of your enrolling in law school, Mr. Adams?"

"No."

"Would you call yourself a disobedient son, Mr. Adams?"

"I'd call myself a man who saw his preferred path in life, when his—father—saw a different path for him."

"Mr. Adams—" Elmer Cole, clearly cautious now, glanced back at Ferrell, who was leaning one elbow on the defense table and burning Pat with his eyes. "Isn't there a deeper reason why your father disapproves so strongly of your friendship with Miss Harrington?"

Cole's defense strategy suddenly unrolled before Pat. What Cole would ask him next. What Cole would ask Mil, to expose her in the daylight of open court. How Cole would provide the jury with a reason why Pat would concoct a story to smear Ferrell.

"No," Pat said.

Elmer's mouth opened and shut, and he might have asked another question, but a bellow from Farrell interrupted him. "The kid's a goddamn liar!"

Judge Browning was giving his bench what for with his gavel, but Ferrell didn't care. He was pounding the defense table with his fist and making as much racket as the judge with his gavel. Two rivals in having things their own way. It seemed to Pat that people were running from every corner of the courtroom, most of them converging on Ferrell—the bailiff, one of the sheriff's deputies, a couple of men Pat didn't recognize, all shouting at Ferrell, while Ferrell shouted obscenities at Pat and did his damnedest to get untangled from his chair leg so he could get up and charge at Pat.

The jurors were on their feet, the better to see what was happening. Pat hadn't thought he could feel any worse. Now what? A mistrial? A start all over from the beginning?

Now the sheriff's deputy had a choke hold on Ferrell, forcing him to his knees and handcuffing him, while the bailiff stood over him with an upraised chair, and Judge Browning found Ferrell in contempt of court and in almost the same breath declared the court in recess—"You fellows are finished with your witness, aren't you?" And Clarke and Cole nodded.

Pat could step down. If he could see to do it. He did see George Clarke turn from the prosecutor's table, looking worried, but Pat kept walking, one foot after the other, until he came to the double doors and walked out of the courtroom and found himself face to face with Mildred, in the hat and dress she had worn to Albert and Evangeline's wedding. Of course she had come to give her testimony as the next witness on George's list.

"Mil," he said. He was beginning to see her point of view. These unexpected face-to-faces of theirs were killing him.

"Pat," she said, "I want to tell you, not right now, but—"

"I'm not doin so well right now, Mil."

Before his eyes, she changed from Mil his gun-shy girl to Mildred the horseback-riding nurse of Plum Creek.

"Sit down and put your head down," she said, and without knowing how he got there, he was sitting on the bench where he had waited earlier.

"I have to be in court," Mildred was saying, "but—"

"Court's in recess."

"Oh." She sat down beside him. "I said, *put your head down!*"

George Clarke was there. "Pat, we'll get you home—"

"No, we won't," said Mildred. "Mr. Clarke, if you've got your car here, we'll take him to Good Samaritan."

"I think his coat and hat are hanging up in the county clerk's office," said Harry Fallon, "and I'll just run and get them for him."

"You think you can walk, Pat? If you can't, Harry and I can—"

"I can walk," he said. But he couldn't.

24

"What do you want to do, Elmer?"

"What I *want* to do is walk off and forget I ever heard about this damned case."

The county prosecutor and the defense attorney sat across the prosecutor's desk from each other and smoked their tailor-mades.

"There's what you want," George Clarke said absently, "and what you get."

"I used to hear that a lot when I was a kid."

"Guess we'll have to talk to the judge. The man's clearly not fit to stand trial."

"Agree with you there. He damn near tore the jail apart when they wrestled him down there this morning. Cussing Pat and cussing me for not asking what he told me to ask. If we could get him down to the state hospital, maybe, where they could straitjacket him if they had to—whatever the hell they do down there, plug their maniacs into electric sockets if they have to—"

George Clarke nodded.

"And George. Attorney-client privileges and all, but I couldn't have brought myself to ask Miss Harrington in open court what Ferrell told me to ask her. I feel bad enough about what I asked Pat."

"Decent of you, Elmer."

"What I asked Pat. Whether Ferrell had deeper reasons for feeling like he did about Miss Harrington. And Pat said *no* under oath."

"I think Pat probably heard *better* reasons when you asked him that."

"That's probably what he heard," Elmer Cole agreed. "In fact, that's what I meant to say. Got my words tangled up."

The two men stubbed out their cigarettes and shook hands.

Pat opened his eyes and saw a familiar white ceiling and said, "Damn it to hell."

Then he turned his head on a pillow that felt all too familiar and saw Father Hugh kneeling in prayer by the window.

Father Hugh finished praying and rose and came to sit by Pat's bedside. "You scared the hell out of all of us, Pat. And now I have to watch myself. I'm picking up too much of your cowboy patois from hanging out with you and Albert."

"Our what?"

Someone laughed from the other side of Pat's bed.

"Is it still Monday?" he asked.

"Yes," said Sister St. Paul, "although it's Monday afternoon now."

He guessed Monday afternoon wasn't too bad. "How soon are you going to let me outa here? And where did Mil go?"

"Mildred went home with Renny. And we'd rather keep you overnight"—Sister St. Paul and Father Hugh both laughed when Pat let his face show what he thought of that idea—"but once you drink the broth and fruit juice I've ordered for you and show me you can stand on your feet without feeling faint, we'll let you get dressed and Doctor will discharge you."

"And then we'll turn you over to Josie," said Father Hugh.

"I promised Albert I'd ride with him when he rides his bronc on Saturday," Pat remembered.

"Saturday? Maybe," said Sister St. Paul, "if you behave yourself, for once, and drink more broth and fruit juice when Josie tells you to. Josie says she doesn't think you've eaten in a week. Or longer. Doctor and I looked you over thoroughly—"

"Yes," said Father Hugh, "and at their leisure, since, at the time, you couldn't object—"

"—and we think all that's the matter with you is trying to starve yourself to death. That and being boneheaded. Why, Pat?"

"I wasn't trying to starve myself to death, Sister. I wasn't hungry, and food stopped tasting good. The boneheaded part, I don't know."

"Pat, if you knew what I had been imagining. Fearing."

Father Hugh nodded. "Possibly an ulcer, Sister told me. Possibly worse. Possibly a cancer."

When Pat's broth and juice arrived, Father Hugh cranked up his bed, and he sat on one side of Pat's bed while Sister St. Paul sat on the other. And they watched Pat's spoon travel between his bowl and his mouth and back, every sip and swallow. Like two black-and-white sheepdogs, Pat thought, watching somebody drink broth and hoping to get a taste themselves.

Two sheepdogs with one sheep. He guessed he'd given this pair of sheepdogs reason to feel like they had their work cut out for them. He had to think about what he should do about that.

....

"Anything I can tell Mildred for you, if I see her before you do?" said Father Hugh, when he and Sister had turned Pat over to Josie's supervision, along with supplies of broth and fruit juice.

"Yeah. But Father Hugh, if you could—I don't know whether Josie will let me outside the house tomorrow—so if you could tell George Clarke I need to talk to him?"

"Sure."

"If you do see Mil. Tell her I said maybe not."

....

Father Hugh dreaded the drive out to the Harrington ranch, on that goat trail they called a road, and now with snow on the ground. So Josie asked around her neighborhood, and Jerry St. Pierre, father of Joe the haystacker and Sammy the substitute Musketeer, said he wouldn't mind visiting with Renny awhile, supposing he could come up with the wherewithal for gasoline to get there. Father Hugh said he thought he could help Jerry out with the wherewithal, and he and Jerry set out. Jerry, a dark and supple man with an alert face that reminded Father Hugh of Sammy the substitute's face, drove competently but silently and gave Father Hugh ample space to think his thoughts.

Whatever glue had joined Pat Adams and Mildred Harrington, it seemed as indissoluble as any words from Father Hugh about no man separating what God had joined together. Pat and Mildred had been separated for fourteen years, until Ferrell, unlikely instrument of the divine, had set in motion a series of causes and effects like falling dominos through Murray County, from ranch to ranch, from convent to courthouse, from Judge Browning to Sammy the substitute. The air that breathed through Murray County told Father Hugh that Mildred believed herself to be healed of old injuries and living a life she had chosen until the evening Pat Adams crawled out of the hawthorns at Svoboda's crossing and startled her horse. Pat, for his part, had his law degree and the offer of a position with an excellent law firm and was headed back to Missoula.

And then Ferrell.

Father Hugh saw a line of smoke rising from the stovepipe at the shack and another line of smoke rising from the chimney at the cabin. So Renny and Mildred both were home. Work eased on a ranch at this time of year, Josie had explained. Work picked up again at calving time in early March, and then no rest until after shipping cattle in October.

Jerry parked his truck by the cabin and said he guessed he'd amble down and see what Renny was up to. "Lemme know, Father, when you're ready to leave."

Father Hugh knocked, and the cabin door opened on Mildred in her men's clothes and moccasins and her braid falling over her shoulder, surprised to see him and as unsmiling as always.

"She never smiles," Evangeline had told Father Hugh. "I don't know why; she just doesn't. Don't worry about it, Father. It doesn't mean she isn't glad to see you."

"Please come in, Father."

He ducked under her low doorframe, loosening his coat in the welcome warmth of the blaze from her fireplace, and saw she was automatically setting out cups and pouring coffee.

"Oh, thank you."

"Let me take your overcoat, Father, if you can stay a little while."

Of course, Mildred would have recognized Jerry St. Pierre's outfit and supposed Jerry had upcoming work to talk over with Renny.

Father Hugh sat, at her invitation, in one of the leather chairs in front of the fire and sipped his coffee and smiled at her without expectation of a smile in return, and he caught her up on a little news about Sister St. Paul and Sister Boniface, whom he knew was Mildred's friend, and about Josie.

"She has a new young woman doing her laundry and cleaning for her. Dottie Archambault? I think she's a cousin of Evangeline's."

Mildred nodded. "Dottie, yes. I think she's about eighteen now. I wouldn't have thought Josie would let anyone help her, although . . ." she trailed off.

"I think Dottie has to hurry to keep ahead of her. And I think Pat hired her."

A silence. A crackle from the fire when a chunk of firewood broke, and otherwise a ranch silence that held a presence of its own after even the modest city sounds of Fort Maginnis. The ranch silence would take some getting used to, Father Hugh thought, as he watched Mildred and waited. Although he had only been a priest for a few years, he still knew he was seeing a young woman who needed to talk.

"I never did testify," she said.

"No, and now it looks as though there won't be a trial. The prosecutor and the defense attorney are going to try to persuade the judge that Ferrell isn't fit to stand trial."

He described Ferrell's outburst in the courtroom as it had been described to him. "And a worse one, apparently, when they tried to get him down to the jail. And no alcohol as an excuse this time. He'd been in jail and dry for over three months."

"What will happen to him?"

"He's got to be kept locked up. George Clarke thinks the state hospital is likely. He'd be sedated there, straitjacketed if necessary, with a court order to keep him there until he can demonstrate his sanity."

Mildred was watching him over the rim of her cup with grave hazel eyes. Father Hugh said, "Pat's fine."

Mildred set down her cup and brought the coffee pot from the stove and refilled both their cups. He saw that her hands were shaking.

"Renny's advice," she said, and for just a moment Father Hugh thought she might smile or cry. "Renny told me either to tell him hello or tell him goodbye and to get the hell out of my life, one."

She looked stricken. "Father Hugh, if I said goodbye to Pat and told him to get the hell out of my life, he'd do it."

"Yes," Father Hugh said. "He would."

"Father, I couldn't bear it!" She was crying now. "Never to see Pat again, after—" she gulped and went on. "And yet I can't—how can I—Father? Did you see Pat's ride?"

"No," Father Hugh said, "but I've heard about it enough times. First from Albert. All the world has been talking about it, or at least, all of Murray County has."

Then, to give her some space, he told her about the scene between Pat and Sister St. Paul in the rectory kitchen, which he and Albert and Sister Boniface had enjoyed so much, and Mildred was shaking her head at the picture of Father Hugh and Albert and Sister Boniface—even Sister Boniface?—laughing at Pat.

"I think Sister Boniface is coming out of her shell, just a little," said Father Hugh. "I can tease her a little now. Mildred, did you hear the story of Sister Boniface's cowboy?"

"Sister Boniface has a cowboy?" she asked, as Josie had before her.

"Well, she used to have one, but Evangeline has him now," Father Hugh said, and then he took pity on Mildred and told her the whole story, beginning with Albert Vanaartsdalen on the convent doorstep, inquiring of Sister Boniface if Mildred was there.

Mildred just shook her head. All that she had missed. She set down her cup, which was in danger of slopping over, and lifted her chin, much as Sister Boniface had. "Father Hugh, I did see Pat's ride. And I—Father, I don't understand why, but watching that ride, I was terrified, even though I didn't have time to be terrified." Words were tumbling out of her that took Father Hugh considerable concentration to link together. The centaur. The horse-man, who had brought back all the old horror—"I had to relive it, Father! As though they were doing it all over again to me, and I was a thing again, a jerked-around thing—and oh, Father, I can't do that again!"

He listened to the story he already had heard from Sister St. Paul and let Mildred vomit out the ugliness and purge herself of it as she hadn't been able to do with Sister St. Paul or Josie. Good word, *centaur*, he thought. Another good word, *catharsis*. But he didn't speak them. And he listened and listened until Mildred ran dry of words and tears and the ranch silence returned to the room, broken only by a crackling of a log, which reminded Father Hugh, and he got up and put another chunk of firewood on Mildred's fire and gave her his handkerchief.

"Sorry, Father."

"Don't be." He thought for a minute while she dabbed at her face and wiped her nose. "So, on the one hand, you can't tell Pat goodbye because you can't bear to lose him. On the other hand, you can't tell him hello because you dread the pain the horse-man brings with him."

He reached across and took her hand. "What I think, Mildred?"

Her eyes implored him.

"I think Pat is the man who can help you through this if you can let him do it. You already know he's a patient man. He's never hurried you, has he?"

"No—except I know he wants me, and I can't—"

"Pat wants you enough to let you take your time, Mildred. Even when he doesn't want to."

She dabbed at her face again, her eyes gone distant.

"A start would be to let Pat talk to you. And you tell Pat what you've told me."

"I don't think I can. Not now."

A jab of wind against the cabin roof. More snow was expected, according to the Fort Maginnis newspaper.

"Would you like me to talk to Pat?"

"Would you, Father?"

He nodded and rose then and carried her cup and his to the kitchen and came back and put on his hat and overcoat, and he thanked Mildred for the coffee and held her in his arms for a moment because she seemed to need it.

"What Pat told me to tell you when I asked him. He said, tell Mil that he says maybe not."

And he was surprised to be rewarded with Mildred's smile.

25

Jerry St. Pierre dropped Father Hugh off at the rectory, and Father Hugh paid him for his gasoline and offered to pay him for his time, which Jerry waved off. Father Hugh thanked him, and Jerry drove off with the beams from his headlights still weak in the darkening afternoon. Father Hugh turned to the rectory door and noticed an oddly shaped bundle on the doorstep. He touched it experimentally with the toe of his shoe and jumped back when it squawked at him and lurched and bumped around on the doorstep.

What in the—Father Hugh stopped himself in time. He gave the bundle another tentative kick, which set off a burst of frantic activity and more squawks.

Something in that bundle very much wanted to get out. Father Hugh picked up the bundle by a corner, which proved to be the mouth of a feed sack that had been roped shut. Holding the bundle at arm's length while it squawked and thrashed, he carried it to the convent for reasons obscure to himself. Afterward, he wondered if he had felt a need for backup when he released whatever was in the bundle.

Sister Boniface opened the kitchen door when Father Hugh knocked. She looked less surprised than interested when the bundle squawked at her, and she loosened its rope a bit so she could look inside.

"Oh," she said, and tightened the rope and tried to give the bundle back to Father Hugh, who didn't want it back. "Someone wanted to thank you for something you have done for them, Father, and so they have left you a stewing hen."

He stared at her. "Why would I want a stewing hen?"

"To cook for your dinner, Father."

Father Hugh looked from Sister Boniface to the bundle, which she had forced back on him. "What do I—"

"First you take the chicken to the backyard and chop its head off," said Sister Boniface. "When it stops kicking and flapping without its head, you bring it back to the kitchen and scald it in boiling water. Then you pluck its feathers, being careful, Father Hugh, not to leave a mess of wet feathers around the kitchen. And then you singe the chicken over a flame in the stove to get the pinfeathers out. And then—"

"Sister Boniface," said Father Hugh. He could see how much she was enjoying herself, and he knew he deserved every bit of what she was giving back to him. "Sister Boniface, will you please kill this chicken for me?"

"No," she said, "but I will show you how to kill it, Father Hugh. And then I'll scald it and pluck it and singe it and dress it. I'll soak it in cold water tonight, and tomorrow I'll cook it for your dinner. I suppose that cowboy of mine is out at the ranch with his wife, but you might invite Pat Adams to dinner with you and try to flesh him out a bit."

She put on her cloak and hood and led Father Hugh to the backyard of the convent, where in the fading afternoon light he saw a tree stump with a hatchet stuck in it. Sister Boniface pulled the hatchet out of the stump and handed it to Father Hugh. Then she took the bundle from him and pulled out the chicken as it struggled and squawked. With one hand she held the chicken on one side of the stump, and with her other hand she held its head and stretched its neck across the stump. Then she leaned back to give Father Hugh some swinging room.

"Chop its head off, Father Hugh. Right there below its head. We don't want to waste the neck meat." And when he averted his eyes, "Don't miss, Father Hugh! I don't want my hand cut off!"

Still he wavered.

"Kill the chicken, Father Hugh!"

Prayerfully he swung his hatchet.

. . . .

George Clarke endured a few days of wrangling about Ferrell Adams's fate with Judge Browning, who seemed to waver between summary execution—"Take the old son of a bitch out into the sagebrush and shoot him!"—and declaring a mistrial and starting over—"Tie the old bastard hand and foot and gag him and roll him into court in a wheelchair!" Lately, however, the judge seemed to have become more open to committing Ferrell to the state mental hospital, especially after George Clarke gave him a written opinion from Dr. Riggio at Good Samaritan and read to him a description of a device known as a Bergonic chair, also obtained from Dr. Riggio.

The judge was intrigued. "Sounds like one of those electric chairs they've installed in some prisons now. I don't think we've got one down in Deer Lodge yet. How do they work?"

"I really don't know," George Clarke said. "I suppose they plug them in somewhere. The point is, Judge—" And how many times had he or Elmer Cole used that phrase in the last two days? How many times had he or Elmer tried to distract Judge Browning from what he really wanted to do, which was to waste everyone's time by inveighing endlessly against the old son of a bitch who had pounded the defense table with his fist in competition while the judge was beating his bench with a gavel?

"The point is, Judge, Ferrell Adams never again can be allowed to endanger the community."

"I suppose you're right," the judge admitted, and Clarke and Cole exchanged glances and wondered if they dared breathe in relief yet.

George Clarke finally found a free evening and dropped by Josie's house to see how Pat Adams was doing. Josie greeted him with her overflow of chatter, poured coffee for him and Pat, and found work to do in the kitchen, and Pat looked up from his book and got up to shake Clarke's hand.

"What are you reading now? You must have finished *Vigilantes*."

"Oh yeah, long way back. This is *Rawhide Rawlins Stories*, by Charlie Russell."

"The painter? I didn't know he wrote stories. Have you ever met him?"

"No. I think Albert met him, just after the war. The Vanaartsdalens say it's Albert in a watercolor Russell painted, but I've never seen the watercolor, either."

"So. You're looking better, Pat."

"Yeah. I drank more broth in the last few days than I ever expected to drink over my lifetime. But Josie has put me back on solids now, and I think she'll let me go back to work tomorrow."

"Josie."

"And one thing I did, George. I moved Ferrell's money out of that Bank of the Mountain States of his and over to the First National."

"Where I bank, myself," said Clarke. "I haven't necessarily heard anything bad about Mountain States."

"No."

Both men reflected on banks and bankers. Their enthusiastic lending of money to homesteaders during the good years. Then the drought and the failure of crops and the precipitous drop in the price of wheat, and the following foreclosures that left the banks with no cash and worthless land. Then the bank closures. Was worse to come?

"That sheriff's deputy, Milton Bill? The reason he came down to Murray County was that he'd been working in a bank in Havre that closed its doors," said Pat. "And I said Ferrell's money just now. I never did find my mother's will, if she had one. But it was her money Ferrell had in his name."

"Well," Clarke said. There didn't seem to be much else to say. "At least he didn't spend it all."

"No. He let his cattle starve to death instead."

A pause. Clarke was turning his topic over in his mind, when Pat, being Patrick Adams, spoke it straight out.

"George. What you said about bodily harm trumping the old story. Monday morning in court it didn't. Elmer Cole asked me if there wasn't a deeper reason for the animosity between me and Ferrell, and I, in that instant, saw where he and Ferrell were taking Ferrell's defense. What Ferrell must have told Elmer to ask, and what Elmer was going to ask me next, and what he was going to ask Mil in open court. And under oath I said no."

A longer pause.

"I decided I'd be disbarred before I'd hurt Mil in public."

"Pat," Clarke said. "Elmer and I got to talking. Elmer's a good man, and he made some decisions of his own that morning. And he and I shook hands, and as far as we're concerned, that's the end of it. If the judge ever asks us, we know what we'll tell him."

Clarke scoured his face with his hand. "Ferrell didn't do himself any good with that outburst in court. Judge Browning is furious about it, and about the fight the sheriff's boys had with Ferrell to get him back in a cell. They finally had to call the doctor to give him a shot to calm him down. We aren't there yet, but the judge is coming around to agreeing that Ferrell isn't fit to stand trial."

Pat nodded. His face still looked drawn, Clarke thought.

"And Harry and I are hoping you're still planning to work for me as soon as we can clear up this goddamned mess."

"I'm countin on it, George," said Pat, and gave Clarke something close to a Pat smile.

"Good." Clarke stood up to leave, shrugging into his overcoat and picking up his hat from the table. He wanted to ask Pat if he was getting anywhere with his girl but wasn't sure how to frame it. Instead, he shook hands again with Pat, thanked Josie for the coffee when she peeped around the kitchen door, and took himself home, hoping like hell he could get some sleep and have a better day tomorrow than the last several days had been.

Father Hugh left his chicken with Sister Boniface and went home to the rectory. From the steps of the rectory, he noticed one of the neighbor boys wheeling around on his bicycle as though he had nothing much to do.

"Sidney," Father Hugh called, "do you know where Josie Archambault lives? Over in the Métis settlement?"

"Sure."

"You feel like earning a little change by biking over there and leaving a note for Pat Adams? He's boarding with Josie."

"Okay," said Sidney, sounding enthused at the mention of a little change. He waited while Father Hugh scribbled a note to Pat, and it wasn't long before Sidney was back and smiling as a little silver found its way from Father Hugh's pocket to Sidney's palm.

"He says to tell you, sure!" Sidney reported.

Father Hugh let himself into the rectory and hung up his hat and coat. Mrs. O'Shea had left a light on for him. She had set a place for him in the dining room, and he supposed she was around somewhere. He entered his study and leaned back in his chair and snapped on his desk lamp, enjoying the luxury of instant electric light. He even had a telephone in the rectory, which Mrs. O'Shea guarded, although the list of numbers he could call was limited. No telephone in Josie Archambault's house, for example, or in most of her neighbors', and none of the ranches.

He'd followed up on Sister Boniface's suggestion that he invite Pat to share his chicken dinner with him. Now he stretched his legs and lit a cigarette, feeling a little weary after his hours of jouncing with Jerry St. Pierre over country roads and his visit with Mildred.

Sister Boniface. Father Hugh wondered if *Kill the chicken, Father!* would entertain as many people as *Sit on his goddamn head, Father!*

Maybe nobody else heard it.

Maybe Sister Boniface would find it in her heart not to tell anyone. But he knew he deserved it if she did.

"Sister Boniface," said Sister St. Paul, "I hear Father Hugh dropped by the convent this afternoon."

"Yes, Sister. He wanted me to show him how to kill a stewing hen somebody had left on his doorstep for him."

"Hm."

Not exactly the tale as told to Sister St. Paul by two nursing sisters who happened to be returning from their hospital shift at a fortuitous time.

Sister Boniface carried the chicken, now stewed and nicely arranged on a platter, to the rectory, where Mrs. O'Shea said it looked very good indeed and that she would add winter vegetables and a gravy made from the jar of stewing water Sister Boniface had brought along. And in due time Father Hugh and Pat Adams sat down to their chicken dinner.

Father Hugh thought that Pat looked less gaunt, his face not so strained, after nearly a week of Josie's aggressive dietary regimen, and he nodded to himself when Pat accepted a second helping of chicken and vegetables and gravy, which indeed were very good.

"Are you going riding with Albert tomorrow?" he asked.

"Sure. Want to come along? Maybe we can find you a horse."

"I'm afraid I've let too much work stack up," Father Hugh said, and Pat gave him a look from across the table but said no more about horseback riding. The housekeeper brought them each a slice of dried-apple pie and poured their coffee, and soon, replete, Father Hugh and Pat retired to Father Hugh's study, where they stretched their legs and lit cigarettes. Father Hugh poured them each a glass of chokecherry wine from a jug he kept on a shelf behind his old Latin textbooks and mistakenly believed Mrs. O'Shea was unaware of.

"I gave Mildred your message," he said, and saw the light in Pat's face at the mention of her name.

"Yeah?"

"And she smiled at me."

"Guess that's something."

"And something else. She talked to me, Pat, and I think she got it all out. Maybe for the first time ever. What she's been bottled up with, I hate to think about, Pat."

Pat was leaning forward in his chair, his face naked.

"And I understand more about her bottling up than I did, though it took me a while. She's got physical scars, Pat"—*Sister St. Paul thinks I may never be able to conceive again*—"and she's got invisible scars that are worse. She told me that Renny advised her to tell you hello or to tell you goodbye, and she can't tell you goodbye because she can't bear to lose you again, and she can't tell you hello because of what she's afraid of reliving."

"God."

"Yes."

A car turned a corner and drove past the rectory, headlights flashing against the windows in Father Hugh's study, the sound of the motor fading as the lights disappeared. The sounds of town. In some ways, Father Hugh reflected, the ranch silence was deafening by comparison.

"I told her I thought you were the patient man who could help her through it, Pat."

Pat was turning his glass in his hand. Dregs of wine, reflection of light when the lamp caught the glass. Turn, turn.

"Guess I'll have to be that man."

26

Pat and Albert saddled Socks and the flea-bitten gray colt, and Pat watched from his saddle as Albert mounted the gray colt and trotted him around the corral a few times.

"Didn't buck much yesterday, either," Albert said. "I think he's pretty much got over his idea that he can buck me off."

Pat leaned from the saddle and lifted the bar and opened the gate and rode through and held it open for Albert and the gray colt. A touch of Albert's spurs, and the colt took his first steps into open prairie with a saddle and a rider on his back.

The colt's eyes rolled back, trying to see Albert. He sidestepped and snorted, and Albert growled at him and reined him down and then touched him with spurs, and the colt settled down and moved out. Pat shut the gate and spurred Socks to catch up.

Snow lay in drifts around the roots of the sagebrush. The sky was pale blue and transparent, and sun dogs shone like miniature rainbows from each side of the sun. The sound of the horses' hoofs on frozen ground was as crisp as drum taps. Pat in Stetson and silk scarf and sheepskin coat, Albert in Stetson and silk scarf and mackinaw, riding through the white puffs of their breaths and the horses' breaths. It was too damn cold to be riding horseback, but Pat and Albert planned to stick it out for an hour and ride back to the ranch house and thaw themselves out and ride for another hour after dinner. If Albert could get in eight or nine saddlings on him, the gray colt would pass for a green broke horse.

"Have to wonder what Ferrell did with the rest of his horses."

Albert shook his head. "Frank and me each had a couple horses to use, and them horses was here, and Frank too, when I left.

Wouldn't a thought Frank would run off with them, but if he decided to go back to Blaine County, I spose he had to have a way to get there."

"Spose so."

Pat rode easy in the saddle, freeing his thoughts while his body fell into the rhythm of the horse and the tap of hoofs. He'd be back soon enough, he knew, if anything spooked Socks or the gray colt. A jackrabbit bounding out from under a sagebrush, a rag fluttering from a barbed wire fence, insignificant to a man, could scare even a horse as good as Mildred's Smokey into terrified flight.

Same way with his own tentative daydreams, Pat thought. Wouldn't take much to jerk him back from them. Still, he'd found himself thinking ahead for the first time in quite a while. Himself working in the county prosecutor's office, if George Clarke ever got the question of Ferrell and his trial settled. Maybe getting enough moisture in the spring that he could buy a few head of heifers, gradually restock the ranch. Albert and Evangeline managing the ranch for him . . .

"Evangeline doin all right out here, so far from town?" he asked Albert.

Albert grinned, "She's been doin fine, up to now. But she's got the house all scrubbed and polished enough to suit her, curtains hung, God knows what all, and now she's got time on her hands. We talked about getting one of her sisters or maybe her cousin to keep her company."

"Sounds good to me," Pat said.

What Father Hugh had told him about Mil last night had set his thoughts dancing around her. The patient man had damn tough work ahead for him, but maybe. Maybe. Then what? He didn't dare daydream further.

"About time we went to the house," said Albert. "I'm damn near froze to a chunk a ice."

They rode back to the ranch buildings and tied Socks and the colt in the horse barn, out of the worst of the cold, and walked back to the house. Evangeline was keeping a hot dinner ready, canned beef stew and fresh bread and a pie she'd made from dried serviceberries soaked back into succulence. Pat and Albert thawed out and ate Evangeline's good dinner and rolled cigarettes and smoked them, and then they bundled up again and mounted Socks and the gray colt for another ride.

"I think he'll make a saddle horse," said Albert afterward, as he and Pat walked shivering back to the house so Pat could thaw out again before he started back to town. "Next thing, see if he's got any cow sense."

Pat nodded. "He's got good action. Good quarters under him. You going to ride him alone tomorrow, Albert?"

"I talked to Evangeline about getting on Socks and riding with me. Either that or working the colt in the corral on neck-reining. Any chance of you riding with me next Saturday?"

"Should be."

"Appreciate it."

Pat drove away, and Albert and Evangeline agreed he looked a whole lot better than he had a week ago.

Pat drove back to town in the last of the afternoon daylight with his thoughts scattered. Evangeline, the Métis girl, as good as anyone on horseback and riding with Albert on his colt. Evangeline's unmarried sister or cousin staying out at the ranch to keep Evangeline company, and the lonesome cowboys who soon would be turning up as Albert and Evangeline's visitors.

What Father Hugh had told him about Mil and the horse-man.

Pat's own memory of his ride was seeing what had to be done and knowing Pink could do it and he could do it. Reaching the shack in what had seemed no time, sweeping the baby and the woman up on Pink with him, and turning Pink for their final run—and God, the feeling. The charge of his own blood. An exuberance he'd never felt. Not in combat, not in the arms of Veeve. What could he do but let it out in laughter?

Now he tried to see his ride through Mil's eyes. The horseman—himself, Pat—the roan horse and the rider reflecting red from the fire and thundering through flames toward her. All that male force and energy hurtling toward her.

"Where do I start?" he'd asked Father Hugh.

And Father Hugh said, "Maybe you could write her a letter?"

Pat spent the rest of Saturday evening and most of Sunday on his letter, tearing it up and starting over, and on Monday morning he stopped by the post office and mailed it, which made him a few minutes late for work. He parked his truck in the courthouse parking lot and almost reached the marble steps when George Clarke's receptionist, Betsy, burst out the doors.

"Pat! Oh, Pat! Thank heavens! Mr. Clarke sent me to watch for you. Something terrible—Ferrell's run off—Judge Browning finally signed the order, and they were taking Ferrell out of his cell to handcuff him and put him in a state car—oh, Pat!" She ran out of breath and started over. "He got a choke hold on one of the deputies before they could handcuff him, and we don't know yet if he killed the deputy. They've got the doctor down there now— and nobody knows where Ferrell went—"

"Betsy," said Pat, "you tell George to call—"

But George Clarke himself suddenly was there. "Ferrell's got the deputy's gun, Pat."

"Where he'll go," said Pat. "Get a couple of the city police over to the convent. A couple more to Josie Archambault's house, and get whoever is handy to run up and down Josie's street, warning folks. And call Father Hugh—there's a telephone in the rectory—and ask him to drive out to the ranch and warn Albert and Evangeline, just in case Ferrell decides to go home."

"Pat, where are you going?"

"To the other place he'll go if he can."

Pat was running for his truck. Thankful he'd fueled it. Thankful he'd hung the two-fifty Savage on its brackets in the rear window instead of leaving it in the saddle scabbard. He spun out of the parking lot and turned for the county road, driving as fast as he dared on gravel and keeping an eye out for another driver behind or ahead of him. The way people left their keys in their ignitions, even in town, made it easy enough for Ferrell to find transportation.

God, Mil. What was he going to do, living forty miles from her?

Mildred finished her Monday morning laundry and pinned her wet sheets and towels and underwear and Levi's and shirts to freeze-dry on the backyard clothesline. She emptied her tubs and mopped the kitchen floor and decided that as long as her kitchen range was fired, she might as well start her bread instead of waiting until Wednesday. She kneaded her dough and turned it into a buttered bowl to rise under a dish towel, thinking that at the rate she was going, she would run short of tasks by the end of the week. And she hadn't heard more about testifying or not testifying.

She was washing the flour off her hands when she heard the sound of a truck being driven too fast and braking to a screeching stop below her cabin, and she reached for a towel just as Pat Adams, carrying a rifle, burst through the door and into her kitchen.

She stood with her mouth open and her towel dangling and thought that if this was an apparition, it was a different sort of apparition from her usual ones.

"Mil. Is everything all right here?" His voice was hoarse.

"Yes," she said. "Why wouldn't it be?"

He didn't answer. Instead, he seemed belatedly to remember that he was standing in her kitchen, after all, and he took off his Stetson and hung it on a nail.

"Sorry," he said. "But if I have to tell you to get up to the loft, Mil, you get up to the loft."

He was looking out her kitchen window, leaning from side to side to see as far up and down the road as he could. Left the window, opened the door and looked out and shut it again, and went back to the window.

"Pat," Mildred said. "Will you please tell me what is going on?"

Pat looked at her as though he had forgotten she was there and then looked out the window again. "Here he comes," he said. "Looks like he's stolen himself a REO. Wouldn't a thought he knew how to drive one. Get up to the loft, Mil."

"No," she said.

Pat gave her one quick look, because the woman behind him suddenly was Mildred the horseback-riding nurse of Plum Creek, and she was holding her kitchen hatchet.

Then he cracked open the kitchen door. If Ferrell had the deputy's gun . . . And Ferrell was extricating himself from the REO, wearing nothing but the slippers and coveralls they'd given him to wear in jail, and when he turned and saw Pat, he pulled the big revolver out of the front of his coveralls and laughed. "Whaddya think you're goin to do with your toy gun? Shoot somebody with it?"

Pat levered a bullet into the chamber of the Savage and walked across the porch and down the steps, with the rifle at the ready. "Lay the gun down, Ferrell."

Ferrell advanced another step, the old bull confronting the young veteran of the Meuse-Argonne. He laughed again.

"You're too damn yellow to shoot me, Pat. You *mama's boy!*"

"Not one more step, Ferrell. Lay the gun down."

"I'll break you in half," Ferrell said.

Ten feet from Pat, Ferrell laughed, deep in his throat, and raised his foot, not for one more step, but to hurtle himself at Pat, and Renny Archambault fired his rifle from the steps of the shack.

27

"I knowed you'd do it, Pat," said Renny. "I didn't want you to hafta do it."

Mildred, watching with her hatchet from the top of the steps, saw not a handshake between the two men nor an exchange of shoulder punches but an embrace.

"Hafta wonder, Pat. Was Ferrell's idea to off himself the way he thought would hurt you the most?"

"Making me kill him? Maybe. Wonder if he went down thinking he had."

"Thing to do now," said Renny, "is roll him up in a tarp—I got one in the barn—and load him in your truck and take him to Fort Maginnis. Give him that much dignity."

"Yeah."

"Best thing for me is turn myself in."

Pat nodded, and Mildred made a sound, and both men looked up.

"Mildred, go back inside or at least put a coat on, afore you freeze."

"His attorney will take care of him, Mil."

"Pat, you know damn well I don't have cash for a lawyer."

"The one I'm thinking about works free."

"Let's get it done," said Renny. "Get Ferrell in the back of the truck, anyway, and sit somewhere warm to figure out what else. Mildred can get her town things together—"

"What are you talking about? I can't go to Fort Maginnis—I've got bread rising!"

Pat and Renny stared at her. "How long does that take, Mil?" said Pat.

"An hour for the loaves to rise, another hour to bake, and I've got wash on the line."

Renny shook his head, and Pat dug out his pocket watch. Not quite ten o'clock. Hardly seemed possible. He'd arrived at the courthouse in Fort Maginnis a little after eight.

"Hell, let her bake her bread and bring in her wash. If Guy Temple wants to know what took us so long, we can tell him Mil had to bake her bread. Maybe we can get Mil to go with us to Guy's office and bring her hatchet with her."

"Sounds like a plan to me."

"While her bread bakes, I'll help you load Ferrell, and then I'll saddle Smokey and ride up to the Svobodas and ask Stan to come after the horses and the milk cow until we can see farther down the road. What, an hour and a half up there, half an hour to thaw out with the Svobodas, an hour and a half back? You can sack up the chickens while I'm gone, and the chickens can visit Josie's chickens. And we can take the dogs with us if they don't mind riding in back with Ferrell. We can be in Fort Maginnis before the county offices close."

Mildred wandered back into the cabin and stoked her stove and greased her bread pans and shaped her loaves and set them to rise under a dish towel. She wasn't doing too badly as long as she was doing something so familiar that she didn't have to think about it. How she'd feel when she started to think was another question.

She saw Pat ride past the cabin on Smokey, hunched against the cold and headed for the Svobodas. He was riding Renny's saddle, for the stirrup length, she supposed. She had been startled by Pat when he burst into her kitchen with his rifle, but not as assaulted and helpless as the horse-man had left her.

Like a dog that had eaten poisoned bait and vomited it up, she had vomited words all over poor Father Hugh. Often the dog that vomited up the poison died anyway. So far she felt a little numb at seeing Ferrell Adams reel and go down, and she remembered the day she had fantasized about shooting Ferrell in the back, picking the exact square in his plaid shirt where she wanted to hit him.

She knew in her bones that Pat would have shot Ferrell if Renny hadn't shot him first, and she wondered, as Renny had, if Ferrell hoped Pat would.

In case Stan couldn't get down for the livestock before tomorrow, Renny pitched hay for the cow and calf and for Pink, and he pitched hay for Smokey when Pat rode him back. Then he took gunnysacks to the chicken house and caught the squawking, flapping chickens and sacked them and tied the sacks shut and laid them in the back of Pat's truck, next to Ferrell in his tarp. He didn't know if Josie wanted more chickens, and he thought these girls were past their laying prime. Maybe take them to the convent as stewing hens, maybe one or two to Father Hugh, and start over with pullets in the spring. If there was a starting over.

Ferrell Adams. Hard to know what to think. Himself, Renny thought he'd have picked the clean shot to the head over life in the state prison or the state hospital. The clean shot to the head more than the old devil deserved.

Pat Adams. He seemed solid on his feet so far, considering what he'd seen and had to do and almost had to do during the last few hours. Pat took his punches and rolled with them and got up again, but Renny had to wonder. Sometimes it seemed like some force was trying to find out just how many punches Pat Adams could roll with. Keeping count, like.

Mildred. His little girl.

Renny saw that Mildred was bringing in her clothes from the lines in stiffened, boardlike stacks. He quit his woolgathering and rigged a shelter of blankets next to the cab for his dogs, and he hung his rifle, to turn over to the sheriff, above the Savage in Pat's rear window. Then he brought a jar of hooch and a change of clothes up to the cabin and warmed himself over Mildred's kitchen range until she pushed him out of the way so she could lift out her loaves and tilt them in their pans to cool.

He poured hooch into his cup and topped the cup with coffee. Not much else to do or think about, he decided. At least, no point in thinking about it.

Knew it was starting to sink in.

Pat rode down the creek trail at a stiff trot, past the cabin, and down to the barn, where he unsaddled Smokey and brushed and grained him and tied him in a stall. He saw that Renny had pitched hay and broken the ice on the water tanks, so he closed the barn door and the gates and walked back to the cabin, where he found Renny drinking coffee that smelled more like hooch and Mildred wrapping loaves of bread in dish towels and stacking them in a flour sack.

Pat hung his hat on a nail and loosened his silk scarf to hang around his neck and poured himself coffee and got as warm as he could while Mildred finished fussing with her bread loaves and Renny looked faraway, and then Pat retied his scarf and put his hat back on and carried Mil's suitcase and her black bag out to the truck to join the chickens and the dogs and Ferrell in his tarp for the drive to Fort Maginnis. Mildred put out her fire and picked up her sack of bread loaves, gave a last look around her cabin, her home, and steered Renny out the door and down to Pat's truck, where she gave him the bread, a three-foot white pillar, to hold on his lap and block his view. She got into the cab from the other side and scooted under the steering wheel to sit by Renny. And then Pat, stamping his feet against the cold, got in the truck and started it, and they were off.

Twenty miles short of Fort Maginnis, they met a black Murray County Sheriff's Department car, and Pat honked and pulled over and saw the car from the sheriff's department make a U-turn and pull up behind him. He got out and met Sandy Duncan and Milton

Bill and, the three of them shivering against the stiff prairie wind, told Sandy what had happened that morning at the Harrington ranch.

"The hell," said Sandy. "So you brought him with you? Better take him to Ted Norman's. He's the county coroner now, and he works out of what he calls his funeral parlor, used to be the undertaker's."

Pat nodded. "I'd tell you not to bother driving all the way out there. We got the livestock seen to before we left. But there's a strange REO sitting out there, which Ferrell drove there, and somebody's probably in a boil over it."

"Guess we better go out and one of us drive it in. You'll go up and talk to Guy Temple after you drop Ferrell off?"

"Ferrell and maybe the chickens. But yeah, we'll talk to Guy before the day's out."

Milton peered through the cab window, and Mildred reached over and rolled it down for him.

"Renny," said Milton, sticking in his head, "what are you holding on your lap?"

"Bread."

Milton shook his head and pulled it out again, and Mildred rolled up the window.

George Clarke's office, with extra chairs dragged in from his conference room. George Clarke himself, tilted back in his desk chair, and Sheriff Temple across from him in the visitors' chair. Harry Fallon, of course, and Elmer Cole. Pat Adams and Renny Archambault and Mildred Harrington, who was wishing she had changed to a dress before she came to town and was trying to sit unnoticed in a corner.

Betsy, scurrying around with fresh coffee and cups borrowed from offices up and down the second floor of the courthouse.

"How's your deputy?" Clarke asked the sheriff, and Guy Temple shook his head.

"Doctor thinks there's a little bone broken in his neck from Ferrell's choke hold. Depends on whether or not it hit a nerve. Have to say, at least that new doctor the sisters got for themselves now is—" Temple looked around the faces in the office and didn't finish his thought.

"What did the judge say?" asked Harry Fallon, and Clarke, who had just returned from Judge Browning's office with his signed order of release on personal recognizance for Renny, shook his head.

"*One* of the things Judge Browning said was, if he'd been the man with the rifle out there this morning—well, no. Let's leave it at that. I think Judge Browning is pleased that at least Ferrell doesn't pose a danger to the community now. In particular, that attack on poor Dwight is not sitting well with the judge."

"Of course, there's a legal procedure now," Clarke added.

A tap on the door, and Father Hugh let himself in. He scanned the faces around the office and found Renny's and went to him.

"Renny."

Renny raised haunted eyes to the priest. "Father," he said. "We left you a couple a stewing hens in a sack at the rectory."

No one present in George Clarke's office understood Father Hugh's reaction to such a simple statement. However, after what seemed to be a brief inner struggle, Father Hugh said, "Thank you, Renny."

And George Clarke said, "Use the conference room, Father," and Father Hugh helped Renny to his feet and guided him into the conference room and closed the door.

It looked to Pat as though Josie was in danger of having an overflow of company. After the meetings had ended in George Clarke's office and in his conference room, Pat asked, "Where would you rather stay tonight, Renny? With Josie or with Father Hugh?"

"With Josie."

"Sounds good," said Pat. "I'll get a few of my clothes from Josie's and hit Father Hugh up for a bed and sleep at the rectory tonight."

Mrs. O'Shea, going to the door and finding a sack with two stewing hens on the doorstep, decided the most merciful act on her part would be to carry the hens down to the convent herself. At the convent, she enjoyed a visit with Sister St. Paul over coffee before she returned to the rectory, smiling to herself.

Sister St. Paul promised herself, on the first opportunity, to explain to Father Hugh that Sister Boniface was a Montana girl, born and raised on her father's ranch. Shy, yes, like so many children on isolated ranches who never saw strangers. But she had plenty of spine.

"Mil," said Pat, later that evening, "I wrote you a letter and mailed it to you this morning."

They were sitting in the cab of Pat's truck, parked outside the convent. Mil, who had been sitting in the middle of the seat, hadn't moved over when Renny got out, so she was very close to Pat in the cooling cab, and Pat didn't like to move, himself.

"It'll probably reach my mailbox by Thursday," she said. "Maybe you can tell me what you wrote."

"I'll do that," said the patient man, though something had lurched inside him. "Maybe not out here in the cold?"

"No. Pat, what will happen to Renny?"

"Right now, he's free on what they call his own recognizance, meaning he can do whatever, stay with Josie, go back to the ranch, as long as he's on hand the next time he's needed, which will be at the inquest. My view, the best thing for Renny right now is Josie. Also my view, the likeliest outcome is justifiable homicide. But these things can drag out, Mil."

The ping of cooling metal. Frost flakes spinning around the light above the convent door.

"Couple things we need to talk about. I don't like to leave the horses and that cow too long with Stan having to find feed for em. If you want to go back to the ranch tomorrow, I'll drive you out and bring em back to you. If you want to stay at the convent for a while, I'll put a stock rack on my truck and haul em up to Albert's. Any case, you'll need to be on hand for the inquest. As I will."

"Pat? I don't know what I want to do."

"Tomorrow is tomorrow, Mil. Sweetheart—"

"Today is starting to sink in, Pat. I need some time."

Then he did open the door and step down from the cab and permit himself the brief touch of her hand to help her down. He lifted her suitcase and black bag from the back of the truck and walked her to the convent door.

"Good night, Mil."

"Have some dinner, Pat," said Father Hugh, the sole resident of Murray County who thought dinner, not supper, was a meal eaten in the evening. "Mrs. O'Shea left plenty."

It seemed to Pat that all his friends were urging him to eat. But when he smelled the plate of canned pork and boiled beans the rectory housekeeper had put in the oven to keep warm for him, he found himself actually hungry, and he tucked in while Father Hugh drank coffee and watched him eat. When he finished, Pat rinsed his plate and followed Father Hugh into his study to smoke and swirl a glass of wine in the luxury of warmth and a cushioned chair.

"You got Renny settled?" asked Father Hugh.

And Pat said, as he had to Mildred, "My view, the best thing for Renny right now is Josie."

"A hard thing for a man to have to do," said Father Hugh.

"Yeah," said Pat, whose experience in doing such things went far beyond Father Hugh's.

"I thought Mildred seemed easier with herself this afternoon. She smiled at me again."

"I was afraid she might fold on me, but I tell you, Father Hugh. When I told her to take cover, she told me no, and when I looked around, she was holding a hatchet."

"Somehow that doesn't surprise me."

"No, and it's the damnedest thing. I can look at Mil, and she'll run like I'd taken a shot at her. And then Ferrell shows up, and she's ready to take him on with a hatchet."

"Has she talked to you?"

"She's friendlier. I have some hopes."

Pat yawned, and the two young men finished their wine and stubbed out their cigarettes and climbed the rectory stairs, Pat to the bed Mrs. O'Shea had made up for him, where he stripped to his underwear and fell asleep almost instantly, and Father Hugh to his own room, where he prayed on his knees for some time.

28

Mildred decided she would rather stay on at the convent than go back to the ranch alone, with no chores to do, so Pat telephoned the county clerk's office from the rectory and explained his absence and set out before sunrise on a complicated trek. First out to Albert's, as Pat had come to think of the ranch he now owned, where the sun was just breaking and where Albert helped him fit a stock rack on his truck and invited him to thaw out over a quick cup of coffee.

"And eat one a Evvie's cinnamon buns, Pat!"

They'd had quite a day out there, Albert told Pat. "The way Father Hugh came burnin in, Pat, you mighta thought somebody was after him. Guess he had reason to think somebody might be. He and I talked about breaking the glass outa the gun cabinet. But then he tried one a the doors, and you'd left it unlocked, Pat. And I took the twenty-two, and Father Hugh took the shotgun—"

"I told Father to give me the shotgun and go back to town," Evangeline interrupted, "but he wouldn't go."

Albert grinned, "She sure did. But Father Hugh and I guarded the place until late afternoon, when Sandy Duncan showed up and told us what had happened. Hell of a thing, Pat."

"Yeah. Bad all the way around. The doctor's concerned Dwight Johnson might not make it, and even if he does, Dwight might wish he hadn't."

"I didn't know that. Hard to figure. All Dwight went through in 1918, and Ferrell does that to him. And I tell you, Pat. You come across the key to that gun cabinet, you might let me have it so we can keep it locked. No big hurry, but we think . . ." Albert lost his place in what he was saying, and Evangeline smiled, and Pat caught on. Quick work, Albert.

Pat dug out his key ring and passed Albert the key and punched him on the shoulder, and he kissed Evangeline on the cheek and thanked her for the coffee and cinnamon bun. And then he girded himself against the weather in sheepskin coat and gloves and Stetson and scarf and headed for the Svobodas.

At the Svobodas, Pat drank more coffee and had a homemade doughnut pressed on him, and Stan told him, "Them horses and that cow are doin fine, Pat; no need to move em unless you want to," and waved away payment when Pat offered it.

"Once you're warm enough, Pat, I'll help you load em."

"Stan, first I have to saddle Smokey and ride down to the Harrington place and collect Mildred's clothes for her—"

"You saddle Shorty for me, Stan," Mrs. Svoboda cut in, "while I'm gettin dressed. Mildred won't want a man goin through her things."

So Pat had company on his ride down to Plum Creek, with Mrs. Svoboda wearing Stan's wool trousers under her dress and a mackinaw and gloves and a heavy wool scarf and riding a chunky little brown gelding. They made their way down the trail to the crossing, with Pat reflecting on how much less complicated his errand would be if there were a bridge over the crossing, where Plum Creek flowed too deep to drive a motor vehicle across.

Finally, they reached the cabin. Pat and Mrs. Svoboda tied Smokey and Shorty, shaggy as bears in their winter coats, to the fence, and Pat built a fire in Mildred's stove and chipped ice out of the water cooler to boil water for coffee. While the cabin warmed, Pat and Mrs. Svoboda thawed, and she went to work emptying Mildred's closet and drawers into flour sacks. Pat put his coat and gloves back on and walked down to the barn and carried a sack of grain on his shoulder to tie on the back of Smokey's saddle. As an afterthought he later was thankful for, he borrowed one of Mrs. Svoboda's flour sacks and stuffed it with clothes for Renny.

Back at the cabin, Pat drank more coffee and rolled a cigarette and smoked it while Mrs. Svoboda finished her packing and then, too much coffee, excused himself to take a leak in back of the cabin. A wonder the stream didn't freeze on its way down, he thought, instead of hissing briefly in the snow and hollowing out a hole of yellow ice.

Pat doused the fire in the stove with the last of the coffee, and he and Mrs. Svoboda, wearing enough clothing for a pair of Eskimos, mounted Smokey and Shorty. Mrs. Svoboda with sackfuls of clothing hanging from each side of her pommel, Pat with the sack of grain tied behind his cantle. Only another hour and a half's freezing horseback ride to go.

Pat backed up his truck to Stan's loading chute, and after they unsaddled Smokey and Shorty, Stan helped Pat load Smokey and Pink and the reluctant milk cow and invited Pat to the house to sit by the stove and drink coffee and eat another doughnut. And Pat accepted, because he was damn near chilled to the bone by now, but he made it quick.

Pat thanked the Svobodas and headed out, hoping he and Stan had snubbed Pink well enough to the stock rack that she couldn't bite or kick the cow. He was driving by headlights now under a darkened sky and across a darkened landscape where the headlight beams cut a tunnel through bleached winter sagebrush and patches of snow. Only because he knew the low hills and draws of the high prairie so well did he know where the grass fire had burned. He detoured around the long coulee that last November had caused him and Albert to reach the fire crew on the south side of the burn instead of the crew on the north side, another happening that had prevented a happening.

Adams ranch buildings in his headlights now. Adams corrals. Albert, running with a lantern to guide Pat backing the truck to the loading chute. The horses and cow unloaded and under shelter. The grain sack from the cab of the truck.

"More grain down at Harrington's, and hay in the barn if you want to take a team and wagon for it," he tried to tell Albert, but his teeth were chattering.

"Pat, you look plumb froze to death. Get up to the house with me and, hell, crawl into the oven if you have to. Maybe you should stay the night."

"Got to work in the morning."

But he was glad for Evangeline's warm kitchen, and he let Evangeline fuss over him. She pulled off his boots and wool socks and rolled up his Levi's and wool long johns, and she poured hot water from a kettle into a basin for him to soak his feet. Pat eased his blocks of feet into the hot water, and he leaned back and opened his coat to the warmth of Evangeline's open oven door. Took her cup of coffee and warmed his hands around it before he drank.

Soon Pat could talk, without his teeth chattering, to Albert, who had been worrying about the Harrington cattle in their winter pasture and whether they needed hay.

"Guess you could take a look for me," Pat said. "What I think, though, Albert. Either the coroner will hold that inquest and Renny and Mil can go back to the ranch if they want to or else Jerry St. Pierre can move out there. Renny's been talking with Jerry off and on, and Jerry's outa work. He'd like to raise his boys out of town, and Jerry's a good hand. He or Renny, one, will get those cattle fed, so you don't have to drive a team and wagon all that way in this weather."

Albert nodded, and Pat didn't mention his own private dream arrangements that he didn't let himself think about in detail. Renny in his shack, the St. Pierres in Mil's cabin, and Mil with Pat.

Pat was as warm as he was going to get. He bundled back up and went with Albert by lantern light to lift the stock rack down from the truck, and then Pat waved to Albert and began the last leg of his trek.

Pat parked in front of the convent and knocked on the door, and when a nun he didn't recognize opened the door a crack, he handed her two sacks of clothes and said, "For Miss Harrington," and ran back to the truck as the nun shut the door hastily against the cold.

He drove to the rectory, teeth chattering, and Father Hugh took one look and said, "Run a hot bath in the tub."

Run a hot bath in the tub. Pat thought he had known what the words meant at one time but had forgotten. Something people living even in small towns did. His landlady in Missoula had had a bathtub, although too many people used it. Now Pat discovered that the rectory bathroom had a real porcelain tub on stately feet and legs, and Pat started water running. Father Hugh handed him in a couple of Turkish towels and a bathrobe made of Turkish toweling.

"I think I have a pair of those slippers they use at the hospital," Father Hugh said, and disappeared.

Pat undressed and piled his many layers of clothes high and slid into a tub of hot water, and oh, yeah. He soaked and felt the cold seep out of his bones and added, to his dream of Pat with Mil, a house with a bathtub and hot water.

The hell of it was, he reflected, Mil liked living out on the ranch with Smokey and Renny and doing her doctoring.

Father Hugh came in with a pair of flimsy white slippers and a bucket of boiling water to add to the tub. "Oh, yeah," Pat sighed, as Father Hugh poured water.

"I was a little worried you might have drowned in here," Father Hugh told him.

"Wouldn't be a bad way to go, in water like this."

"Do you know how long you were on your trek, as you call it?"

"What time is it?"

"Half past eight. No wonder you're cold."

Pat had left the rectory before seven that morning.

"Not too bad," Pat said, "for a man who couldn't walk out of court a couple weeks ago. Although not what Sister St. Paul could call acrobatics."

Father Hugh said, "She might differ with you there. There's hot food in the kitchen when you think you can unsubmerge yourself," and left Pat to pull the plug on his wonderful bath and towel himself and dress in his wool long johns and the bathrobe.

He ate Father Hugh's hot food and rinsed his dishes and joined Father Hugh in his study to smoke and sip wine and tell Father Hugh about trucking Mil's horses and the cow to Albert and about Albert's cautious, well, not for sure, but we think maybe, news.

Later, in his borrowed bed, Pat reflected that he also had gotten Mil's clothes to her at the convent, and frozen as he was at the time, he'd hoped to see her and hadn't.

Maybe tomorrow.

As it happened, he didn't. Pat spent Wednesday morning catching up on his filing and placing telephone calls from the county clerk's office to the funeral parlor and to the Presbyterian manse to arrange for Ferrell's burial in the Protestant cemetery for Friday morning. Pat didn't suppose Ferrell would attract any mourners, but he knew he had to go through the motions for common decency and was surprised when he told the county clerk that he needed still another morning off.

"Hell, Pat, your father's funeral, and under the circumstances? We'll close the office Friday morning."

Under the circumstances, just a graveside service, Pat had told the Presbyterian minister and Ted Norman at the funeral parlor.

"I see your point, Pat," said Norman, "but it's going to be colder'n hell out there."

And it was. Pat, dressed in his dark suit and wearing his sheepskin coat over it, was surprised again at the number of, well, not mourners, exactly, but maybe quiet supporters, who were grouped around the grave that two of Norman's men with pickaxes and crowbars had dug for Ferrell in the frozen sod of December.

The contingent from the county clerk's office. And it looked as though George Clarke had closed the prosecutor's office for the morning, because he was there, along with Harry Fallon and Betsy. Not Albert, not Evangeline—Pat hadn't had time to get word to them. But Pat's new friend Miss Clara Manning, the longtime librarian at the Carnegie Library, was there, as were some faces Pat didn't recognize, perhaps Presbyterians who had known Ferrell when he was a good cattleman and his moods sometimes were sunny. Father Hugh, in black hat and black overcoat, had come from the rectory with Pat and stood beside him, although the other Catholics present were huddled across from Pat and uneasy on Protestant soil—Mrs. O'Shea and Sister St. Paul and Sister Boniface and two nuns Pat thought he remembered as nursing sisters who had laughed at him, all in black cloaks and hoods, and some of the St. Pierres and Josie.

And Mil, wearing a dress and hat and coat.

Six dark-clad men lifted Ferrell's casket out of Norman's hearse and carried it to the grave and lowered it. Pat hadn't thought of pallbearers. These men were Presbyterian elders, he guessed, rounded up by the minister. They stood with everyone else while the minister read the brief service and consigned Ferrell to the dust whence he had come, although in Ferrell's case, more to the chips of hacked and frozen prairie sod.

Done.

Father Hugh shook Pat's hand and embraced him, and the Presbyterian minister shook his hand. Handshakes from George Clarke and the county clerk and others from the courthouse, and some of the men Pat didn't know, and some of the women, and he was moved when one of the women smiled at him and murmured that she had known his mother.

The nuns. Jerry St. Pierre and his wife.

But not Mil. He'd lost sight of her again.

"Pat."

He looked down and saw Josie, and she hugged him. And he lifted her off her feet and hugged her and set her down.

"Pat, come see me. Come see Renny."

"I will," Pat promised.

And Ferrell really was over and done, except for the tracks and scars he left behind.

29

Pat and Father Hugh returned to the rectory, and Pat shared Father Hugh's lunch. He knew Mrs. O'Shea had taken to doubling Father Hugh's servings, and he felt bad about it.

"I gotta do something, Father Hugh. I can't keep bumming a bed and food off you and swilling your wine—"

"Pat, I'm glad to have you here."

"Josie doesn't have room for me, with Renny there, and I've been thinking I should find rooms somewhere."

"Do you really think you can find rooms in Fort Maginnis with a bathtub big enough for you?"

Pat had to laugh. "I've been thinking I should reimburse the diocese for your water bill."

"Pat. Maybe I can put it this way. When I came to Montana from Boston last April, I was—well, as you or Albert would put it—scared as hell. This would be my first parish where I, well, another case of hanging out with you and Albert and picking up your patois, *held the reins.*"

"Another good word for cowboy talk is *lingo*, Father Hugh."

"If you say so. I didn't know a thing about Montana, and everything was strange. And then, too, people often expect a priest to be somber and serious, and you may have noticed, Pat, that somber and serious are hard for me to maintain. And Pat, I was lonely. I can't tell you how lonely. I'd left good friends behind me in Boston, and, anyway, I think what started to break the ice for me was the day Sister St. Paul sent for me and I walked into the convent parlor just after she'd flung a knife at the parlor door, in her outrage. The blade stuck in the door, Pat, a good inch and a half, and I looked from that knife still quivering in the door to Sister St. Paul and thought, there's more to this woman than appearances."

"There sure is," said Pat. And he had to ask, "What was she so outraged about, that she was throwing knives?"

"You and Mildred and Ferrell."

Pat closed his eyes for a minute.

"Remember the night I sat in a chair in the door of your hospital room, and we started to get acquainted? Then we got better acquainted, and Albert showed up. And what can I say? Two young men I could laugh with, and like, and respect—so Pat, don't talk to me about abusing my hospitality, if that's what you think you're doing."

"Father Hugh," said Pat, with the same expression that Father Hugh once had seen him turn on Sister St. Paul, "you said a mouthful. We Montana boys usually don't have that much to say."

Then he smiled his Pat smile at Father Hugh.

"Pat," Father Hugh said, "at least wait until after the inquest and see what Renny and Mildred are going to do. See what you can work out with Mildred."

An exchange of shoulder punches, and Pat went back to work.

On Saturday Pat drove out to the ranch and rode with Albert, and when he got back to Fort Maginnis, he stopped at the meat market and bought a roast of beef and a beefsteak and stored them in the rectory icebox. The roast, he explained to Mrs. O'Shea, was for her to cook for him and Father Hugh, and also a slice for herself, if she felt like one. The beefsteak was a present for a friend.

Pat spent Saturday evening and Sunday morning reading Frank Linderman's *Indian Why Stories*. He shared lunch after Sunday mass with Father Hugh, who did note a smile exchanged between Mrs. O'Shea and Pat. After lunch, in coat and scarf and hat and gloves against the cold, Pat took his beefsteak and the flour sack of Renny's clothes and drove to the Métis settlement along Spring Creek.

"Pat! Pat!" Josie bubbled her greeting. "You come see Renny? What you brung, Pat?"

Renny looked up from his contemplation of the air in front of him and nodded to Pat as Josie led him with his package to the kitchen. Josie exclaimed when she unwrapped the butcher paper, "Pat! You stay, have supper with me? With Renny?"

Her eyes were on the beefsteak, and Pat remembered the ample, if carefully thrift-driven, meals Josie had served him. He suspected her meals had become more frugal without the board money he had been forcing on her.

"The steak is for you and Renny. I think the housekeeper at the rectory has something good planned for tonight."

"You drink wine," she told him, and hugged him again.

Pat carried his glass of wine into Josie's front room. "Renny," he said, and Renny nodded again while his dogs looked up sadly from their mat beside his chair.

"Can't drink that swill of Josie's," Renny said after a while, "and I drank too much hooch one day awhile back, and now I'm off the hooch."

Pat nodded and sipped and waited.

"Didn't show up Friday morning," Renny said. "Couldn't bring myself to. Didn't seem right."

Pat, knowing what was happening with Renny and having had time to meditate on what he'd said to Father Hugh—we Montana boys don't talk much—had concluded that taciturnity and under-statement were not necessarily his best means of expression.

"Renny," said Pat, who had never spoken a word to anyone at home about his battlefield experience, "I don't know that I've ever told you much about the Meuse-Argonne in 1918?"

Renny shook his head, and Pat told him about what Albert once had described to Father Hugh as quite a bit goin on right then, like Powder River, let er buck, including an experience of

Pat's own that had led to one of the things on ribbons in a hidden drawer he did not mention to Renny.

"Once in a while, something a man could kinda smile about. We had a Blackfoot in our unit, by the name of Big Man, who counted coup one time. Big Man sneaked up on a German soldier and rapped him over his helmet with a stick with a knot on the end, and when the German soldier spun around, Big Man shot him dead. Wouldn't a believed it if I hadn't seen it."

Renny shook his head. "Counting coup among the Hun? You think that's how he seen it?"

"Maybe. I do know old Big Man fought like a wildcat, all the way through the Meuse-Argonne, until the November armistice, and he made it out alive. And Renny, if there ever was a man who had a reason to despise the U.S. Army, it was him. Big Man lost most of his family on the Marias River back in 1870 when Major Baker attacked their camp."

Pat swirled his wine in his glass and sipped, while Renny thought his thoughts and Josie, seated behind Pat and not missing a word, made a small sound of distress.

"We killed other men because we had to, Renny. I killed other men because I had to. And I woulda shot Ferrell that day if you hadn't shot him for me first."

"Sunk into me, what I done," Renny said. "Not right away, but gradual like."

"How it happens."

"Appreciate it, Pat."

Renny looked beyond Pat, to Josie. "What did Pat bring you, Josie, to make you sound so excited about?"

....

Sunday dinner at the rectory. Oh, the aroma of roast beef with mashed potatoes and gravy made from the drippings.

....

The coroner's report on the death of Ferrell Adams reached the county prosecutor's desk by mid-December, and George Clarke read through it and noted the salient points. A side shot to the head that passed through both frontal lobes, fired from approximately fifty yards away. Death instantaneous. A thirty-aught-six-caliber bullet recovered from Adams's skull.

Straightforward enough, George Clarke thought. He telephoned Ted Norman and asked him if he thought he could round up a coroner's jury and get the inquest into the death of Ferrell Adams scheduled before Christmas.

Mildred, to give herself work while she waited for the inquest, gathered bits and pieces of white nursing habits, most of the pieces salvaged from the convent ragbag, which she patched and seamed together, and she joined whichever nursing shift at Good Samaritan could use her. It felt odd to her, working at the direction of a floor supervisor after so many years of making her own decisions and acting on them.

Her work with Dr. Riggio in surgery she found the newest and most interesting, because of course she hadn't been doing surgery in the Plum Creek country, or even observing it. She assisted Dr. Riggio in an appendectomy and two hernia repairs, and Dr. Riggio asked Sister St. Paul, "Who is the new nun? The shabby one?"

"A shabby new nun?"

"She's the only nun I've ever seen with patches on her nursing habit. She's very competent."

"Yes, she is competent," said Sister St. Paul, finally understanding whom Dr. Riggio was talking about. "She's a graduate of our diploma program, but she's not a nun. Her name is Mildred Harrington, and she's staying at the convent temporarily while she waits for a judicial matter to be settled."

Then she told the doctor from St. Louis about the horseback-riding nurse of Plum Creek, which amazed Dr. Riggio almost as much as Father Hugh had been amazed when he first met Mildred.

"She provides mostly midwifery and first aid."

Sister St. Paul decided to withhold what she knew about Josie Archambault's traditional concoctions that Mildred sometimes drew on.

"You should get her to tell you about her work during the flu epidemic. Riding horseback from ranch to ranch, sometimes driving that rattletrap old truck. And oh, yes, sometimes her emergency work. Doctor, do you remember Patrick Adams? The young man you took out of traction and fitted with a walking brace? Mildred is the one who set his bone and splinted his leg and brought him to us."

"She did good work there," said Dr. Riggio thoughtfully, although he had to wince at the thought of what the experience of having that bone set must have been like for Patrick Adams. And he took to requesting Mildred Harrington in surgery when he operated.

Like Pat, Mildred allowed herself a tentative starting-over dream. A return to the ranch, a gathering up of loose ends. New pullets in the chicken house, the milk cow freshened, Mildred's garden planted. Renny living in the shack again with his dogs. New babies to help into the world. Spring rains. Was it possible?

Did Mildred want it to be possible?

She circled the edges of that thought, cautious as an antelope drawn by its curiosity to the fluttering white handkerchief of the waiting hunter. Not that Mildred had seen an antelope, the antelope herd having been slaughtered by hungry homesteaders who themselves had since starved out, but she could visualize an antelope's taupe and white grace, the curve of her neck, the sudden swivel of her head on that neck, her huge eyes and sensitive ears and prongs of horns. Mildred played for a time with the idea of an antelope returning to the high prairie and finding what? Loneliness, she supposed, and the year-round cycle, year after year of grazing and scorching sun, the early darkness of fall and the deeper darkness of the subzero winters. Rain in the spring, or rainless spring and dry summers.

What did Mildred want to be possible? The antelope paused, sensing the white-handkerchief waiting game of the patient man. The threat of the horse-man lurking within him.

....

Ted Norman thought it could just be done. A day at most. Get it behind them. They'd begin with the medical report, he told George Clarke. Then they'd hear Renny Archambault's testimony that, yes, the rifle now in the possession of the sheriff was his; that he had fired it at Ferrell Adams; and that, yes, he had intended to kill him. Hear Guy Temple's testimony that the rifle in his possession had been turned over to him by Renny Archambault. Hear from the sheriff's deputies and maybe Betsy Anglaterra. Hear the testimony of the two eyewitnesses, Patrick Adams and Mildred Harrington.

What else? Did they want to bring in Ferrell's June 5 attack on Pat Adams? Or Ferrell's threats on July 19, which Father McHugh had prevented him from carrying out? Or Ferrell's lethal attack on poor Dwight Johnson?

Ferrell had been armed, George Clarke pointed out, although he was wearing nothing but slippers and jailhouse coveralls. The wonder was, he hadn't frozen to death before Renny had a chance to shoot him.

Clarke could imagine a juror wondering why Renny Archambault and Patrick Adams, together, couldn't have restrained him. True, Ferrell had been carrying poor Dwight Johnson's revolver, but did he intend to use it? Sounded to Clarke more like he had a physical assault in mind.

Ted Norman said he imagined there were some sheriff's deputies who might have a thing or two to say about restraining Ferrell Adams. The two men kicked the question around until Clarke said he was going home to get some rest and think it through.

"What it comes down to," Norman pointed out, "is that my jury will find a verdict, one way or another, and then it's up to you, George, as you well know, whether to charge Renny Archambault or not."

30

Mildred, returning to the convent after a long and almost certainly unsuccessful surgery, found Sister Boniface in the kitchen, washing the dishes from the nuns' supper. Sister Boniface poured Mildred coffee. "No! For heaven's sake, sit! You look worn to a frazzle, Mildred, and I'm nearly finished here."

Mildred sat in her makeshift and now blood-spattered nursing habit and watched Sister Boniface dry the last of her dishes and hang up her dish towel and empty her dishpan. The predictable routines of the convent, from matins to meals. Prayers and meditations. Nursing shifts. Teaching. Cleaning and laundry, mending and praying.

"You always look so happy, Sister Boniface."

Sister Boniface smiled, "Oh, yes."

Surgery had its predictable routines, too, until the unpredictable happened.

The woman was middle-aged and overweight and frightened. Her husband, who had driven her to see the doctor, was middle-aged and scrawny and angry.

"Gettin to where she's no use to me, Doctor!"

Dr. Riggio sent the husband out to fume in the waiting room and tried to get the woman to tell him what the trouble was that brought her to him, but she blushed and cried and couldn't speak. Finally, Dr. Riggio asked one of the nuns to fetch Miss Harrington, who he thought was working a shift on the second floor that day. When Mildred, in her patched-together nursing habit, tapped on his door, Dr. Riggio rose and went to speak to her in the corridor, where he briefly explained the situation he had on his hands, and Mildred nodded.

Dr. Riggio paced the corridor once or twice after Mildred slipped into his office and closed the door behind her, and then he cadged himself a cup of coffee from the nurses' station and thought about the young woman, Mildred Harrington, who never smiled. A story there, the doctor supposed. She had lovely hazel eyes, though.

In the doctor's office, the weeping woman looked up and said, "Oh, Sister!"

Mildred didn't correct her. "Mrs. Johnson?"

She held Mrs. Johnson's hand and asked her about herself, and Mrs. Johnson said, yes, she and the mister had been hanging on, but it was hard. No rain for so long, and now such late rain and snow, but maybe. Maybe next year. She and the mister lived on a little truck farm down on the crick, just below Fort Maginnis, and they had a good well, they were lucky there, and of course crick water. It was hard, Mrs. Johnson said, and Mildred looked at the hand in hers and thought how many hands of women she had seen with their fingers bent and stiffened and their skin scarred and roughened from their years of hard work.

As it turned out, Mrs. Johnson and the mister had raised three children, but one of the grown sons and the grown daughter and her husband—"They decided they had enough, Sister. And they packed up and moved to Seattle to see if it weren't better out there, and of course they taken them grandbabies with em."

A common enough story. How many times Mildred had heard it. The young moved away because they could, and the middle-aged hung on and grew older.

And there was more. Mrs. Johnson began to cry again. "I still say three, Sister, but one of em—poor Dwight, Sister, you hear what happened to poor Dwight?"

Mildred, who of course knew all about poor Dwight Johnson and had helped to give what care they could to him, held the sobbing woman in her arms and thought about invisible tracks and scars that ran deeper than the skin, and finally, she coaxed Mrs. Johnson to admit to her current trouble, which was that she'd started bleeding *down there*, years after she'd thought she was done with all that. And worse.

"Oh, Sister, it hurts me so bad, so terrible bad, when he does it to me."

"I thought of sending her down to Billings, when Miss Harrington told me the story she'd gotten out of her," Dr. Riggio told Sister St. Paul, "on the chance they could do more for her in Billings. But the Johnsons had no money, of course, and I thought it likelier he'd take his wife back to the what—the truck farm, they called it—and watch her die. Or I could operate and hope to take out enough to help her."

"So you operated. And it doesn't look good for her."

"No."

"I did have a chance to visit for a few minutes with Miss Harrington," he went on. "Incredible. I had no idea people lived like that. I told her how much I could use a surgical nurse like her, but she says she's going back to Plum Creek after the inquest. Seems a shame."

Sister St. Paul, who naturally had ferreted out some of Dr. Riggio's own story from him—the beautiful dark-haired Jewish girl in St. Louis and the objections raised by his Catholic family—was silent for a time. "Mildred made a choice once, Doctor. She could have converted and taken the veil, but she decided instead to return to Plum Creek and live that life, out there . . ."

Too much Sister St. Paul didn't feel up to explaining to the doctor from St. Louis, not right then. "Now she can return to Plum Creek and turn herself into a living legend, the horseback-riding nurse whom I suppose some will be thankful for and some will remember after she's gone. Or . . ."

Dr. Riggio waited while Sister St. Paul thought of the long talk she'd had with Father Hugh.

"Or she could say hello to a patient man."

....

Ted Norman scheduled the inquest for Tuesday, December 22, and he rounded up his jury while George Clarke rounded up his witnesses. And a banjo-playing man named Jake Pence dropped by Josie's house on his way back to the Plum Creek country and told Renny they'd scheduled a dance at the Cottonwood community hall for December 26, and any chance Renny could play the fiddle?

"Got high hopes I can," Renny told him, "and some hopes of getting my little girl to go to that dance with me."

....

The news of that dance and that hope breathed its way through the air of Murray County and had reached the ear of the patient man, who now sat, dressed in his dark suit, in what usually was the viewing room at Ted Norman's funeral parlor and waited to testify at the inquest into the death of Ferrell Adams while very aware of the presence of Mil, seated behind him.

Mil, who hardly more than a week ago had sat beside Pat in the cab of his truck and talked to him, not for long, but *talked* to him, now for whatever reasons of her own wasn't talking to him. Pat had seen her walk into the viewing room, now the court of inquest, with Renny and Josie and Father Hugh, who probably was chauffeuring everyone around, and Pat had looked away, afraid that his hunger for her would show in his face and spook her even worse. What he'd done to his brown-haired girl to keep her so spooked for so long.

A number of spectators had gathered, many of the same faces Pat had seen at Ferrell's funeral. Father Hugh. Jerry St. Pierre. The county clerk. Some of the pallbearers. The woman who had told Pat she remembered his mother.

George Clarke, who had reviewed Ted Norman's list of jurors and of course knew every name, had decided to go with his short list of witnesses, with a couple of additions. Now the coroner called Dr. Riggio, who attested that Dwight Johnson had later died of his injuries and then reviewed the medical evidence and the process by which he'd removed the bullet from Ferrell Adams's skull.

Renny Archambault came trembling up to swear his oath in the clothes he'd worn to see Evangeline married and that Pat Adams, in a providential afterthought, had brought to town for him.

"Is this your rifle?" the coroner asked him, and when Renny nodded, the coroner added, "You have to say it out loud, Renny," and let him sit down while Guy Temple also identified the rifle in the chain of evidence.

First Milton Bill and then Sandy Duncan described the fight in the jail and what had happened to poor Dwight Johnson. More medical evidence regarding Dwight's death. Betsy Anglaterra recalled her conversation with Patrick Adams on the courthouse steps, where she'd told him about Ferrell Adams's attacking Dwight and breaking out of jail.

"Patrick Adams."

For the second time in less than a month, Pat swore to tell the truth about the man he could bring himself only to call Ferrell Adams. Confronting Ferrell at rifle point in front of the Harrington cabin. What Ferrell had to say. The revolver in Ferrell's hand. Then the rifle shot from the direction of the shack.

"What did you do with the revolver, Pat?"

"Left it in his hand. Then we rolled him up in the tarp and loaded him into my truck."

"Some background to all this, Pat?"

Ferrell's crowbar attack. Ferrell's dumping Pat in the hawthorns at Svoboda's crossing. Ferrell's charging into Josie Archambault's house. His threats.

A self-contained Mildred Harrington, who never looked at Pat but confirmed what Pat had told the coroner.

Renny again. "Did you intend to kill him, Renny?"

"Yes." And Renny did look at Pat.

"I believe we're finished here," Ted Norman told his jury after he let Renny sit down again, and he escorted the jurors back to his own office to confer on their verdict. Everyone waited, and after about half an hour the jurors filed back into the viewing room, where the foreman told George Clarke they were recommending a verdict of justifiable homicide to him.

In the foyer of the funeral parlor, Pat happened to run into Jerry St. Pierre, who was waiting for Renny.

"He's back there on his knees to Father Hugh," Jerry told him.

"Maybe you can give him a message for me, Jerry? Tell him I took Pink and Smokey and the milk cow over to Albert's for him?"

"Sure. I'll tell Renny. Guess he and Mildred will probly be headed that way," Jerry said wistfully, having his own reasons for hoping the patient man prevailed. He added, "Now that we got this stinking mess behind us."

"I guess so," said Pat, who hoped to hell the stinking mess was behind them.

As it happened, Renny had underestimated Sister St. Paul's comprehension of Michif, which she had heard for so many years among the older Métis parishioners and which, of course, was heavily French based. What Sister St. Paul knew, Father Hugh usually came to know. Now he blessed Renny in the coroner's office and helped him to his feet and thought of old sorrows, which Father Hugh had decided to go on knowing nothing about. Nothing Father Hugh could do but pray about the old sorrows, anyway, unless someday Renny brought himself to speak of them.

Jerry St. Pierre had waited in the foyer with Josie and Mildred until Father Hugh and Renny finally emerged from the coroner's office. Jerry passed along Pat's message, and Renny nodded and pondered the complications of rural travel, what with no bridge over Plum Creek.

"Maybe the best way, Jerry," he said. "If you could take Mildred and me home. That way, I could put the stock rack on my truck and drive the long way around, maybe takin Mildred with me so she wouldn't be alone out there without a horse if she needed one. Then I can load up them horses Albert's been keeping, and the cow, and bring em back."

Jerry nodded. "That'd work."

....

"Mildred?" said Josie. "You want go back Plum Creek? Not stay in town for Christmas?"

"Yes," said Mildred, although she saw the concern in Josie's black eyes. "Yes, I want to go home."

....

The antelope left her delicate tracks where the snow had drifted around the roots of the sagebrush on the high prairie. Lifted her hoofs high in places where the snow had drifted deep around the edges of thought. Skirted the dark edges where the horse-man kept himself, although the antelope feared the horse-man less and less. The antelope knew a thing or two about being killed off and coming back.

....

A snowbound Plum Creek, a freezing cabin. Mildred started a fire in her stove and changed, shivering, from her town clothes into Levi's and shirt and moccasins to help Renny and Jerry St. Pierre carry in supplies from the back of Jerry's truck, while Renny's excited dogs ran back and forth with them in the snow. Then she watched as Jerry and Renny got back in Jerry's truck, which Jerry backed around and drove down to the shack where Renny's truck was parked. Jerry waited to make sure Renny's truck would start, which it took a while to do, but eventually Mildred saw white puffs of exhaust from it. And Jerry waved and drove away, and that was that.

Home again. Her home unchanged since she left it, except for empty drawers and empty spaces in her closet where she hadn't yet put away her clothes.

Pat's hat, still a silent presence beside the clock on her chest of drawers. Pat's letter to her that had waited for her so long. Her name in Pat's handwriting on the front of the envelope. Mildred sat by the fire that crackled in her stove and gradually warmed the cabin, and she held Pat's letter without opening it, until finally she set the unopened letter back on the brim of his hat and went about unpacking her clothes and putting them away.

And then she had nothing to do.

She pulled a book from one of the glass-fronted bookcases in her front room and poured herself a glass of warm water and sat in one of the leather chairs by her fireplace, where she'd kindled another fire, and thought she might read for a while. Instead, her thoughts wandered.

She had decided to return to Plum Creek as a way, she supposed, of not exactly saying goodbye to Pat, or saying goodbye to him while pretending not to. Instead, she was back in the limbo where she'd been in church while Evangeline and Albert were getting married.

"Pat," she said aloud, and the antelope lifted her inquisitive muzzle, pausing at the dark edge where the horse-man kept himself.

What if she'd . . . what if . . . What if she'd listened to what Dr. Riggio at Good Samaritan was saying and understood he was offering her another choice? A choice that didn't necessarily blast the hopes of the patient man?

Her fire had died down, and her windows were darkening to black mirrors. Mildred lit her lamp and put another chunk of wood on her fire and decided she would ride along with Renny when he went to bring the horses and the milk cow back from Albert's, probably three hours over there and maybe closer to four hours returning, what with hauling the horses and the cow, and come back to a freezing cabin, rather than spend the day alone without even a horse if she needed one.

Strange how much she felt the isolation, when she hadn't expected to.

Strange, too, with Ferrell Adams so recently dead and buried, how quickly people were referring to the Adams ranch as Albert's. Pat took the horses out to Albert's, Renny had said. We gotta bring the horses and the milk cow home from Albert's.

31

"I'm playin fiddle at a dance over at Cottonwood, day after Christmas," Renny told Mildred while she helped him steady the stock rack as he lifted it and fit it on the truck. "You better put a dress on and come along, Mildred."

"Oh, no," she said, although she dreaded staying home alone. "Thank you, Renny, but I have way too much to do."

He scowled at her. Of course he knew she had nothing much to do, but he didn't say anything, just looked her over to make sure she was dressed warmly enough to suit him.

Mildred leaned back in her seat as Renny drove up their teetering road, on snow over frozen ruts, to the county road, which hadn't been ploughed and had a surface mostly of flattened and frozen snow for the truck to slide around on and try to keep its traction. Renny had to gun the motor to make it up a slick hill, and once, he had to back up and make a second run at another slick hill.

Well, the roads were what they were, and Mildred and Renny never had to talk to be companionable. Mildred let the sound of the motor lull her and let her thoughts drift to another community dance. Maybe out at Beaver Creek? Maybe in February or March of 1922? The flu epidemic by that time would have sated its appetite for victims, and Mildred, who had come home to help Renny tend to those victims, had returned to Fort Maginnis to complete her final year at Good Samaritan for her diploma and then returned again to the ranch.

Mildred's father was dead by then. He'd died just before the epidemic hit, and Renny had brought him to Fort Maginnis in the back of a truck for a frozen-ground funeral. How the world seemed to circle around on itself. Mildred sighed at the thought of the two old range bulls, Ferrell Adams and Thaddeus Harrington, now buried on opposite sides of the Protestant cemetery in Fort Maginnis.

The dance. Not that long ago. Renny must have taken her. Renny probably was playing the fiddle at that dance too. Mildred had finished her nursing program at Good Samaritan, and by the time of the dance, she would have had a couple of years to turn herself into the horseback-riding nurse of Plum Creek.

That dance. The Beaver Creek community hall. Kerosene lanterns and a coal stove and a bandstand with a piano to try to keep up with the fiddle. Mostly square dances, a few waltzes, the butterfly polka, and almost always a Virginia reel. Mildred hadn't danced—she never did, although she had been taught the waltz steps with the other girls at the Catholic high school. She had been watching the dancing from a corner by the cloakroom, when the community hall door opened to a whoosh of cold air and the energy of several young men, and one of them was Pat Adams.

Pat saw Mildred, turned, and trapped her by planting his hands against the wall on either side of her.

"Mil."

Whiskey on his breath. The young men did that, never mind the law, passing a bottle of moonshine or bootlegged whisky from hand and mouth to another hand and mouth in the darkened pasture where automobiles and buggies and wagons were parked. Music filtering from the community hall. Lighted windows. The Beaver Creek boys always were wild.

"Mil."

Pat, trapping her between muscled arms. His fair hair, his blue eyes that wouldn't let go of hers. The familiar lines of his face, mouth, neck, and shoulders. His nose not quite right, never properly straightened since the last time she had seen Pat's face and it was streaming with blood. The smell of whiskey. For the first time, she felt afraid of him.

"Let me go, Pat."

"I'll never let you go, Mil."

The face at Pat's shoulder was not Ferrell Adams's, but Renny's.

"Let her go, Pat."

Something changed in Pat, as though he'd suddenly sobered. He straightened and let his hands drop from either side of Mildred. "Sorry, Mil. Sorry, Renny," and he was sloping off to find his friends, only a little unsteady from the whiskey.

"Come over and sit by the bandstand," Renny told her. "We're almost done playing, and then we'll go home."

The laughter of young men. One of them probably was Albert, Mildred thought now. Singing.

—*I'm wild and woolly and full of fleas,*
and never been curried below the knees—

Renny stopped in Fort Maginnis for fuel and kept driving. Soon the road was rising to the high prairie, wind-scoured snow and drifted snow. Winter sagebrush, winter sky. For some, the low line of gray hills and distant outline of blue mountains that circled their horizon was enough. I never lost anything on the other side of those mountains, a rancher was apt to say. Got all I need right here.

Like Albert Vanaartsdalen, Mildred thought. Albert had finished a couple of years of high school and gone to cowboying for Ferrell Adams, and following his war years, here he still was.

Father Hugh, now. How much of the world he had seen, although of course his vocation guided him. And yet somehow, Father Hugh and Albert had—Mildred couldn't think of the right way to describe it—Father Hugh and Albert had made friends, she guessed. As simple as that.

Finally, with the sun a shrunken hole burned into the sky directly above, Renny was driving into the Adams ranch yard.

Albert's ranch yard, as everyone was starting to think of it, and here came Albert himself in mackinaw and dirty Stetson, riding a flea-bitten gray colt.

Albert swung down from the colt as Renny stepped out of the cab, and they gave each other the ranchers' quick handshake. "Hell, go right up to the house, Renny. Evvie's got coffee on the stove and dinner on the table, and I'll be up as soon's I take care a my horse."

Back in the cab, Renny put the truck in gear and drove the few yards, and Mildred saw the house she last had seen by headlights fourteen years ago. A story and a half of shingles and gray siding and narrow windows. What passed for a big house in ranch country.

A house where Evangeline beamed a greeting from the front door. Evangeline would have swept out any troubling cobwebs from this house. Evangeline was hugging Mildred and bubbling with welcome, as Josie would have. "Renny, Mildred, take your coats off. Lemme have em. Come into the kitchen where it's warm. I got coffee on the stove."

And here was Evangeline's sister Marguerite, who had stood up for Evangeline at her wedding, not as effusive as Evangeline but nearly as tall. Rita, everyone called her.

And now Albert, come up from the corrals in his Stetson and mackinaw, with his nose reddened from the cold and the rowels of his spurs jingling as he walked to the stove in his undershot bootheels and poured himself coffee.

"Take off your spurs and your hat and stay awhile, cowboy," Evangeline told him, and Albert took off his hat and hung it up and kissed her.

Mildred thought she was seeing the way people were supposed to live and love. Was it years of hardship that turned a bride into the crying and unlovely woman whose uterus Mildred had assisted the new doctor in surgically removing, even as she and Dr. Riggio saw the surgery was next to useless? What accounted for the woman's underfed and angry husband? How Mildred hoped Evangeline always would bounce and giggle and Albert always would be ready to kiss her.

More laughter at dinner, about the cowboy who had ridden by the house and spotted Rita. Now the cowboy rode by the house often, and it looked like Albert was going to have to ride out and talk to him.

"And tell Pat," Albert said, "that I got a letter with a Chinook, Montana, return address on the envelope, and it was from Frank. Frank said he decided he'd rather hang as a horse thief than leave them horses to starve. Said to let him know if we looked to have moisture in the spring to do any good."

After dinner Albert and Renny bundled up again and went out to load the horses and the cow, and Mildred, over Evangeline's protests, washed the dishes while Rita dried.

"You girls don't hafta wait on me! I'm fine!"

Mildred's hands stilled in the dishwater. Evangeline's bloom. Mildred turned, "When are you due, Evangeline?"

Rita began to laugh, while Evangeline blushed.

"The middle of August," Evangeline said.

"You know what they say," said Rita. "Nine months and ten minutes!"

The dishes finished, Evangeline wanted to show Mildred her house. Yes, it was Evangeline's house now, Mildred thought, which Evangeline had exorcised of more than cobwebs with her scrub brush and polish and bleach. Mildred thought she had never seen a house so clean. Evangeline led her through rooms with sparkling windows and shining floors. Curtains at the windows—she and Josie had found curtains in a box, Evangeline told Mildred, and washed and ironed them and hung them up. She told Mildred how, when she and Josie had asked him, Pat told Evangeline and Josie that the furniture belonged to the house.

Pat.

A bedroom, now Albert and Evangeline's bedroom, where a tall fair-haired woman with a face like Pat's once had fled, probably to plug her ears against what was happening in the next room.

That next room, where a rolltop desk had replaced a flat-topped desk.

All cleansed and exorcised by Evangeline.

Well, with some help from Father Hugh, as Evangeline explained. "That day he burned the road getting out here? After we heard what had happened at your ranch—Renny—Father Hugh said, as long as he was here and had some holy water in his automobile, which first he had to thaw out. And then he sprinkled it in every room, and he spoke in Latin, though I can't understand any of it."

"No," said Mildred. "I've forgotten most of it too."

"Mildred," Evangeline said. "Been needin a chance to tell you."

Albert and Evangeline and Father Hugh, the Three Musketeers. Sammy the substitute, and how fast that kid could run. How fast Father Hugh could run.

"Mildred, we love Pat," Evangeline said, "and one day Pat and I got to talking . . ."

The French girl he called Veeve—how he had left chocolate with her and had no way of knowing what happened to her, but *All I want in this world is Mil.*

"Evangeline," said Mildred. "I don't know how."

"Mildred, it's—well, Father Hugh explained to us what the Latin at our wedding meant—the part about being one flesh? It really is, Mildred. Me and Albert, we go to bed at night and—it really is one."

Mildred realized Evangeline was trying to tell her about the sweetness of the flesh.

Renny was at the door, waiting for Mildred. He and Albert had the horses and the cow loaded, and he was ready to start the long cold drive home.

Christmas Day. Evangeline and Albert and Rita had big plans. Driving in to Fort Maginnis and staying the night. Josie. A Christmas tree. Attending Christmas mass.

Mildred warmed a little canned ham for her and Renny's Christmas dinner, with potatoes and carrots from her root cellar. She had embroidered a linen shirt for Renny, and he had carved for her a graceful little figure of an animal from a chunk of light wood he'd come by.

32

Renny, the man of few words, stood in Mildred's kitchen in his wool shirt and boots and pants with suspenders, holding his beat-up old felt hat in his hand because he would no more keep his hat on his head inside Mildred's house than he would spit on her floor. Big dark-skinned, dark-eyed Renny, who looked so much like tiny Josie. Quick on his feet in spite of the pounds he'd put on over the years. Hair and beard more grizzled than when she'd first known him. When? She'd always known him. She couldn't remember a time when there had been no Renny.

"Are you my sidekick that helped me carry soup when two-thirds a Murray County was down with the flu? Fed em and bathed em and emptied slop and boiled up Josie's tea for their pain?"

She stared at him.

"Are you the best goddamn midwife in the county, hell, likely in the state?"

"Renny—"

"Mildred, I'm tellin you. You either get out of them pants and moccasins and put on a dress and stockings and real shoes, or I'll do it—" he broke off. "No, I won't. I'll go get Josie to do it for me."

He glared at her, clapped his hat back on his head, and slammed the door behind him.

....

A girl like you shouldn't have the brass to show her face again, her father had told her.

Mildred baked a cake and frosted it to take to the dance supper that would be held at midnight. She filled the galvanized tub with hot water and bathed with her sheet pinned around her neck.

Then she dried herself and put on clean underthings and a slip and garter belt, and she drew on her silk stockings, one and then the other, and gartered them. Her good navy shoes. The blue silk dress the nuns had given her when she graduated from high school because they wanted her to have a graduation present like all the other girls. A dress she had never worn.

She had washed her hair the day before, and she shook out her heavy braid and brushed and combed her hair and rebraided it and wound the braid around her head and pinned it.

What else. She had a small necklace of pearls and pearl earrings that had been her mother's. But Mildred's ears never had been pierced, and she already felt like a costumed imposter without adding a necklace. She looked at her face in the small mirror in the kitchen and saw that her hair was smooth and her collar straight.

One of the lowered-voice women's stories, told after a glance around to make sure the men weren't near enough to hear what men's ears should not. A girl who lived—where?—in Hilger, Mildred thought. One of the little towns that had risen out of a patch of prairie to provide the homesteaders with a general store and a post office, a railroad depot and maybe a lumberyard where they could buy sawn boards and tarpaper to build their shacks. And—stealthy glance, voice even lower—this girl had given birth to a baby without being married. She and her baby had gone on living with her mother and father. But she kept indoors, and no one ever saw her again. The baby, it was told, lived to be three or four years old and choked to death on a slice of apple.

Mildred put on her coat. Took a last look around her cabin, her home. Pat's unopened letter on the brim of his hat. Mildred asked herself the question she'd forbidden herself to ask. Was it possible she hadn't opened his letter because she would rather he tell her what he had written?

Renny brought the truck around to pick her up, looked her over, and nodded. Told her to button her coat and put her scarf and gloves on. It was thirty degrees below zero out there.

33

The Cottonwood community hall was a long and narrow frame building, sided and shingled some years ago by the men of the Cottonwood community, with steps up to a little roofed entryway. A path had been shoveled to the steps. Renny parked the truck in a shoveled space where a few cars and trucks already were parked with more arriving. Probably there were saddle horses with loosened cinches in the barn behind the hall.

Renny, carrying his fiddle in its case, came around to help Mildred down from the high cab in her unfamiliar heeled shoes and walked with her to the hall with a good grip on her arm as though he thought she just might break and run. Inside the hall an oil stove radiated heat, and kerosene lanterns hung from hooks in the ceiling and shed circles of light on the dance floor. A cloakroom near the door and a counter at the opposite end of the hall where supper would be spread at midnight. Behind the counter, a kitchen with a stove and a water cooler and shelves of heavy white crockery. In the little storage room off the kitchen was a bed where the babies would sleep while their parents danced.

Renny walked Mildred to the counter to set down her cake, and then he walked her to the other side of the dance floor where he had spotted the Svobodas. Mrs. Svoboda beamed at Mildred and patted her knee and told her that little Joey was doing just fine and sleeping in the room off the kitchen. Agnes Svoboda and several other children ran and slid on the dance floor, which had been made slick with powdered wax, and Renny climbed up on the little bandstand and started tuning his fiddle with Miss Cole at the piano and Jake Pence, who played his banjo when he wasn't calling square dances.

More people were crowding into the hall, a whole community eager to take a break from winter and have a good time. Mildred knew many, maybe even most, from bone setting and childbirth, bandaging and soothing, and, God knew, the terrible, terrible flu. Maybe Renny was right, and she could relax and take a break from winter like everyone else and enjoy watching people dance.

But no. Because checking his sheepskin coat and Stetson at the cloakroom and walking to the side of the dance floor was Pat.

Pat in a white shirt and new Levi's. Lantern light falling on his fair hair. Behind her numbness, she noted mechanically, professionally, that he had walked in without a sign he'd worn a brace so recently. Walking just fine, walking like Pat.

Piano and fiddle and banjo struck up a schottische, and couples rushed to the dance floor. It might be thirty below zero outside, the forecast might be bleak, but inside, there was a thunder of shoes and boots on polished boards, whoops of pleasure, spinning colors of women's skirts, exuberant spill of notes from the banjo, racing melody of the fiddle, and the piano holding it all together in the joy of dancing, dancing, dancing.

Pat saw her.

How could he not spot her? A woman in a blue dress sitting alone, one of the few who weren't dancing. Oh, a few elderly women with their heads together, probably criticizing the dancers, a pair of old men having a chance to compare snowfall with each other and ask how their hay was holding out. The dance ended, the music changed to a two-step, and couples changed partners. Mildred saw Mrs. Svoboda dancing with one of the Bartas and Agnes and another little girl dancing together in a corner. Once, she thought Pat was about to walk around the dancers to her, and what could she do? Where was an escape?

He didn't. He stood on the other side of the dance floor with his thumbs hooked in his belt loops and watched her as she watched him. Occasionally, a man who knew him stopped and punched his shoulder or shook his hand and talked to him for a minute or two, asking him how he was doing, she supposed, but Pat's eyes always returned to her.

The two-step ended. Jake Pence stepped up to call a square dance, and partners formed in squares of four couples to follow his calls.

"Shake a big foot and keep time to the fiddle, and when you have swung, remember my call—swing your partner and promenade all!"

Mildred thought that if she went to the water cooler in the kitchen and poured herself a glass of water, she could sip the water and tell herself she was doing something. Or maybe the coffee was ready.

She threaded her way between chairs and behind dancers until she reached the counter. She didn't dare to look back. Everyone but her was dancing or visiting. Another square dance had formed. "Ladies round ladies!" bellowed Jake, "and the gents don't go!"

No coffee yet, but she went behind the counter to the kitchen and took one of the heavy glasses from a shelf and ran water into it from the cooler.

"Mil."

The weight of the glass in her hand.

"Mil, will you please let me talk to you?"

The feel of water cooling the glass in her hand. If only she could be invisible.

He was standing very close behind her. His voice low. "What I did to you, Mil. I made you pregnant. And that was why they hurt you. And if there was anything I could do to change it—any damn way—but there isn't. All I can do is tell you I'm sorry. And I am. I'm sorry, Mil. And do we really have to have this conversation while you've got your back turned to me, Mil?"

Stamp and thunder of square dancers, quiver of dance floor under their energy and zest. A break from winter and a good time, a good time, a good time, a good time, a good time!

"I'm not fourteen anymore!" she burst. "You don't even *know* me! And I don't know you!"

A pause.

"Um—what do you want to know about me, Mil? What my favorite color is? I'm real fond of blue."

Damn Pat! He always could make her laugh.

She turned, and there stood Pat in his white shirt and Levi's, belt and boots. He smiled at her. Pat's smile.

"Why are you apologizing to me?"

"Father Hugh told me to."

That did it. She set down her glass and put her hand over her mouth to hide what it wanted to do, which was to smile back at Pat, and she edged around him toward the dance floor. She thought he might try to catch her hand and stop her, but no. He walked beside her while the fiddle and piano and banjo began a sweet slow waltz with a melody she often had heard Renny playing in the night.

"Will you waltz with me, Mil?"

The least conspicuous thing she could think to do was to let him take her hand and hold her waist and waltz with her on the dance floor, although she knew they were drawing eyes. Patrick Adams waltzing with Mildred Harrington! People asking each other if they knew the story. She couldn't breathe—she couldn't stand it. She tore away from Pat's arms and felt something in herself tearing as, even knowing every pair of eyes in the hall were following her now, she bolted and ran for the door.

Ten feet outside the door of the community hall, she paused, wrapping her arms around herself. Now what? It was thirty degrees below zero out here, she realized. She could freeze. A path had been shoveled as far as the parked vehicles, with snow banked on either side. She could walk to Renny's truck and sit inside the cab, where the metal would make it even colder than outside, and she shivered to think of it.

She heard the community hall door open behind her. A long oblong of gold light spread past her, carrying with it a burst of polka music from fiddle and banjo and piano before the door closed again, the light vanished, and the music faded.

"Mil."

The sky full of soundless stars. A clear night and all the colder for its clarity.

"Mil," Pat said. "If what you want . . ." His voice sounded slow and disconnected from what he was saying. "If what you want is for me to go away—go away somewhere, where you never have to see me again, so I can't cause you any more distress, any more pain—all you have to do is say so."

She couldn't answer.

"If that's what you want me to do, Mil, you have to tell me so."

Never. See. Pat. Again.

"No!" she cried. She turned and saw that he had followed her outside without his coat, in his shirtsleeves, and somehow the ten feet of shoveled path between them had dissolved, and he was holding her and searching for her mouth with his mouth, and she was hugging him back with her teeth chattering.

"Sweetheart," he said, into her hair. "Mil. It's colder than hell out here. Come back inside where it's warm."

"Everyone will stare."

"Let em."

He held her with one arm and opened the hall door into what felt like an explosion of lantern light and heat from the oil stove. The polka must just have ended, because everyone was standing on the dance floor, and now they all were looking at her and Pat. Stricken with embarrassment, she tried to hide her face in Pat's shirt, but he had his hand in her hair and wouldn't let her. Pat looked around at the circle of faces and smiled his smile that lit up the room and with his free hand gave them all a high thumbs-up.

And suddenly, she and Pat were being swarmed. Men were shaking Pat's hand and slapping him on the back, and women were hugging Mildred and kissing her on her cheeks. Women whose babies she had delivered. Mrs. Svoboda, Mrs. Barta, Mrs. Knutson, Mrs. Naylor, Mrs. Barber, Mrs. Danvers. Women whose children's scrapes and bruises she had patched and bandaged and bones she had set. Women she had nursed through the flu and whose children she had nursed. So many.

On the bandstand, Renny said something to Miss Cole at the piano, and she nodded. Jake grinned and tipped his banjo in agreement, and they began to play again the slow sweet waltz from the Red River country, the country where Renny's people came from. And Pat took Mil in his arms and waltzed with her, just the two of them on the dance floor for several measures before other couples joined them, and then others, until Mil and Pat waltzed in the midst of a whole community of waltzers. And she found herself safe at last, and Pat kissed her on her forehead and smiled at her until she smiled back at him.

The antelope lifted her inquisitive muzzle, and the horse-man cantered up to her on hooves that broke through the crust of snow. He reached a hand toward the antelope and drew his finger along the line of her taupe-and-white face, the swell of her cheekbones, and her long fine nose and mouth.

Epilogue

Love and laugh, Pat and Mil. Love and laugh while you can, Albert and Evangeline. Ahead lie years of sparse rain, while the rest of America enjoys the prosperous 1920s, and then will come the crash of 1929 and the Great Depression, which you may hardly notice after the drought and desperate dry years of the 1920s. You'll hang in there. You'll say goodbye to Josie and Renny and, yes, to Sister St. Paul. Father Hugh will continue with you for many more years, graying but still laughing, and so will Sister Boniface, who has learned to laugh. Then will come World War II, born from the blood the Montana boys shed fighting in the Meuse-Argonne during October and early November of 1918.

A LaFountain will be the mayor of Fort Maginnis one day. A LeTellier will be the county prosecutor of Fort Maginnis one day.

And in a new century, a granddaughter of Albert Vanaartsdalen's will call her eldest daughter on a cell phone—how could Pat and Mildred or Albert and Evangeline have imagined such communication—and ask her if *Powder River, let er buck!* means anything to her, and mother and daughter will be brought to tears by their family heritage and Albert's granddaughter's research.

After she ends her conversation with her daughter, Albert's granddaughter, who is no longer young and whose preoccupation is with words—the beautiful way the words meet each other and kiss or bristle, the way the words echo each other and sometimes double back in a reprise, and sometimes, like the antelope, leave delicate footprints where they have circled the edges of thought where the horse-man waits—Albert's granddaughter will gaze for a long time at a framed print that hangs just outside her study door. It is a print of the watercolor the Montana artist Charles M. Russell painted of Albert in 1919 in which Albert has just roped a steer and has thrown his weight into his opposite stirrup to counterbalance the force of the steer hitting the end of his rope.

Every detail just right. Russell was famous for getting his details just right. Albert's spare cowboy frame, his undershot bootheels, the rowels of his spurs. Although—his granddaughter can't tell, because of his pose whether Albert has taken his dallies or tied his rope.

Albert's granddaughter vows to do her best to give voices back to Pat and Mildred and Albert and Evangeline and to listen to them laughing with their friends and cherishing their love for each other. And as best she can, to get every detail just right.

Pat. Mil. I'm thinking of you.

Lightning Source UK Ltd.
Milton Keynes UK
UKHW012258270221
379365UK00015B/574